MUSE SQUAD
The Mystery of the Tenth

Also available from Chantel Acevedo

Muse Squad: The Cassandra Curse

MUSE
SQUAD
The Mystery of the Tenth

CHANTEL ACEVEDO

BALZER + BRAY
An Imprint of HarperCollins *Publishers*

Balzer + Bray is an imprint of HarperCollins Publishers.

Muse Squad: The Mystery of the Tenth
Copyright © 2021 by Chantel Acevedo
All rights reserved. Printed in the United States of America.
No part of this book may be used or reproduced in any manner whatsoever without
written permission except in the case of brief quotations embodied in critical
articles and reviews. For information address HarperCollins Children's Books, a
division of HarperCollins Publishers, 195 Broadway, New York, NY 10007.
www.harpercollinschildrens.com

Library of Congress Control Number: 2021932058
ISBN 978-0-06-294772-7

Typography by Joel Tippie
21 22 23 24 25 PC/LSCH   10 9 8 7 6 5 4 3 2 1

First Edition

For Didi

Chapter 1
ARACHNOPHOBIA

My room looked like it had imploded. There were items of clothing draped on every surface—my dresser, the doorknob, the door itself, my sister's new microscope (an adoption day gift from our twin brothers), and even on my sister.

"Callie, this is entirely unacceptable," Maya said, a long sock dangling over her face.

"Sorry!" I said, snatching it away. "I can't figure out what to pack for New York." I was out of breath and sweating. It was summer in Miami and the air-conditioning in our house had conked out that morning. Even my elbows were damp.

Maya glanced at her own suitcase, already packed and propped up by the door, ready for our flights tomorrow morning. She was heading to Space Camp in Huntsville, Alabama. Meanwhile, I was going to New York City to spend a month with my papi; my stepmom, Laura; and my new baby brother, Rafael Jr. My brothers were staying in Miami to earn money to buy a used car. At least, that was the excuse they gave. Papi had asked them to visit, too, but they'd said no right away. The truth is, when Mami and Papi broke up, the twins got really angry at Papi for leaving, and a part of them was still mad.

Maya's summer sounded infinitely cooler than mine. While she would be learning about space and gravity and actual *rocket science*, I would be stuck in a small walk-up apartment in Queens, staying in the baby's room while the baby slept with Papi and Laura in a cradle by their bed.

"I wish I was going to Space Camp," I grumbled.

"Since when do you want to be a scientist?" Maya said. "Because astronauts are scientists first, you know."

I didn't have to take long to consider it. Science was Maya's thing. Did I even *have* a thing? I thought of my best friend, Raquel, who just knew she wanted to be a performer. What did I want from life? I had no clue. Whenever anybody asked me, "What do you want to be when you grow up?" I nearly always just shrugged. Could a person make a career out of hanging out with friends, eating snacks, and watching television?

I don't think so.

"Why the face?" Maya asked me. "I'm sure you'll have

plenty of a-*muse*-ing adventures this summer."

"Stop it," I said, rolling my eyes. Maya was the only person in my family who knew I was one of the nine muses. It's supposed to be a secret, but *you* try keeping information from your genius sister!

There have always been nine muses, and usually, they're grown-ups. But now, for the first time ever, *four* of us are kids. We're the Muse Squad, which is a silly name, but we've gotten used to it. I'm the Muse of epic poetry. It sounds a little boring, but isn't as it turns out, because epic poems are about heroes, which means I am a hero-maker.

Maya was right. Something interesting would probably come up this summer. But the thing was, I hadn't heard from the other muses in ages. Nia was trying out for a gymnastics club team in Chicago. Mela's mother had bought her theater passes for the summer, and she was catching every tragic play she could, and Thalia had volunteered to be a junior librarian at the British Library. They were all pretty busy with non-muse activities.

As for the other muses, the grown-up ones, I hadn't heard from any of them either. Usually every few weeks our leader, Clio, would call us to headquarters—which was in London, England, at the Victoria and Albert Museum—either for training or missions. Maybe things were quiet in the summer. Did muses go on vacation? I didn't know. But the silence made me nervous. It made me feel as if something was *up*.

"Earth to Callie," Maya said, snapping me out of my thoughts.

"Sorry, Mission Control. We've got a problem. I'm panicking," I answered her, then slumped on the floor on top of a pile of a sweatshirts and tees. It was so hot, I couldn't concentrate.

Maya smiled. She liked it when I called her Mission Control, and I liked to imagine her there, behind panels full of technology, solving important scientific problems. Maybe she could solve my problem, too. Without asking, she started plucking different clothing items off the floor and the furniture, folding them deftly and sliding them into my suitcase for me.

"No need to panic," Maya said, cool as can be. "When I was in foster care, I had to pack up a lot. You don't really need to take too much. Plus, you'll want room in your bag for all the souvenirs you're going to buy me," she joked, rolling a pair of jeans like a burrito. Maya had started wearing her hair like Princess Leia—in two buns over her ears—and they bobbed a little as she packed, like a pair of loose headphones.

"Why aren't you sweating?" I asked. I was drenched. The ceiling fan was spinning, but it was really just moving the warm air around. It felt like a giant was blowing his hot breath on us.

Maya giggled, lifting the bottom of her T-shirt a little. There, duct-taped to her stomach, were three ice packs.

"You won't be laughing when it's time to pull those off," I said.

Maya's smile slipped a little. "Climate change. We all have to manage somehow." Last fall, before Mami adopted her, Maya had won the county science fair with her project—a plan to address sea-level rise in South Florida.

It hadn't been an easy win. The competition was tough. Plus, a rogue muse who happened to be our evil science teacher, Ms. Rinse, and her three siren minions, did their worst to try to stop Maya from succeeding. Maya doesn't know it, but she's a Fated One—meant for great things thanks to that massive brain of hers, which means she's under the protection of the muses.

Maya zipped up my suitcase and said, "Voilà! All packed. Now can we please go to the mall where the temperatures aren't trying to kill us?"

She'd done it. She'd packed my suitcase. Sometimes Maya saved *me*.

"Vamos," I said, "we'll ask Fernando and Mario to take us."

Maya crossed her fingers *and* her eyes. She was right. We'd need all the luck we could get if we wanted to convince the twins to be our ride to the mall.

"Bros. My bros. My wonderful brothers," I called down the hallway. Mario popped his head out of his bedroom.

"What do you want?" he asked.

"The answer is no," Fernando added from inside. The twins would be seventeen soon, but Maya and I usually had them beat when it came to maturity.

"Please?" Maya squeaked, her hands clasped under her chin and her eyes doing their best puppy dog impersonation.

Mario blinked. "Well—"

"Don't you give in," Fernando barked. I could hear their favorite video game, Underwatch, blaring away.

"It'll be nice and cool at the mall," I said. "We won't even bother you. You can spend the whole time at Gamer Place."

"Air-conditioning, air-condiiiiiitioning," Maya sang, the perfect backup.

"Fine," Mario said.

"Ugh. You always fall for it," Fernando said, shutting off the game. The truth was, they *both* always fell for it. When we'd gone before the family court judge in May to make Maya an official member of the family, the judge had given my brothers a big speech about what it meant to have a new little sister. And though it kind of bugged me that he was giving them the whole "men of the house" talk (I mean, let's be real here. I'm in an all-girls-*with*-ancient-powers squad, and my mom is the head of the house, no question), my brothers had taken it to heart. That meant Maya got away with a lot when it came to them, the big softies.

As for me, unlike Maya, I was old news. Just last week, they'd covered my bed in a hundred sticky notes that read "dork." It took all my willpower to keep from "inspiring" them to drink a ketchup milkshake.

Because that's what muses do, we inspire people. If we wanted to, we could convince just about anyone to do something truly awful. But muses aren't about that villain life. Besides, we have a bunch of muse rules we follow:

1. A muse always trusts her instincts.
2. Muse magic is just love, concentrated.
3. A muse never uses her magic against her sisters.
4. Inspiration knows no borders.
5. All people and places are worthy of magic.
6. A muse must always keep her identity a secret.
7. A muse is a person on whom nothing is lost.
8. A muse is no better, or worse, than the heroes she inspires.
9. Muses are goddesses. And don't ever forget it.

They're good rules, but lately, I've been coming up with my own. Like Callie's Muse Rule #236: Your brothers are idiots, but you love them anyway.

Still, when I saw my bed covered in sticky notes, and Maya's pristine and untouched, it hurt my feelings. I almost said something to them, but then I just . . . didn't. That's been happening a lot lately, too. Whenever I try to tell somebody about my *feelings*, my eyes get all watery and stupid, and I absolutely hate crying. Mami always says, "All feelings are valid because you feel them. That's the point." But I don't know about that. Sometimes my feelings seem pretty ridiculous, even to me.

"I'm getting one of those food court cookies the size of my head," Fernando was saying as he tied his laces.

"For sure," Mario added.

"Mmm," I said, my sweet tooth coming alive.

"I hope you brought your own money, 'cause I'm not sharing," Fernando said. My pockets were empty and I let out a groan. Sweet tooth deactivated.

Maya pointed at her purse and gave me a wink. She'd gotten lots of adoption day gifts from our extended family, mainly in the form of spending money. Our great-aunt Carmen gave her a hundred bucks. All I ever got from her at Christmas and birthdays was socks.

Sometimes it pays to be the new kid. Literally.

Mario and Fernando had gotten permission to take Mami's van, and we piled in. The air-conditioning was working, and we blasted it into our faces while Mario turned the radio to the reggaeton station.

Maya and I sang along to song after song the whole way to the mall. It was our last day together in Miami, and I wanted to make the most of it. First, we'd go straight to the food court for some ice cream (pistachio for Maya, plain chocolate for me), then we would make our way to Pop! Mania and see if they had any *Zombie Beach* merch for sale. *Zombie Beach* was a new horror show set in Miami. We'd seen the first season twice already and were halfway through our third viewing. I watched most of it through my fingers, covering my face every time a zombie crashed into the room and ate someone's face. Maya was fearless, though. For some reason, the bloodier the scene, the more she laughed. Mario and Fernando were that way, too, and they teased me about being so chicken.

I was just thinking about how my brothers had always been brave about that kind of stuff when Mario let out a bloodcurdling scream.

The van swerved, tilting up onto two wheels before slamming back down and going into a spin. My seat belt cut into my shoulder, and I watched as Fernando's head smacked the passenger door window. Maya curled into a ball in her seat, her hands clamped onto her hair buns. I could feel myself trembling all over, and I think I was saying, "No, no, no, no, please," out loud, but I can't be sure. The steering wheel spun wildly on its own. Mario needed to get a grip . . . literally!

I tried to summon my muse magic, but the instant tingling on my skin that came with the magic? It didn't happen. Again, I willed my magic to come, but it just wouldn't. After what felt like a million years, the van rolled onto the grassy swale on the side of the road and finally stopped.

Mario was still screaming.

"What happened?" I shouted, clicking off my seat belt. Maya was already clambering toward the front of the van, while Fernando was holding Mario by the shoulders and shaking him.

"Sp-sp-spiders!" Mario spluttered, and then I saw them—hundreds of tiny, nearly transparent spiders, crawling on the dashboard.

Fernando made a strangled sound, slamming his baseball cap over the crawlers again and again until they were still. Then he swept them into his hat and threw the whole thing outside.

Mario whimpered, his hands covering his face, his shoulders shaking. It broke my heart.

"Hey, bro," I said softly, laying a hand on Mario's head. I tried to call my muse magic one more time, waiting to feel my fingers going numb, and my hair standing up at the root a little, like it always did.

Nothing happened. "Don't panic," I whispered to myself.

"Too late," Mario answered, hyperventilating now.

Thinking maybe I could nudge the magic along, I pictured Mario taking deep breaths, calm and brave, like he normally was. The picture in my mind grew sharper and more defined until Mario stopped shaking.

Had my magic worked? Or was Mario just back in control of himself?

"I don't know what happened. I've never been funny about spiders," Mario said after his breathing returned to normal. "But there were so many, and they started getting on my hands." His voice was firmer, and he was smacking his own cheeks a little, like a person trying to wake up from a dream.

"Good job," Maya whispered to me.

"Um, yeah," I said softly. I rubbed my hands together, and they felt normal. No tingling. It was definitely my turn to panic. Where had my magic gone?

"That was nuts," Fernando said, running his hands through his hair. He took a look at his cap on the ground outside and shivered.

"M-maybe we should go home," Mario said, and we didn't argue.

"Want me to drive?" Fernando asked, and Mario nodded, so the boys traded places. I watched as Mario checked the van for damage (there was none), then came over to the passenger side, his eyes darting back and forth over the grass, checking for more spiders.

That's when I saw a different spider in the distance. This one was very large, black, and furry. It had crawled onto a traffic cone, perched at the very top.

I nudged Maya with my elbow. "Do you see that?"

Maya squinted. "The traffic cone?"

"No, what's on it."

Maya squinted harder. "Nothing's on it, Callie."

When I looked again, I saw that Maya was right—the spider was gone. I rubbed my eyes and leaned back in my seat. Clio had once told me that muses saw the world a bit more magically than others did. In fact, I had once spotted a nymph in the River Thames. It was possible that the spiders that had scared my brother weren't just any old arachnids. But there was no way of being sure.

My brain was racing all the way home, thoughts pinging back and forth, but nothing feeling like it made any sense.

I looked at Mario, drumming his fingers on his thighs to music. He was his old, chillaxed self again, but we were all very quiet. Nobody was in the mood to talk about what had just happened. We stopped at a red light, and I watched as a man standing on the sidewalk spit his gum onto the ground.

"Ugh. Litterer," Maya said in disgust.

Narrowing my eyes and staring at him, I called my magic again.

Everything was still as the world seemed to slow down before my eyes, but still, my magic didn't come. The man didn't move. In fact, we watched as he dug into his pockets and threw some crumpled receipts on the ground.

"He's the worst," Fernando said from the front seat.

My breath started to hitch.

"You okay?" Maya asked.

I shook my head.

"That was pretty scary back there," she added, resting her head on my shoulder. "But I wouldn't worry anymore. The odds of that happening again are astronomical."

Maya may not have been a muse herself, but she had a way of making people feel better that was pretty magical.

Outside the van windows, the man on the sidewalk pressed the crosswalk button repeatedly. I steadied myself, remembering that I'd used my imagination when Mario was freaking out, and he'd calmed down. Maybe it was a coincidence, or maybe . . .

I pictured the litterer bending down, retrieving his gum, and throwing it into a trash can that was only six feet away from him.

Just as the picture finished forming in my head, the man licked his lips, dug into his pocket for yet another receipt, bent down for the gum, and sailed it into the trash can with an elegant toss. Then he picked up the other receipts he'd let drop.

I frowned. Had I done that? Was I summoning my magic differently now?

"Three points, bro," Fernando said.

"You're two for two," Maya whispered.

That had been easy. I hadn't had to *call* my magic so much as *imagine* it. Was that a thing all muses did eventually? Had I, like, leveled up or something?

I was just thinking about all that when my muse brace-let started to heat up, hotter and hotter, just as Fernando slid the van into our driveway back home.

Perfect timing. The muses were assembling and I hated being late.

Chapter 2
MUSE SQUAD REUNITED

"Home so fast?" Mami asked as we filed into the house. We were still pretty shaken, but one look from Fernando warned us not to say anything. If Mami found out Mario had almost crashed the van because of spiders, we'd all get an endless lecture, and they wouldn't be allowed to drive the van ever again.

"Traffic was bad, so we decided to turn back around and come home," Mario said.

Thankfully, Mami was distracted. She'd hauled our suitcases out into the living room and was busy refolding everything. Good thing, too, because my muse bracelet was basically on fire.

"Run," Maya whispered, then mouthed, *I'll cover for you*. I never told her that she really didn't have to. Clio, the Muse of history, could hold back time for a bit while we were having our meetings. If Maya knew that, she'd break her brain trying to figure out the physics of it—some things you just keep to yourself.

I crawled under my bed, where there were still at least a dozen sticky notes from my brothers' prank. The jerks knew I sometimes crept under my bed "to think." The last thing I noticed before closing my eyes was the word "dork," written in thick black marker, over and over again.

When I opened my eyes, I saw a familiar pair of pink sneakers with hand-drawn smiley faces on them.

"Hey, Thalia!" I said, wriggling out from under the Great Bed of Ware, which was one of the treasures of the V and A Museum, and my entrance point.

"'Sup, dork," Thalia said, bursting into laughter as she reached out and pulled a sticky note from my hair.

I growled and snatched the note away. "My brothers—" I started.

"Always liked those two," Thalia finished. She would. She was the Muse of comedy, after all, and nobody enjoyed a good prank like Thalia did.

Before I could say anything else, I saw Nia, the Muse of science, and Mela, the Muse of tragedy, coming toward us. Mela was wearing an Elizabethan ruff around her neck. It was a fancy collar, basically, and she'd obviously gotten it from the dress-up room. Nia was clanking around in a vest made of chain mail.

"Hey, dork!" Nia said.

"Come on," I complained, "that's the second one," while Thalia pulled yet another sticky note off my shoulder.

Mela looked me over very seriously. "No more dork signs, I promise," she said.

Nia had an app on her phone that could calculate the possibility percentage of success or failure of any action based on the position of the stars, and she could use her magic to inspire scientific breakthroughs, inventions, or even, you know, breaking the law to save a captive whale. That last one had actually happened last fall.

Mela could make a person cry in a snap—not just sniffling cries, either, but full-on sobbing. Mela also loved country western music, probably because so many of the songs were sad. I sent Mela an old-school poster of Taylor Swift, back when she sang country, all the way to New Delhi for her birthday in April. She sent me a teary thank-you video that made me all sniffly and sensitive for hours.

"Muse Squad, reunited," Thalia said, then started singing, "And it feeeeeeels so gooood."

"Clio hasn't called us in ages," I said, and the others nodded.

"Anybody know why we were called today?" Mela asked.

The rest of us shook our heads. "We're always the last to know anything," Nia grumbled. She was right. The other five muses usually got the scoop from Clio, our leader, before we did. Nia, Thalia, Mela, and I were twelve years old now, the youngest muses in history. It was cool, but sometimes it felt as though the other muses didn't quite know what to do with us.

"I wonder if it has anything to do with the spiders," I thought.

"Spiders? Did you say spiders?" Mela asked.

"I said that out loud?"

The others nodded.

"Oh. Well. My siblings and I nearly crashed the car because of them," I explained, and realized that my legs were actually still a bit shaky. It's funny how a scary thing can still feel scary in your body long after it's happened. "I need to sit down," I said, and sat on the Great Bed of Ware, which was a no-no, since it was so old and priceless.

Thalia got a delighted look on her face and clambered on, too. Mela and Nia followed, and the bed creaked under our weight.

"Steady on, mates," Thalia said.

"What do you mean spiders nearly caused a car crash?" Nia asked.

"Mario was driving. They appeared out of nowhere on the dashboard and freaked him out. He swerved, and it nearly tipped the van over, but we were okay. The thing is, Mario isn't scared of anything. Not even *Zombie Beach*!"

"I *cannot* watch that show," Mela said with a shudder.

"I know, right?"

The Great Bed made a groaning sound and we all grew very still.

"It's survived for over four hundred years," Thalia said, patting the bed. "It can handle four twelve-year-olds."

"Go on," Nia said.

I took a deep breath. "The weird thing is that once the spiders were out of the van, I could have sworn that I saw another one, a big one, sitting on top of a traffic cone. I think it was staring at me."

"That *is* weird," Mela said.

"I thought so, too. Then my bracelet started heating up, so I figured the meeting was about the spiders." I didn't mention the other thing that had happened—how my magic had changed. Mami always said that a person's body belongs to nobody but them. This change in my magic felt like that, like a personal thing, and a secret I should keep for a while.

Just as we all began to climb off the bed we heard a snap underneath us. We yelped in surprise. The Great Bed seemed to have dropped half an inch.

"Get off, get off, get off," Mela was saying in a whisper, as if a loud voice might finish the bed off entirely.

A moment later, we were all standing around the Great Bed, which looked a little bit disheveled, but not very different from before. I smoothed the red-and-gold bed-spread with my hands, erasing our butt prints, and hoped it wouldn't crush me when it was time to slide under it to get back home.

Because there was no way I was telling Clio that we broke the Great Bed of Ware.

We made our way to the theater, where we held our meetings. Outside, it was midnight in London, and the lights glimmered through the museum windows.

"Spiders are terrifying," Mela said as we walked.

Nia gagged. Thalia laughed. Mela shivered all over.

"But just because you saw creepy spiders, it doesn't mean anything magical is up," Mela said. "Mario likely just got scared."

"People get frightened all the time," Thalia said kindly, her hand on my shoulder.

I took a deep breath. "You're probably right." We were quiet the rest of the way to the theater. I was still a little nervous, though. Last fall, my science teacher and three of my classmates had turned out to be evil mythical beings. It was the kind of experience that was hard to shake, and more than once since then, Maya had accused me of "seeing shadows everywhere."

But wasn't muse rule number one that a muse always trusts her instincts?

My instincts were telling me trouble had eight legs and was coming straight at us.

Chapter 3
THE MYSTERY OF THE TENTH

We entered the small theater where we usually held our meetings. Normally, the theater played fifteen-minute programs about medieval church construction or the gardens at Kensington Palace, but today, the projectors were turned off.

Clio, the Muse of history, stood at the front of the room beside a podium. The other grown-up muses sat together in the front row. We sat just behind them.

"Thank you all for being here," Clio began. "My apologies for not holding more regular meetings this summer. Things have been a bit complicated."

Those of us in the second row looked at one another. "Complicated"? That was never a good word to describe anything.

Clio stacked and restacked papers on the podium, and

if I didn't know any better, I would think she was anxious. But Clio was never anxious. She cleared her throat. "I'd like to ask Paola to join me."

Paola, Muse of the sacred, rose from her seat, jingling as she went. Paola was short. Latina like me, but Colombiana instead of Cuban. She wore long patchwork skirts, with shiny, thin chains circling her waist. Small bells hung off the belt, and they rang when she moved. Her dark hair was always up in a bun. Carefully, she stepped up to the podium.

"Two weeks ago, early in the morning, I came to headquarters for a bite to eat. You all know how much I love the cafecito they serve here. With a scone, ay que rico," Paola said, going off topic. Clio nudged her. "Ah, sí. I was in the café, when I heard a clock chiming. It was the muse finder."

Clio had shown me the clock last year. Whenever a muse retired or passed away, the muse finder clock went to work seeking the one who would replace her. It's a beautiful clock, with a globe held up by muse figurines. When a new muse uses her magic for the first time, the globe spins and spins, and then points to where the muse can be found. Clio told me that when the clock found me, the globe spun for eight hours, and that it had never done that before.

She'd said, "There's more goddess in you than the rest of us." I didn't know what that meant. I really didn't feel special, but what had happened with my magic earlier made me nervous, and also a little bit excited. My magic had worked differently. Maybe that's what happened to all the muses when they got used to their powers. There *was* one other weird thing about me. Muses didn't inherit their roles. It was all sort of random. But my tia Annie was the Muse of epic poetry before I was, and when she died, there were only eight muses for a long time.

That is, until the clock found me.

Clio said that Tia Annie went to Mount Olympus before she got sick—but Tia Annie never told the other muses what she'd gone to ask for. Was it for her health? That didn't seem like something she'd do. If Tia Annie had made that trip to see the gods, it wouldn't have been for herself.

Sometimes I wondered if she'd asked the gods to make me a muse in her place.

And I wondered why she would ever think that was a good idea.

I saw Tia Annie after she died. There's a portal to the other side here at the V and A. It's an old dog tomb, of all things. Last year, I crawled inside and met Tia Annie—or her spirit, I guess. She helped us defeat the sirens and Ms. Rinse. But she also said not to come looking for her again.

I have so many questions.

Plus, I miss her a lot.

The bells tinkling around Paola's waist brought me back

to the present. "I went to the clock gallery and saw that the clock was spinning and spinning. And then it stopped," she was saying.

Tomiko interrupted, "Where is it pointing?"

"New York City," Paola said.

"Queens, to be specific," Clio added.

I gasped. Queens! I'd be there tomorrow, staying with my dad in a neighborhood called Corona.

"Will the new muse be old enough to vote?" Elnaz asked snarkily, and I heard Mela huff beside me.

"None of you are asking the right question," Clio said.

That's when Nia raised her hand, clearing her throat.

"Nia?"

"There are nine of us. Nobody has quit or retired. So why would we need another muse? That's the question," she said.

Silence fell over the room like a wet blanket.

Clio nodded. "Excellent question, Nia." I watched Elnaz sink in her seat a little bit. Clio shut off the projector. "Thank you, Paola," she said, and Paola took her seat, jingling as she went. Clio folded her arms and took a deep breath before continuing.

"There have always been nine muses. Just nine. The clock has only chimed *after* a muse has quit the job or died. Never before," Clio said.

I felt a chill all of a sudden, so I rubbed my arms. It didn't help.

Tomiko's hand rose in the air, shaking a little.

"Tomiko?"

Tomiko cleared her throat, looking pale. "Does this mean the clock has turned prophet? Is it saying that one of us is going to—"

"I don't know what it means," Clio interrupted. "Let's not jump to conclusions, everyone."

Elnaz's hand went up next, sturdy and straight as an arrow. "What if the rules have simply changed? Where there were once nine, there will be ten. Simple."

"Not simple," Etoro said softly. "The rules of the gods do not change. Never has a god or goddess altered their mind once they've made it up. We are meant to be nine. Somehow, nine we will be."

My imagination raced on to places where I did not want it to go. The muses were my friends. The Muse Squad, especially, were some of my best friends. If one of them got hurt, or worse . . .

Clio interrupted my thinking, thank goodness. "The mystery of the tenth is our primary mission. It may be the biggest mission the muses have ever had. But let's not dwell on dark thoughts. There are answers to our questions and we must seek them out. To that end, I've been to Queens many times this summer, have followed up on all unusual cases of people performing acts of heroism, and cannot locate the new muse. All we have is a general indication that *somebody* in New York City has been identified by the muse finder clock, but no idea who or where this person might be."

"Aren't you going to New York, like, tomorrow?" Nia whispered to me.

I nodded.

"Convenient," Mela added, overhearing us. Her headphones rested around her neck, and she twiddled with the cord. They were new ones—super shiny, with a mirrorlike surface. Every once in a while, Mela would use them to check her lip gloss.

"Muse Squad time," Thalia said, rubbing her hands together.

My heart started racing. Suddenly, going to New York for the summer didn't feel like a drag. It felt like a job. A really important one. There was a mysterious tenth muse to locate, and my Muse Squad friends would be coming along for the action.

"It will take some time to plan our next steps, so I ask for your patience," Clio said. A wrinkle formed between her eyes, and her mouth was turned down farther than usual. "We will get to the bottom of this."

A loud bang resonated through the theater, startling all the muses. For a moment, I wondered if the Great Bed of Ware had fallen completely apart.

"That sound brings me to my next announcement," Clio said with a sigh. "You may have wondered why we haven't met in a while. What you are hearing is a construction crew beginning the process of dismantling the museum flooring. All of it has to come up, thanks to mold, so the V and A is closing for the next few months. Which means headquarters is changing places, and I've been drowning in paperwork."

"Oh no," Thalia said. She lived just around the corner, in Kensington.

The rest of us perked up. New headquarters? They could be anywhere! Egypt! Moscow! Hong Kong! Athens!

"Don't keep us waiting," Etoro said from her wheelchair in the front of the room. She'd been fanning herself throughout the meeting and whispering now and again to Paola.

"Of course," Clio said. "It seems to me that our current, shall we say, mystery makes our choice obvious. The next time we meet will be in the New York Hall of Science, in Queens."

Suddenly, everyone was talking at once, putting in entrance point requests—"No closets this time," Mela shouted, having once been stuck with a custodian's supply room as her entrance point—asking about time zone changes, and how far Queens was from Times Square.

Clio clapped her hands to quiet us. "I realize that you will leave today's meeting full of questions. But please know that I believe you all belong here, that you are the muses the world was meant to have." Clio looked at each of us, then she smiled. But it was the saddest smile I'd ever seen on a person. Maybe Clio was thinking that our group of nine wouldn't be *the* nine for much longer. My throat tightened. "We'll see one another in New York soon," Clio said, and passed around a plate full of brownies.

Mela, Nia, Thalia, and I chewed our brownies and talked with our mouths full as we left the theater.

"So I'm terrified. Anyone else feel that way?" Thalia said.

Nia shook her head. "Not me. I trust Clio to figure it out."

Mela handed half her brownie to Thalia. "I've lost my appetite," she said. "I'm only twelve. I have a whole life to live," she muttered.

Thalia slung an arm around Mela's shoulder. "Hey, I know tragedy is your thing, but maybe settle down a bit?"

"But what if one of us is in danger?" Mela asked.

"Then we have to protect one another," Nia said.

A thought sprang to mind, and I blurted it out before I could stop myself. "What if one of us is . . . broken? Like, not *meant* to be a muse."

The others stilled. We could hear the construction crews working on the V and A, and our own breathing.

"You are all thinking very loudly right now," Thalia muttered.

"Haven't you ever wondered?" I asked. "That maybe you didn't belong here? That the clock picked you by mistake?" These were secret thoughts, ones I'd never said out loud, though I'd been thinking about them from the beginning, when Clio first told me I was a muse. It felt good to say them now.

"All the time," Nia said. "Remember last year, when I couldn't get my magic to work without an app?"

Mela nodded. "Me, too. Back in January, remember? When I ruined the meeting because I couldn't stop thinking about my favorite TV show being canceled, and then everybody started crying?"

We all turned to look at Thalia.

"What?" she said. "I'm funny, I make people laugh. Confidence, people! Know what I mean?"

You could have heard a fly buzzing in that room.

"Fine," Thalia said after a beat. "I'm always afraid my jokes will *bomb*, and then everyone will know I'm a fraud. Now we're all properly miserable. Happy?" She plopped down on a nearby eighteenth-century throne and wiped her eyes.

That made me feel a lot better. They'd all had doubts about their place among the muses, too. All this time, I thought I'd been the only one having those feelings.

I thought about my magic, and how it was different now. "Okay, so we've all doubted ourselves. But . . . have any of you felt your magic changing lately?"

Mela looked at Nia, who shrugged. Thalia just wiped

her nose, then cleaned her hand on the throne's upholstery.

"Nope," Mela said.

"Me neither," Nia added.

"Same old, same old," Thalia said, and sniffed again. "Has *yours* changed?" she asked.

"Um, no. No. I was just wondering," I lied. How could I explain the way that my magic had gone from an easy-to-explain buzzing feeling on my skin to complex pictures in my brain, pictures of what could be?

I could see it just then, an image of the three of them, confident and cheerful, forming in my head. I willed it away, the way you can sometimes stop yourself from sneezing. I didn't know if this new ability was something I should be experimenting on friends with.

"You all right?" Nia asked, noticing the face I was making.

I was making an "I'm stopping myself from sneezing" face.

"I'm good," I said as I felt the magic drain away. But my friends looked so bummed out. They needed help. I was always good with a pep talk, even without magic.

"Here's the thing," I started. "We know we have magic. We've used it to inspire people like Maya. And how awesome is she? Super awesome. We are muses, and we are meant to be muses. This tenth muse thing—well, we'll just figure it out. Like we always figure stuff out. Together."

"Hear, hear," Thalia said, still a little sniffly.

"Well put," Mela whispered.

"Message received," Nia said. "The pity party ends now."

Thalia rose from the throne and gave it a little pat. "I'm still rather sad, though. We have to leave the V and A. I'll miss you," Thalia said to the suits of armor in the hallway, and to the tapestries on the wall.

"You live here in London. You can visit when the museum is open again," Nia said.

"Yes, but not *magically*," Thalia whined.

"I've never been to New York," Mela said, excitement in her voice.

"Me neither. But that will change tomorrow, I guess," I said.

We parted ways in front of the Great Bed of Ware. It looked lopsided.

"I think it's safe?" Nia said. She was still wearing the chain mail from the dress-up room. "But just in case." She pulled off the heavy vest and wrapped it around me.

"Here," Mela added, and shoved a knight's helmet on my head. "Don't get crushed."

"I won't be able to bring these back," I said a little sadly, my voice muffled behind the armor. So I took everything off again. "I think I'll be okay."

We hugged, and I watched as the others went their

separate ways to their own entrance points. It would be the last time we'd use them, and that made my eyes sting. Stupid tears. I hated them so much.

I thought of a new muse rule.

Callie's Muse Rule #347: Tears are annoying and dumb. Avoid if at all possible.

I wiped my eyes and walked over to the nearest window, which looked out at the courtyard below. There was a round pond, which was Thalia's entrance point. I watched until I saw her jump in the water and disappear. She'd end up in her bathtub back home. From here, I had a good view of the café, too. Nia wandered in, and I knew she'd be stepping into the beautiful fireplace that would take her to her own fireplace in Chicago. As for Mela, she was elsewhere, sliding behind a unicorn tapestry that would send her to New Delhi, behind the curtains in her living room.

My eyes wandered over to a wall near the café. I couldn't make out the letters of the dog tomb, which read TYCHO. But I knew that if I opened up the tomb, I'd find the portal to the other side, where Tia Annie was, guarding the source of muse magic. We called that magic the searchlights, because that's what they looked like.

We were leaving the V and A. I was leaving Tia Annie.

She'd told me not to come looking for her again.

She'd *told* me.

But this was my last chance to see her. Maybe she knew

about the tenth muse. Maybe she knew if one of the muses was in danger.

I glanced back at the Great Bed of Ware. "Sit tight," I said, as if the bed could hear me. Then I made for the stairs, the courtyard, and a dog's grave.

Chapter 4
PACKING UP THE V AND A

It was dark out, and even though it was early June, London was cold. Grass crunching underneath my feet, I made my way to the Tycho tomb.

I'd avoided the courtyard and the tomb ever since I saw Tia Annie for the last time. Her advice had helped us defeat the sirens. It was enough to know that Tia Annie, who had died when I was younger, existed beyond this life. The first time I saw her on the other side, I had pulled off the little plaque with the long-dead dog's name on it to reveal a wide green space and a lake that went on forever. There, on a boat, was my tia Annie. We had talked. She had given me advice. She even had given me a big hug and called me Callie-Mallie, like she used to.

Then she'd told me to go and not look back. I'd been good, following her advice, and totally avoiding the courtyard, mainly because it made me so sad to think that Tia Annie was there, just on the other side, and she didn't want me to seek her out.

But here I was again. I rested the tips of my fingers on the edge of the plaque. It was still somewhat loose, wiggling when I used just a little bit of force. My heart was pounding, and my knees shook. What if this time I went to where Tia Annie was and couldn't come back? What if she got angry with me?

"Oh, Tia Annie," I whispered. "I wish you could come out of there and be alive again."

I pulled the plaque off the wall, and there were poor old Tycho's bones again, in a pile off to the side. Last time, I'd pushed the back of the tomb to reveal a sunny, grassy plain, with water in the distance. Tia Annie was somewhere over there, on the other side.

I extended my arm into the tomb. My fingers grazed the back wall. I pushed.

Nothing happened.

I tried again, hitting it harder, but the wall wouldn't give.

"What are you doing?"

Startled, I fell backward, landing on my butt. Clio stood there, looking down at me. She held out her hand and I took it. Then she lifted me to my feet.

"Sorry," I said. "It's just, we're moving headquarters and—" I stopped. I had a good reason for what I was about to do, but I still knew it was wrong.

Clio held my hand. "Grief. It doesn't go away entirely. Some days, you think you've forgotten that you've lost someone important, and other days, it's all you can think about. It comes and goes, like a wave. If you're loved, and if you love, grief is a thing you'll experience eventually. It means you're human, Callie."

I wiped my cheeks, hating every single tear. Like I said, I cry more than I used to. Was that part of growing up? Because it was the worst.

"What was the last thing your aunt Annie said to you in there?" Clio asked.

"She said, 'Now go, Callie-Mallie.'"

Clio thought for a minute. "Something tells me you haven't done as you were asked. Part of you is still inside that place, with Annie. But she's not there. She's here," Clio said, pointing her finger at my heart.

I sniffed. "Cheesy," I said, but appreciated it anyway. I laid a hand on the plaque. "I did want to ask her something. Just one question, for me. I wanted to know what she asked of the gods on Mount Olympus."

"Hmm. She would have told you last time, don't you think, if she thought it was a thing for you to know?"

I didn't have an answer to that. Clio was probably right. "Tia Annie came to me in a dream. Twice," I said. That had been before our last meeting, though.

"Well then, if she wants to give you an answer to that

question, you can bet she will. Now, I have an office to pack. Would you like to help?"

I froze. The only time I'd spent one-on-one with Clio was when I'd been in trouble.

"Um. Okay," I said, and followed Clio back through the museum.

Clio's office was a mess. Every drawer of every file cabinet was open. Cardboard boxes covered the floor and her desk. And here and there, plates with chocolaty crumbs littered the empty spaces.

"You sure do love to bake," I said.

"My mother was a wonderful baker," Clio said. "It reminds me of her." Her voice broke a little on "her."

Waves. I thought of how Clio had just described grief, and took a guess as to why she suddenly sounded so sad.

Clio handed me a big, dusty box and pointed at a shredder in the corner. "Shred the files in here, please, and I'll get started on my desk drawers."

The box was heavy and musty. I set it down on the floor and sat cross-legged beside it. The papers inside were yellowing. Some were held together by rusty paper clips. All the writing was in Greek, and there were no photographs. The shredder made a loud whirring noise as the pages went through it, spitting out paper noodles on the other side.

It helped to do a boring job. It cleared my head a lot, so that I wasn't thinking about Tia Annie or having to say goodbye to the V and A, which I'd grown to love.

I was reaching into the box for the last file when my fingers brushed cloth. Clio was underneath her desk, working at a drawer that was jammed shut and muttering angrily to herself. I grabbed the cloth and lifted it.

It was heavy, like a rug had been folded into the bottom of the box.

But it wasn't a rug. It was more like a tapestry, similar to the ones that hung all over the museum.

Except this was the most beautiful tapestry I had ever seen. As I opened it up, the tapestry seemed to grow larger in my hands. I could have sworn it wasn't much bigger than a tablecloth when it was inside the box, but now, out of the box, it seemed to be wall-sized.

In fact, I could barely lift it.

"Magic," I whispered. Clio didn't hear me. My fingers trembled as I laid out as much of the tapestry as I could. The enormous cloth had five pictures on it, each image set off by metallic thread that glittered in the dim office light. There was a scene in the center, and then four others taking up the corners. I smoothed my hand over the central image to get the wrinkles out and took a good look.

The central image was of a gorgeous woman wearing a golden helmet, facing off against a man with long, flowing hair, holding a trident. He looked like Ariel's dad from *The Little Mermaid*. *Poseidon*, I thought. The god of the sea. But who was the woman? Then I noticed that she held a spear and she was pointing it at a little tree, full of fruit. As for Poseidon, the end of his trident was buried in the ground, and water was pouring out.

The picture to the left caught my eye. It was pretty plain. Just two snowcapped mountains. But the snow really seemed to sparkle in the light, and I could swear that looking at it made me a little chilly, like I was on that mountain.

The next image showed a tall stork with white feathers, its wings outstretched as if it were about to take off. The bird was surrounded by a bunch of guys holding swords, and the look in their eyes told me that they would be having stork stew for dinner.

There was another bird in the next scene. A crane maybe? It was flying through the sky, and it was crying, tears streaming down its beak. But here was the weird thing—the bird had hair. Really long, pretty brown hair. I touched my own wavy hair, and noticed it was snarled, which was pretty much a permanent thing with me. I never met a hairbrush I didn't eventually snap in half.

The final picture depicted another weeping figure. This time it was a man—by the look of his crown, he was a king. He was sitting on a cliff, sobbing. Below him were many people who appeared to be flailing about in the water. The man looked so sad that my jaw started to ache, the way it sometimes felt when I might cry. It got so bad I wondered if Mela was nearby, using her magic on me.

The tapestry was beautiful. In fact, it was so beautiful that it made me a little dizzy looking at it. But it also made me nervous in a way I couldn't entirely explain.

Suddenly, I heard a gasp. "Where did you find that?" Clio asked in a whisper.

I let go of the tapestry. "In the box with the files to be shredded," I said really quickly.

Clio shut her eyes and tilted her face to the ceiling. Her nostrils flared. I'd seen that look before on my mom. It was a look that said, "Your room better be clean this time, Callie, or so help me."

But I hadn't done anything wrong, had I?

"I can't believe that Athena's tapestry was in that dusty box all these years," Clio said with a sigh.

"Athena? As in *the* Athena?"

"Daughter of Zeus, Dread Goddess, goddess of wisdom, courage, war, et cetera, et cetera." Clio approached the tapestry, holding it up to take it in. "It's been lost for ages. Deadly thing," she whispered as she looked at each panel.

I took two huge steps backward. "D-deadly?"

Clio nodded. "Well, technically that's not the right word. Arachne wasn't exactly killed."

I took another step back. I had no idea who this Arachne was. "Who's that?" I asked.

The tapestry fell out of Clio's hand. "Honestly, you don't know?"

I shook my head.

Clio started muttering in Greek. Probably something about how much I still had to learn.

I waited for her to finish. When she did, she took a steadying breath before explaining.

"Arachne was a regular girl, about your age. She was marvelously skilled at weaving and boasted about her talent all the time. Arachne wasn't wrong. She truly was the best weaver the world had ever known. But the gods never liked to be bested at anything, and Athena, goddess of wisdom and war, and so many other things, was also the goddess of woven arts.

"They held a weaving competition. Athena and Arachne both worked at their looms, and when they were done, the people who had been watching declared that Arachne's tapestry was the finer of the two.

"However, instead of saying, 'No, no, Athena's is better,' as was expected of her as a human facing a god in a contest, Arachne simply said, 'Yes, I know.' In her rage at being so disrespected, Athena tore Arachne's tapestry into four pieces and flung them to parts unknown. Then she turned Arachne into a spider, so that she might learn not to be so proud but could continue to weave as her heart desired. Webs instead of tapestries, of course."

Clio ran her fingers over Athena's cloth. It really did feel deadly all of a sudden. But I needed to know more. "What do the pictures mean?"

Clio waved me over, and I approached cautiously. "The center image is a contest between Athena and Poseidon, held in order to determine who would get to name the great city of Athens. Poseidon presented the people with a gift of spring water. Athena gave them the olive tree. The people went with olives, and the city became Athens forevermore."

Athena liked contests, I guess. But only if she won them. "Go on," I said.

Clio pointed at the two mountains. "These mountains were once people. A king and queen who dared compare themselves to Zeus and Hera, the king and queen of all the gods. So the humans were turned into mountains as a punishment for their pride."

I was sensing a theme. "How about this one?" I asked, tapping the picture of the stork.

"Another queen. Gerana was her name. She claimed to be prettier than Hera, so she was transformed into a stork. And her own people hunted her down." Clio moved on to the other bird, the one with the hair. "This crane was once a girl named Antigone. She was from Troy."

"Let me guess. She was really into her hair," I said.

"Indeed," Clio responded. "She compared it to Hera's."

"Hera didn't like that and turned her into a crane, right?"

"You're getting it," Clio said. "What do you think of the last image?"

This was the one with the crying man, weeping on a cliff while the people below flapped about in the sea. "I'm guessing he angered Hera," I said with a shrug.

"Not this time. This king did not keep a promise to his friend, who then cursed him. So Apollo drowned his fifty daughters."

"Whoa," I said. "First of all, fifty daughters? And second of all, I didn't know the gods were so . . ." I paused. I was suddenly scared. "The daughters were innocent. I didn't realize the gods could be so mean."

Clio made a sound like "hmm" in the back of her throat. "I suppose the tapestry was a warning against having too much pride. Arachne should have been paying attention."

"Hubris," I said. It meant having excessive pride. I'd run into that myself last year. Everybody knew bragging wasn't great, and nobody liked conceited people. And yet something bugged me about the Arachne story. "But Arachne was right. Her tapestry was the best one. She won fair and square."

"The gods are the gods," Clio said. "They require deference." I must have given Clio a really blank look, because she added, "Deference. It means respect. And humility. The gods demanded it once."

"Then the gods weren't being fair," I said before I could stop myself. I wrapped my arms around my chest, half expecting to be struck by lightning or something. "Just because they were in charge, that didn't give them the right to be cruel," I said in a whisper. I remembered what Etoro had said at the meeting about how the gods never changed their minds. What kind of people didn't admit it when they were wrong? It just didn't seem fair.

You're a goddess, too, a voice whispered in my head. Not *a* voice—*my* voice. And suddenly I wasn't so sure I wanted to be on the same team as Hera, Athena, and Apollo.

"This was long ago," Clio tried to explain further.

"But it doesn't make it right," I said.

Clio finished folding up the tapestry. "You are correct. Just because something we know is bad *now* happened many years ago, doesn't mean it wasn't bad *then*, too." She closed the dusty box and wiped her hands on her pants. Then she came over to me and put her hands on my shoulders. "But we are here now to make things right."

I didn't realize it, but my arms were still tight across my chest.

"Clio, I should probably get going," I said. "Lots to pack back at my place, too. The Big Apple awaits!" I said, trying to sound cheerful.

Clio patted my cheek softly. "Of course. You've got a big summer adventure ahead of you. Here, take a brownie for the road." She wrapped one up in a napkin for me, and I slid it into my pocket for later. "I've got lots to do, too. Including fixing the Great Bed of Ware," she said with a wink.

"Oh," I said, my stomach sinking a little. "You know about that?"

"I know lots of things. Run along now. I'll see you in New York." With that, Clio returned to the messy piles all over her office, and I started toward the door but then stopped again.

"Clio, did you mean what you said about how all of us muses are meant to be here? To be muses? Even if the muse finder clock chimed?"

Clio looked at me with those sad eyes again. "Yes, Callie. I believe this with all my heart."

"Then why is there a tenth muse? It doesn't make sense."

Clio looked thoughtful, then she shrugged. "We'll have to wait and see what answers we can find on our own."

My eyes rested on Athena's tapestry, and another idea came to mind. "What if it's a test, like the weaving contest? What if the gods are testing all of us? Or one of us?"

Clio straightened the files on her desk into a neat column. "A test can be passed or failed," she said, then looked at me. "And I won't let us fail, I promise you."

Walking back to my entrance point, I tried to really focus on my surroundings, saying goodbye to the V and A in my head. But I couldn't concentrate. The Arachne story and everything I'd heard about the gods' punishments kept cutting in. I felt nervous all over.

I got to the Great Bed faster than I'd hoped. I patted its scratchy bedcover, grabbed on to one of the wooden posts, and whispered, "Goodbye, Great Bed. I'll miss you," before blinking back tears (stupid, stupid tears) and sliding underneath.

As I closed my eyes, I remembered four things that made me even *more* nervous:

I forgot to ask Clio what had been on Arachne's tapestry—the *winning* tapestry.

I'd just had two freaky spider-related things happen to me in less than three hours.

There was a chance one of the nine muses wasn't going to be a muse for much longer.

This time tomorrow I'd be in New York City.

Chapter 5
LOST IN LAGUARDIA

It was my first time flying. When the plane took off, I gripped the armrests tightly. Before I knew it, Miami was just a map far below me, the highways marking off the city into grids. Every house was a small shoebox, and in the distance, the blue ocean sparkled.

The flight attendant, a blond woman named Roxy, came by every so often to check up on me. Roxy was the kind of grown-up who perched her hands on her knees to ask a kid a question. "How old are you?" "What's your favorite school subject?" "Ever been to New York?" She brought me cookies and a soda, and even though I turned twelve in May, she gave me a little pilot's pin to wear, then booped my nose.

I watched an episode of *Zombie Beach* on the plane (through my fingers, of course), and then dozed off, waking up with a jolt when the plane landed and every-body started clapping. I clapped, too. We'd made it. I was in New York!

But when I got off the plane, I couldn't find Roxy. She was supposed to walk with me to the exit once we landed at LaGuardia Airport, but in the crush of passengers, I lost her. Panicked, I got onto a courtesy shuttle and ended up in Terminal B. It felt like I was going in circles, pushed around by people and their rolling luggage. I couldn't even hear myself think! Airline employees on microphones kept saying things like "We board by group," and "Sorry for the delay," and "This flight is overbooked," and every time one of them talked, people shuffled about, shoving me out of the way.

Mami had said, "Don't be nervous. Read the signs over-head. Call your papi when you land."

I'm here, I texted Papi.

Yay! he texted back. Exit your terminal. I'll be waiting for you there.

Oh-oh, I thought. Which terminal? Where was the exit again?

I can do this, I told myself.

I sat in a corner and blew out great big puffs of air, trying to stop myself from panicking. I pulled out my phone, but now I didn't have any service. Waving my phone around in the air didn't help either. I scanned the signs overhead. Where were the exit signs, anyway? They read "Gate 24," or "Ground Transportation," or "Baggage Claim," but not one said "Exit This Way."

How do I get out of here? I wondered. A woman with a toddler on a leash glanced at me on the way to the restroom. Without thinking, I pictured her helping me out, hoping she would.

The woman stopped, turned around, hoisted her little boy onto her hip, and approached me. "Need help?" she asked kindly.

I silently thanked the gods for magic and the kindness of strangers.

"Yes, please," I said. "How do you exit this terminal?"

"Follow me," the woman said with a wink. Over her shoulder, the toddler blew wet raspberries at me, and I crossed my eyes at him. "Voilà!" she said, pointing at the exit. "Now where are those toilets," she muttered to herself, and rushed back into the terminal.

Flooded with relief, I took a good look around. I saw Papi before he saw me, his dark eyes scanning the crowd for a girl in a Yankees hoodie.

"Papi!" I called out, and my dad turned his big eyes on me.

"Callie!" he said, and came running. He put his heavy arms around me and hoisted me a few feet in the air. "My girl. How I've missed you!"

I had forgotten what he smelled like (ink and tobacco), and how strong he was (very), and how his rumbly voice shook something loose in my chest. Oh, Papi. I hadn't realized how *much* I'd missed him.

And you know what?

It felt like home.

Papi and I took a bus from LaGuardia to his house. Actually, the bus dropped us off directly in front of the Hall of Science—our new muse headquarters! I could see it just past a stand of tall trees, thick with leaves. Off to one side there was a rocket, as tall as a building. Beside that was the museum itself, with the words "New York Hall of Science" in big silver letters above glass doors.

"We live just down the block," Papi said, tugging me away from the museum. We turned off 111th Street and onto Forty-Ninth Avenue. I kept my eyes on the signs, trying to remember the street names. Papi and Laura didn't have a car, and I knew that if I wanted to get around, I was going to have to walk, ride a bus, or get on the subway like a real New Yorker.

"So this is Queens?" I asked.

Papi nodded. "Yes. And the neighborhood is called Corona. When we visit Manhattan, we can catch the 7 train at 111th Street station just a few blocks that way." He pointed vaguely to the right.

"Got it," I said, though I didn't really. Not yet, at least. Two-story brick houses lined both sides of the road. Wires crossed overhead, and here and there sneakers dangled by their laces from the wires. The air was hot and smelled a little sweet. Windows were open on some of the houses, and I could hear people talking in Spanish. Off in the distance, one block over, I spotted some shops—a nail salon, a small grocery store, a tattoo place.

If I swapped the brick for stucco, and the tall trees for palms, Corona would be a bit like Miami, I thought.

We stopped in front of a house that looked different from the rest. Instead of brick, this house had wood panels across the front, and they were painted a cheery yellow. The paint was peeling in places, and someone had tied plastic daisies to the railing around the front porch. The flowers were faded and missing a lot of petals.

"Home," Papi said, hoisting my suitcase in the air to climb the porch steps.

I'd never lived in a house with stairs! I already imagined sliding down the banister. And was there a basement? Or an attic that wasn't just a crawl space? Miami homes didn't have any of those things. I started to feel a little flutter of excitement. This was going to be so cool!

But then Papi opened the door, and we were staring directly at a very narrow and dark staircase. "We're on the second floor," he said, leading the way.

"So you don't live in the whole house?" I asked.

Papi made a sucking sound. "You wouldn't believe how high the rents are in New York. We can only afford half a house, but it's still home," he said.

Off to the right was a tight hallway and another door. Beyond the door, I could hear someone laughing while a television game show host told a joke. Those would be the downstairs neighbors, I guessed. If there was a basement, we wouldn't have access to it anyway.

I followed Papi up. The stairs creaked really loudly, and I realized that there wasn't a bannister, or even a handrail. The walls were dingy from people's handprints, too. At the top of the stairs was another door. Papi unlocked it and pushed inside.

"Welcome home!" Laura shouted. She was wearing a paper crown. In one arm, she held my brother, Rafael Jr. In the other hand, she had a fistful of pink confetti, which she tossed up into the air. A glittery banner behind her read "Welcome!" The place smelled wonderful—like onions, garlic, and ground beef simmering in a pot somewhere.

I stepped into the apartment, which was bright, clean, and very modern.

Laura grinned at me, confetti stuck to her hair and the baby's.

"Hi," I said, stepping forward to give Laura a kiss on the cheek.

"I made you a welcome dinner. And we can go get ice cream afterward. You're going to love New York, I just know it!" Laura said.

"This is Rafaelito," Papi said, taking the baby from

Laura and handing him over to me.

"Hey," I said. Rafaelito, not Rafael Jr. So that's what they called him. I had been mad when I first heard about the baby, just like my brothers were. I'd thought Papi would forget all about his Miami kids.

But now, looking at Rafaelito, I had a hard time finding that angry feeling. His eyes were big and brown, and he smiled at me right away, drooling a little on his tiny chin. I nuzzled the top of his head and took a deep breath. He smelled like Cuban baby cologne—agua de violetas. I still had a bottle in my room back in Miami. Laura must have just doused him in the stuff. Rafaelito looked like Papi. I could already tell he was going to have Papi's thick eyebrows, and his sticking-out ears. But his eyes were Laura's, and his hair was a lighter brown than mine and Papi's.

A small, chubby hand came to rest on my cheek.

"He loves you already," Laura said.

I didn't say anything, but I could feel it inside—I'd do anything for this kid.

On the spot I came up with Callie's Muse Rule #427: Baby brothers are worth fighting for.

I handed Rafaelito back to Laura.

"Can I use the bathroom? Wash off the airplane germs?"

"Claro," Papi said. "I'll take your bag to Rafaelito's room."

"We set up a bed for you," Laura added.

In the bathroom, I washed my hands. There was

honey-scented soap at the sink, and the towels were gray and monogrammed in silver with Laura's and Papi's initials. The grout in the shower sparkled. The faucet was sleek and shiny. The house in Corona might have looked run-down on the outside, but the inside was nice, and Laura really had a knack for decorating. I could hear her running the vacuum, already making the confetti disappear. I made sure the hand towel was neatly folded when I finished with it.

I left the bathroom, went down the hall, and found the room I'd be staying in. It was Rafaelito's room, painted in a soft green. There was a forest mural on the wall opposite his crib. A navy blue rug took up the center of the room, and it was so soft that I had to touch it. There, under the window, was my bed.

"Sorry. A pin-pan-pun is all we could fit in here," Papi said from the doorway.

Back in Miami, we had a pin-pan-pun, or a foldaway bed, stored in the garage. Mami said they'd once used it for relatives who'd come from Cuba long ago, back when people showed up unexpectedly and needed a place to stay for a few months while they got themselves sorted in a new country. She said it was called a pin-pan-pun because you could open it up in three steps. Pin! Pan! Pun! And because it creaked in a way that sounded like those words.

Pin! Pan! Pun! went the bed when I sat on it. But it was comfortable in spite of the noise.

"I'm sorry," Papi said again. "The couch might be comfier if you prefer. Or we can get an air mattress. Whatever you want, mi niña."

"It's okay. I'm starving. Let's eat."

Papi smiled, threw an arm around me, and we walked off to the small kitchen, where Laura had prepared a feast. We ate picadillo and white rice, and Laura even put raisins in the ground beef, just how I liked it! There were plantains to eat, avocado and tomato salad, and fresh-squeezed orange juice.

Halfway through the meal, Laura made a toast. "To Callie," she said, holding up her glass.

"Callie. Home in New York," Papi said.

Rafaelito gurgled in his high chair, smashing his hands into his rice.

"Okay. To me, then," I said, feeling a little uncomfortable, but loved and full.

After dinner, Laura loaded Rafaelito up into a baby sling that she wore across her front, a contraption that Papi called "el canguro." And he was right, she did sort of look like a kangaroo carrying a joey around.

We left the apartment and walked a few blocks for that ice cream Laura promised. I was expecting an ice-cream shop, with a long cooler in front loaded with buckets of ice cream in all kinds of flavors. I expected sticky floors and a teenager behind the cooler, ice-cream scooper in hand.

Instead, we stopped in front of what looked like a convenience store. A sign out front read "The Queen of Corona," with neon crowns on top of the Q and the C. Outside the store, fresh flowers sat in buckets of water. Signs in the windows advertised $2.99 bags of coffee, and another sign read: "We Accept Food Stamps."

"Ice cream?" I asked.

"You'll see," Papi answered.

We went inside. It definitely was a convenience store, but not like one I'd ever been to.

"It's a bodega, Callie," Laura said.

I felt something warm brush against my legs. Looking down, I saw an orange tabby cat, purring like an engine around my ankles.

"And that's a bodega cat," Laura added with a laugh.

The place was packed with stuff—there were about forty mops leaning against one another on one wall, a shelf full of candles, three aisles of canned food, an entire corner dedicated to fresh fruit and vegetables, toys on one end of the store, refrigerators packed with drinks against another wall, and a lot more. Who knew such a small place could hold so much?

It was also full of people. Three women chattered over tomatoes, while another two were taking turns sniffing air fresheners. I could hear the rackety noise of dominoes in the air and searched the place until I found a small table in the back, where four men played a game in silence, the tiles clattering loudly as they swirled them around on the tabletop. A couple of kids my age—two boys—were in the chips aisle choosing snacks.

"Callie, over here," I heard Papi call.

I found them in a little room off to the side. There they were, the coolers full of ice cream! And so many flavors. Dulce de leche, and pumpkin, and marshmallow, and café con leche, and banana, and caramel, and apple pie. I'd never seen so many flavors.

"Hard to choose, right?" said a girl behind the cooler.

"Oh. Yeah. It's amazing."

"Thanks," she said. Her name tag read ARI, and she looked about my age. Her hair was very dark, long, and parted down the middle. Her skin was very pale. She wore a black T-shirt and black jeans. And she was wearing lots of black eyeliner, too. The only spot of color was on her wrists, which were full of bright friendship bracelets.

"You work here?" I asked. She didn't seem older than twelve or thirteen.

Ari shook her head. "Just killing time. My aunt owns the place. She's around here somewhere. So what do you want?"

"Huh?"

"Ice cream. Which flavor, I mean. I'll load one up for you." Ari waved a scooper at me.

"Um, dulce de leche," I said.

Papi got the same, and Laura chose banana. There was

nowhere to eat the ice cream except right there in front of the coolers. But Ari didn't seem to mind. I watched as she rinsed the scooper. Then she dried her hands and pulled a half-made friendship bracelet out of her pocket. This one was orange, green, and white. Ari started making knots really quickly, and I understood why she had so many bracelets.

"So, Ari," my father interrupted between bites of ice cream.

Ari looked up, her eyebrows raised.

"You go to Corona Arts Academy?"

Ari put a hand on her hip. "What are you? Sherlock Holmes?"

My heart skipped a beat. This kid just back-talked to my dad like it was nothing. *Nobody* back-talked Papi. Ever.

Then Papi cleared his throat, and he pointed at a back-pack on the floor by the sink. It, too, was black, but it read "Corona Arts Academy" in hot pink letters.

Ari looked to where he was pointing, then smirked. "Wondered what gave it away."

"Are you attending the summer session?" Laura asked. She was still wearing the canguro and was now bouncing because Rafaelito had started to make noises. The bouncing seemed to help.

Ari nodded. "Keeps me busy and out of trouble, my aunt says." She shrugged and resumed making her bracelet.

"Callie here is going to Corona Arts, too. Starting Monday," Papi announced.

I coughed up a blob of ice cream and didn't stop coughing until Laura pounded on my back a few times.

"What?" I asked when I got my voice back.

"Like she said. Keeping you busy and out of trouble," Papi said. "Laura and I work all day. Rafaelito goes to day care. I can't have you home alone for four weeks."

"What?!" I hadn't counted on having to go to summer school, or camp, or whatever this Corona Arts Academy was. And if it was full of strange kids like this Ari, kids who had the nerve to talk back to my father, then I really didn't want to go. Besides, I had an important muse mission. How was I going to get in and out of school when I needed to?

Laura cleared her throat, saying she needed to pick up a salad for tomorrow's dinner, leaving me, Papi, and Ari alone.

"I can stay home alone. I promise."

"No arguments, Callie."

"But Papi," I started.

"You might have fun," Ari put in.

"Nobody asked you," I shot back.

Then, silence.

I wasn't usually that rude, especially not with a stranger. I chanced a look at Papi, and his face was full of disappointment.

"Is that how you talk to people in Miami?" Papi asked, his voice low and serious.

I'm sorry, what? Did he not catch Ari's attitude a few minutes ago?

I walked over to the garbage can and threw out my half-eaten ice-cream cone. "I want to go home," I said.

"Bien," Papi said, throwing out his ice cream, too. "Let's go."

But I didn't mean back to his apartment.

I heard Papi calling Laura's name in the bodega and watched as they went to the cash register to pay for a head of lettuce.

"Hey, Corona Arts isn't bad," Ari said, back at work on her bracelet. Unbelievably, she'd just about finished it. "Here," she said, tying the last knot and handing it to me. The bracelet's colors reminded me of Miami. Green like the trees, orange like the sun, white like clouds, and Mami's rice, and my house. My eyes prickled with tears.

"Like I said, it isn't bad. And the best part is the Student Showcase. At least, that's what the kids at school tell me," said Ari.

"So you're new to Corona Arts, too?" I asked, but Ari didn't answer. She just walked off into the store, trailing her finger over the cans on the nearby shelves.

"Thanks," I said out loud, though I couldn't tell if she'd heard me. I put the friendship bracelet alongside my muse bracelet. They sort of went well together. I tied it off, using my free hand and my teeth.

"Callie, vamos," Papi called.

By now Rafaelito was wailing. Outside the sun was setting, and Laura started to complain about the baby's "witching hour." "Sorry in advance, Callie," she said. "Nobody gets any sleep in our place thanks to him."

Great, I thought. The pin-pan-pun awaited, and with a pang I remembered the Great Bed of Ware, and my own bed in Miami. A police car roared by in the distance, the siren blasting.

Rafaelito cried even harder.

That night, I called Mami, who wanted to know all about New York City.

"I haven't seen much," I started to say, but I could hear my brothers asking for the phone, and Mami soon handed it over.

"How's it going, dork?" Fernando asked.

I bristled. That was one good thing about being in New York—I didn't have to deal with the twins' pranks. "That sticky note joke hurt my feelings, you should know that," I said.

Mario spoke up. "Get tough and get even then."

"Speaking of tough, how's Papi treating you?" Fernando asked.

"Okay," I whispered. "He's making me go to summer camp."

The twins laughed. "Told you to stay home this summer. You could be watching TV all day instead of going to some camp," said Fernando.

I could hear Papi and Laura chatting in the kitchen. "Do you want to talk to Papi?" I asked.

My brothers were quiet for a moment. "No, that's okay," Mario said.

I recalled how they'd reacted when they'd learned our baby brother's new name. Rafael, named after my dad. They didn't say anything, but I know they were thinking it—how come neither one of them got his name? I remembered when Papi left, how Mario and Fernando had teamed up against our dad, shouting at him and, later, refusing to talk with him on the phone.

But my brothers were tough. They didn't complain. If they were feeling some kind of way about Papi, they kept it to themselves to spare Mami and me. I looked up to them, which is why I hated the tears that sprang to my eyes every once in a while.

"Have fun at camp," Fernando added, breaking the silence. Then we hung up.

Papi stuck his head into my room. "Was that the boys?" he asked. I nodded. "Ay, I wanted to talk with them," he said, disappointment all over his face.

"They're busy, I guess," I said.

Papi came over and sat beside me on the pin-pan-pun. It squealed and dropped several inches. He slung his arm around me and squeezed. "I'm glad you're here, Callie." Then he dropped a loud kiss on the top of my head.

"Me, too, Papi," I said.

When he left the room, I searched my feelings. Was it even true? Was I glad to be in New York? In Miami, I knew exactly what to expect. Miami Callie had it all figured out. Miami Callie could sometimes forget that her parents were divorced, or that her aunt was dead, because in Miami, everything was familiar and comfortable. In New York, it was all different. New York Callie was all mixed up, like food that didn't belong together on one plate. Mami would describe it as an "arroz con mango" situation. And in New York, that's exactly what I felt like—a big old dish of mangoes and rice, all mushed together.

What had Mario said? "Get tough and get even." I had nothing to get even for, but I could get tough. I'd be going to a new school in a few days, full of new kids, in a new city. Could I be tough? I really hoped so.

Chapter 6
CORONA ARTS ACADEMY

Getting ready for summer camp was a lot like preparing for the start of a new school year. Over the weekend, Papi and Laura had taken me shopping, and they'd bought me a few new outfits, and a little backpack for my phone, keys, and a just-for-me subway MetroCard preloaded with some money. "Your official New York ID," Papi had said, handing it over.

The night before camp, I'd set out a pair of new white jeans and a plain blue T-shirt to wear, and made sure my bag had everything I needed. It felt good to be prepared, but inside, I was still all rice and mangoes.

Papi, Laura, and I walked over to Corona Arts right after breakfast. Rafaelito sat snug in his sling the whole way. Corona Arts looked like any other school. It was a big two-story building, with a flagpole outside, and "Slow!

Children Crossing" signs up and down the street.

"Why summer school?" I whined. We'd had a great weekend, going to the top of the Empire State Building, visiting Times Square at night when it was all lit up like a carnival, and finally, visiting Grand Central Terminal's whispering gallery. In a tiled area of the station, Papi had stood on one end of an arched wall and whispered, "I love you, Callie." I could hear him clear across the big room near another arch! Papi called it an "acoustic oddity." Maya would have been able to explain how it worked in detail, but I just thought it was super cool.

But Papi and Laura had to go to work now, and summer camp was directly in my future.

"Oh, come on," Papi said. "It's an arts program. You always loved art!"

"Yeah, back when the only thing I had to do was color inside the lines." I was feeling grouchy. Rafaelito was, as advertised, not a good sleeper. He cried all night, and the pin-pan-pun was springy and uncomfortable after all.

"Look at the art," Laura said encouragingly. She was pointing at a pair of sculptures that flanked the front doors. They were papier-mâché bulls, their horns sculpted out of pipe cleaners.

"I'm looking," I said, and left it at that. What I really wanted to say was that I didn't need to go to an arts program, not when I got to hang out with the Muses of dance and music, drama and comedy, science and history, and love songs and sacred hymns *on the regular.*

Well, maybe not so regularly. I touched my bracelet and wondered what the rest of the Muse Squad was up to, and when Clio would call us to our new headquarters. I hadn't heard from anybody in days. And it wasn't just the muses. I hadn't been able to get hold of Maya either, except for last night, when she'd texted me a GIF from the movie *Apollo 13*, along with a big thumbs-up emoji. I guess she was having fun at Space Camp.

Papi gave me a kiss on the top of my head and a little shove in the direction of the front door.

"Dale," he whispered. "Que tu puedes."

I looked back at them. Laura was smiling, Rafaelito was drooling, and Papi had his arm around them both.

You can do it, Papi had said. I took a deep breath, turned around, and pushed open the front doors.

It may have looked like every other school on the outside, but inside, Corona Arts was *nothing at all* like a regular school. Salsa music was blaring from the speakers, and a wide circle of students were dancing a rueda right there in the center of the school. They formed six couples and were dancing together, synchronized, every so often switching partners. It was awesome.

I peered down a hallway and saw students painting lockers—there were landscapes, and portraits, and abstract shapes. They chatted as they worked, dipping into palettes loaded with more colors than I could name.

A loud knocking sound drew me to another set of doors, and when I pushed through them, I saw a theater, and a bunch of kids on a stage, hammering away at sets. They were building a castle, complete with a turret.

And down the center aisle of the theater was a beautiful runner made of bright red and silver thread, with tassels on either end. It sparkled like Christmas. That's where I saw her—Ari—sewing on the last of the tassels.

There's nothing like a familiar face in a new place. I hadn't realized I'd been grinding my back teeth until I saw her. Feeling a bit more relaxed, I went down one of the rows of seats and stood off to the side.

"Hey, Ari!"

"Hey," she said without looking up. "Welcome to Corona Arts. Have you found your poets yet?"

She still hadn't looked at me. How did she know it even *was* me?

"Um, no? Do I need to find poets for some reason?"

I watched as Ari tied the final knot in the fat tassel she was holding. She looked up at me at last and stood, her knees creaking like a grown-up's.

"The poets are your artist group. I saw your name on the class list. From the look on your face, not a first choice, I gather? The other groups were probably full, is the thing. I'm with textile arts," she said, flashing her armful of bracelets at me. "Those kids are set design," she added, nodding toward the people onstage. "There's dance, visual arts, musicians, singers. Then there's the poets." She said that last one with a wiggle of her eyebrows.

"Poets?"

"And you don't even know it!" Ari added, laughing to herself. "Come on."

I followed her out of the theater. We passed the kids dancing the rueda, and even though I couldn't dance, I watched them longingly. That seemed so fun. We marched past the painters, who were now flicking globs of paint at each other. Also, fun. But poetry?

I know, I know. My secret identity was Muse of the epic poem. But that just meant I was good at hero-making. That's what epic poems *do*. They tell the stories of great heroes. It didn't mean I wrote *actual* poems.

Poetry sounded like homework.

And homework is such a pain.

Ari led me to a staircase, and as we climbed farther away from the noise downstairs, everything grew quiet. "Corona Arts has been around for a long time. It relies mostly on rich donors for the supplies, the teacher salaries, the camp scholarships, which everyone is on. Most of the kids here are from Queens. Nobody's paying a lot for summer camp, you know?"

I nodded. Papi was an AC installation contractor. Laura worked as an office assistant at Queensborough Community College. Rafaelito's day care was expensive enough, as were my plane tickets. I thought about Ari's aunt, owning the bodega. I wondered what her parents did for a living.

Ari stopped at a window on the stair landing. It was dirty, so she rubbed off a clean spot with her elbow. Beyond was Queens—all brick buildings and storefronts. Off to the right I spotted the rocket at the Hall of Science.

"I love Queens. It's definitely better than the place I was before this," Ari said.

"Where were you be—"

She cut me off. "And this school has been the best. But there are rumors that the donors are pulling out. That they aren't impressed with what we're doing here."

"How could they not be impressed? Everybody is so talented!"

Ari shrugged. "I've only been here since January, but from what I've seen, I think everyone is really talented, too. The donors are coming to the Student Showcase in a few weeks. It's a chance to show them Corona Arts is worth investing in."

I thought of everything I'd seen so far. And the day was just starting. Ari looked pretty dejected, but there was just something about her. Something . . . heroic.

"But you want to save this school, right?" I asked.

Ari nodded. "I want to save a lot of things."

I pictured Ari at the Student Showcase, the whole school applauding as she held a check with enough zeroes in it to save the school. The picture in my head got clearer and clearer.

Ari's dark eyes met mine. They were shiny, but her stare was intense. She took a step away from me. Then another.

I faltered. "Okay," I said. In my head, the picture of Ari grew more detailed and more vivid. "I bet you can do it. I think you can help save this school, show those donors how awesome this place can be. I'll help," I said, putting as much cheer into my voice as I could.

Ari stared at me for a tick, then burst out laughing.

"You are super, and I mean *super* weird," she said.

"I get that a lot," I admitted. I let the image in my head fade to nothing.

Ari narrowed her eyes at me. "Come on, poet. If you want to help me save Corona Arts, you'd better start your scribbling."

I followed her to a classroom that had only one other person in it. The girl had dark brown hair in a bun, with a pencil sticking out of it. She was wearing a Wonder Woman T-shirt and a pair of jeans. Her head popped up as soon as we walked in.

"Maris, meet your new poet."

"I'm Callie," I said, and waved.

Maris regarded me with a serious expression. "I wish my name was Emily, but Maris will have to do. I'm going to change it when I get older—I decided at the age of six, as soon as I read Dickinson."

"Dickinson?" I asked.

At that, Maris groaned, threw down the pen she was

holding, and stalked out of the room.

"Don't mind her. You just insulted her favorite poet, Emily Dickinson. She'll get over it," Ari said. Then she spun me around and clapped me on the back. "Have fun poem-ing!" she sang as she skipped out of the room.

Here's how my first day at Corona Arts went.

First, I insulted Maris Emad by not realizing that Emily Dickinson was a pretty famous poet. It was just me and Maris in the poet group, and the fact that she didn't speak to me for the first two hours of camp made things pretty awkward.

I met Mr. Theo, our artist group leader, who had us writing limericks all morning. Mine went like this:

> *There was a young girl from Miami*
> *Who wished she was home in her jammies.*
> *She thought poems were cursed,*
> *They're the absolute worst.*
> *In French, the word "friend" is called "amie."*

I'd never thought of it before, but rhyming words with "Miami" was almost impossible. I figured they'd be impressed that I'd done the limerick at all, but Mr. Theo scowled after I read it, and Maris wondered out loud if I wouldn't rather be with the theater kids, "the comedic actors, in fact."

I felt like a jerk, of course.

We had tacos for lunch in the school courtyard, and I watched as the dance kids picked up the rueda again. Meanwhile, Maris sat beside me, complaining about her tenth revision of a poem and how it was "killing her soul."

There was more poem-ing after lunch. Mr. Theo taught us how to write ghazals, which have a complicated rhyme scheme. I think I understood what Maris meant by a poem "killing her soul." She was having a hard time of it, too. Once or twice, if I noticed Maris struggling to get a line just right, I tried to give her a little muse boost. Just the tiniest push, a snapshot in my head of Maris smiling when she got a good idea. Magic usually made me feel like the top of my head was coming off. But this kind? Helping someone find the perfect word, or the best metaphor? That felt like the softest buzz on my skin, like goose bumps, or an unexpected breeze.

We wrapped up the afternoon by sharing our ghazals-in-progress. Halfway through reading mine, my bracelet caught fire. Not actual fire, of course—it just warmed up slowly to the point that it started to sting a bit. I had to get to the Hall of Science!

Clio couldn't have timed it better. A bell rang, announcing the end of the day. "Don't forget to work on your ghazals!" Mr. Theo called as we made for the exit.

I heard Maris grumble goodbye. She was clearly still mad about my limerick. I'd have to make it up to her somehow, but right now I needed to run.

"Bye!" I called back, and raced out the door. Students were clogging up the hallways, and I snaked around them as quick as I could. But when I reached the front doors and pushed outside, I was completely confused.

There were the papier-mâché bulls standing guard on either side of the doors. But which way was the museum again? I looked in the distance for the rocket but couldn't see it from where I stood. Meanwhile, my bracelet just got warmer and warmer. "I'm coming!" I whispered into it, hoping Clio heard me.

I felt a tap on my shoulder and turned around.

"Lost?" Ari asked. There were pieces of bright thread stuck in her hair.

"Yeah. Um. I'm meeting a friend at the Hall of Science. Any idea where that is?"

Ari paused before answering. "Two blocks that way, then take a left. You'll see the rocket straight ahead." Then Ari walked in the other direction, her long black hair swinging behind her.

I took off running, passing a couple more bodegas on the way. One block, two blocks, then I took the turn, and there was the rocket in the distance. School buses were lined up on the street outside the museum, and kids from various summer camps were loading into them after a busy day at the museum.

Inside, kids were wandering about while their teachers

shouted directions, and I managed to sneak past the ticket counter. But now that I'd made it to our new muse head-quarters, I didn't have a clue as to where to go and meet everyone.

Then a tiny voice came through my bracelet.

It was Clio: "Meet in the Great Hall, muses."

I grabbed a museum brochure, located the Great Hall, and headed that way, without pausing to look at any exhibits. Somewhere, muses were popping into the museum via their entrance points. I was wondering where mine would be, and if I'd ever learn the layout of our new headquarters, when I saw the sign for the Great Hall above a set of boring old double doors.

Missing the V and A, I took a deep breath and pushed the doors open.

Chapter 7
GROSS! GROSS! GROSS!

Once inside, I couldn't believe my eyes.

The ceiling was high—it had to be over a hundred feet. And there were about a million pieces of blue glass stuck in the walls, which curved gently here and there. I couldn't spot even a single corner or angle.

It was like being inside a wave at night. Or an alien spaceship.

"Welcome to the Great Hall," Clio said from the front of the room. Eight beanbags sat on the floor in front of her, and she gestured to them.

I was the first to arrive, obviously, but that didn't last long. Tomiko and Elnaz strolled in next, and they both gasped at the sight of the room, too. They were followed by Etoro and Paola, who had similar reactions. Clio was smiling without showing her teeth, which was about as happy as she ever looked, and I knew she was feeling pretty pleased with herself for choosing this place for our first meeting. Tomiko, Elnaz, and Paola settled onto beanbags, while Etoro rolled her wheelchair up to the front near Clio.

Feeling anxious, I looked at the door. I heard the rest of the Muse Squad before they came in. Thalia was laughing loudly, and I heard Nia say, "Control yourself, for the love," when the doors opened up.

"Holy smokes!" Nia said.

"Brilliant!" Thalia said.

Mela was just a few feet behind them, and I watched as she covered her mouth with her hands, her eyes wide. The three of them sat in the beanbags nearest me. I sighed happily. I mean, Maris was nice, and Ari was, well, Ari. But there was nothing like being with friends who really understood you.

"Welcome, muses, to the Hall of Science, and the Great Hall itself. This will be our meeting room from now on. I hope your entrance points were satisfactory."

Everyone started talking at once.

"I got the Hall of Mirrors. Like in a fun house! Cheers for that, Clio," Thalia said.

"I got the rocket! Thanks, Clio!" Nia called out. She was wearing a T-shirt with an otter in an astronaut uniform, the words OTTER SPACE written below. Just about her entire wardrobe was science pun shirts.

"Clio, I'd like to arrange for a change of entrance

points," Mela said. "The preschool playroom is absolutely *not* going to work." Then she leaned over to me and said, "Everything in there is sticky," and made a funny face.

"Where's yours?" Nia asked.

I shrugged. "Don't know. I ran here from the summer camp my dad put me in."

"Look at you, all New York and stuff," Nia said.

"Hardly. I would have gotten lost if not for Ari."

"Ari?"

"I'll tell you later," I whispered as Clio finally got everybody to quiet down.

It was dark in the Great Hall, illuminated only by the eerie light coming through the blue glass. That's why I didn't notice the muse finder clock behind Clio. I squinted and could see that the pointer was still resting on New York. Somewhere out there was the tenth muse, and it was our job to find her. Even if that meant one of us might lose her job. Or worse.

"Recalling our mission," Clio began solemnly, "Paola and I have been in the city for a few days now and are no closer to finding the tenth muse that the clock has indicated. So we'll need a new approach."

Clio switched on an ancient projector, which sputtered to life with a whir. A bright beam of light hit a screen at the front of the room. The image sharpened by the second to reveal an eye dangling from a single slimy strand of eyeball gunk. It spun slowly, the gray iris staring blindly. The white part of the eye was covered in tiny veins, and the hand that dangled it was withered and pale.

Even though my stomach was doing flip-flops, I couldn't look away.

A second, equally withered hand cupped the eye away from sight. Then a third hand appeared and tried to snatch the eye. Just then, the projection stuttered, and the screen went blank.

"My apologies. The projector is a bit of an antique," Clio said as she smacked the machine a few times to get it going again.

"What was that all about?" Nia asked, pointing at the screen.

Clio cleared her throat. "I told you, the projector is old."

"Not the projector," Nia persisted. "The disgusting *eyeball*."

"I was getting to that," Clio said.

"Can we please not talk about an eyeball?" Mela asked in a quiet voice, her cheeks going a little green.

"Yes, the eyeball is vile," Clio said. "But maybe not as nauseating as the tooth," she added, and with another whack, the projector whirred back to life. This time, the withered hand held a black molar in the center of its palm, the nerves still twitching from the tooth's base, and the long roots sharp like fangs.

"Yikes, there's nothing funny about that," Thalia said, "and *everything* makes me laugh." Then she tapped her chin, thought for a bit, and giggled. "Oh, never mind. It *is* funny."

Clio tapped the projector and a third image appeared. Three ancient women were sitting on a park bench, city skyscrapers in the distance behind them, their heads ducked down over knitting. They seemed to be making one very long pink sock.

"These are the Graeae. They share one tooth and one eye among them," Clio said.

"Ew!" Nia said. "Hygiene, people." Nia was meticulous about everything, probably because her dad was ex-CIA.

"They are ancient witches, sometimes known as the Gray Sisters," Clio said.

"Are they evil?" Mela asked.

"Duh," Thalia answered.

"Just because they are gross witches who share eyes and teeth—" Mela began.

"*An* eye and *a* tooth. Singular," Nia put in.

"Whatever. That doesn't mean they are evil," Mela said, crossing her arms and huffing through her nose.

Clio nodded. "Well. They aren't exactly *good*. But Mela is right. They aren't exactly evil, either. They are neutral, so to speak. That eye gives them the power of sight. They know secrets. And see secrets. Nobody can hide anything from them when they have the eye in their possession."

"Would they know the answer to my maths tests then?" Thalia asked, and Clio sighed.

"We normally don't bother with the Gray Sisters. They've been around a long time and no longer seem interested in anything but sunning themselves at the park. We haven't had a need for their particular expertise either. But now that the muse finder clock has indicated a new muse, and we can't seem to find her, our only hope is to try to get the Gray Sisters to help. There are no such things as secrets when it comes to them. We may be able to entice them to help us locate this muse. They live here in Queens, after all."

I sucked in a breath. The Gray Sisters were in Queens!

"The stubborn sisters, more like it," Etoro said, huffing and crossing her arms. I took that to mean that Etoro, at least, had dealt with them before.

"They're capricious," Paola added. "They'll offer advice one day, curse you the next. We need to be careful with them."

"Indeed," Clio said. "They aren't always easy to work with. But they are fond of the innocent, like children." Then she stared at us. I could swear I saw her left eye twitch.

"That's where the Muse Squad comes in?" Thalia asked, pointing her thumbs at all of us.

Elnaz turned around in her beanbag to look at us. "They are a bit creepy, what with the one eye and one tooth thing. Steel yourselves."

Tomiko faced us, too. "But don't stare. Be cool," she added.

Clio nodded. "Remember, they like children. Adults usually only ask them questions when they want to gain something for themselves."

"Unlike children, who are less concerned with ambition, and more interested in curiosity for its own sake," Etoro said, her eyes crinkling kindly at us.

"That means you have an advantage over the rest of us," said Clio. "You'll find them in the arboretum of the Queens Botanical Garden tomorrow afternoon at four thirty. Simply introduce yourselves, then state your question about who the tenth muse is, and hopefully, they'll be in the mood to assist us."

Suddenly, we heard a scream coming from outside the Great Hall. It sounded like a little kid. Then another screamed, and another, until it seemed like a thousand kids were yelling just beyond the doors.

Elnaz was the first to move, followed by Tomiko. I watched as Elnaz pulled a tin whistle from the pocket of her jeans. Paola was also on her feet, and I could hear a little hum coming from her, as if she was practicing scales with her voice. As for Clio, I could see that she was tugging on her left ear, making her trumpet earring twitch.

As Elnaz slowly pushed open the double doors of the Great Hall, the sound of screaming children grew louder. Mela linked arms with me, and I watched as Nia and Thalia held hands, too. Whatever was happening, we were ready.

Thalia was the first to see it—a tiny spider, crawling over Elnaz's foot. Beyond the door, kids were running everywhere, shaking their arms as they ran, or stomping the ground.

"Is that a—" Thalia started to ask when I saw another spider, then another, then more and more, all pouring into the Great Hall.

"Ah!" Elnaz shouted, and started stepping on as many as she could find. But they crawled up her legs.

More spiders poured in, a whole wave of them, clambering on top of each other until they started to seem like some other, giant creature altogether. It was like the day with Mario and the van all over again—a million spiders causing chaos. All the while, my mind was racing with one thought: *This is my fault!* If I'd mentioned the spiders to Clio earlier, maybe this, whatever this was, wouldn't have happened.

I started walking toward Clio, to try to make things right somehow, but she was shouting, "Muses, clear out! To your entrance points!"

The other muses did as they were told, including Thalia, Nia, and Mela, who ran past me, half yelping, leaping to avoid the crawling piles of spiders forming everywhere.

"So freaky! Ugh," I heard Nia shout as she ran by.

"I don't want it, I don't want it," Mela repeated as she ran.

Then Thalia took off, and I watched as she picked a

spider off her wrist and flung it across the room. I sprinted for the exits. I didn't even know where my entrance point was in the museum. The only way out was through Queens, down the block, back to the apartment, through thousands—maybe a million—tiny, teeming, definitely not normal spiders.

Chapter 8
FESSING UP

Somebody had called the police, and now three cop cars were parked in front of the museum, their red and blue lights blazing and the sirens going off at full volume. Museum-goers were still running out of the Hall of Science, brushing past the officers, who stood there, dumbfounded, as more and more spiders crawled through the doors, then disappeared into the wooded park surrounding the museum.

I ran to a bench underneath a large tree and tried to catch my breath. My heart was doing somersaults in my chest, and my legs felt like jelly. Every once in a while, I shivered all over.

Whatever this was, the muses were at the center of it somehow. First spiders showed up in Miami and almost caused a car crash. Then there was an attack at the museum.

On top of all that, the Muse Squad was just given a mission to find the Gray Sisters, which was only the start of a *bigger* mission to find whoever the tenth muse might be. What if it was all connected somehow? The spiders and the tenth muse?

Closing my eyes helped. I knew what I had to do, what I should have done some time ago.

"Clio?" I asked into my bracelet. "We need to talk. I'm outside. On a bench." I didn't hear anything in return, but a few moments later, Clio emerged from the front doors of the museum, carrying a lunch bag. She made her way to where I was sitting, and I scooted over a bit to make room.

Clio opened up the lunch bag and gave me a brownie. "Still warm," she said, and stretched her legs. I noticed a couple of crushed spiders sticking to the soles of her shoes, and I shuddered.

"Is there something you want to tell me?" she asked after I swallowed the bite of brownie I'd taken.

I wiped my mouth with the back of my hand. "Yes. The spiders. It's not the first time something, um, spider-y has happened recently."

Clio listened as I explained about Mario and the van. She didn't say a word, only listened, and I found myself getting more and more nervous as I spoke. My voice was so shaky.

"I'm sorry I didn't mention it sooner, Clio. I really am.

At first, I thought it was just a coincidence. But now this? This is bananas."

Clio hummed in agreement. "It's the whole fruit salad," she said. "Apology accepted."

Clio, making a joke? Everything really *was* bananas.

"What does it mean?" I asked over a mouthful of brownie.

"I have to say that I don't know. It seems to me, given the fact that this *invasion* happened during our first meeting at the new headquarters, that somebody is trying to keep the muses from doing our work."

"And our work is finding the tenth muse, right?"

Clio thought for a moment. "Yes, at this juncture that's our most pressing mission."

"The tenth muse must be really special, I guess," I said, wiping my hands on my jeans, leaving chocolate streaks behind. Laura was going to hate that. "But what's up with the spiders?"

Clio sighed deeply. "The only thing these creatures," she said, pointing at the spiders we could still spot here and there, "seem interested in is disruption and chaos."

The word "chaos" sent a chill through me. Last year, when we'd battled the sirens, chaos had been their weapon of choice. And though the sirens shape-shifted into birds, mainly, they could take any form they wanted, eight legs and all.

"Is it sirens, Clio? Could they be back?"

"I haven't ruled it out." A cool breeze moved through the trees. "Mm, that's nice," Clio said. She leaned back and shut her eyes.

I closed my eyes, too, but my imagination wouldn't settle down. The words "the tenth muse" and "spiders" appeared in my head. They were written on cream-colored banners, dancing in the air like gymnasts' ribbons. Then the muse finder clock came into view, chiming its bell.

"Clio, I'm worried," I said shakily.

She pulled me into a hug. "I know. We all are. I'll do my best to find the answer to all of . . . this," she said, gesturing at everything at once. Clio closed the lunch bag and stood. "Go back home, Callie. I have some research to do. In the meantime, the junior muses have three sisters they need to charm."

"Any tips?" I asked.

"Churros. I hear they like them." Clio winked and marched back to the Hall of Science.

Chapter 9
DRAMA AT THE BODEGA

I walked back to the apartment, remembering the path Papi, Laura, and I had taken that morning. The yellow house looked a bit more cheerful in the afternoon sunlight, but my mood didn't match it.

The fact that Clio didn't know what was going on with the spiders worried me. If she couldn't figure it out, what hope did I have?

I could hear Rafaelito crying from the porch. With a deep sigh, I climbed the stairs, opening the door to find Laura, her hair a mess, Rafaelito howling in her arms, and the smell of garlic coming from the kitchen.

"Smells good," I said, taking my brother into my arms. He stopped crying and started pulling my hair instead. Hard. "Ow, you," I said, and tickled him a bit to get him to stop.

Laura thanked me for taking Rafaelito and rushed into the kitchen. Two seconds later I heard her say, "Ay! I burned the rice." She emerged with a scowl on her face, and a five-dollar bill clutched in her hand. "Here, muñeca. Go get some instant rice from the bodega, would you? And get yourself an ice cream, while you're at it."

"Okay." I settled Rafaelito into his playpen, took the money, and put it in my pocket.

Back down the stairs I went and surprised myself by remembering to turn right to get to the Queen of Corona.

It was empty this time. The bodega cat came out to greet me. I bent down to look at its tag, which read YOGURT. "Hey, Yogurt," I said, scratching behind its ears before walking to the back where the ice-cream counter was.

There was Ari, wearing her Queen of Corona apron, right where I'd hoped she would be. After the day I'd had, a friendly face and yummy ice cream were exactly what I needed.

Except the face behind the counter was anything but friendly.

Ari was scowling at me, her hands crossed tightly over her apron.

"Have fun at the museum?" she asked.

She was definitely not happy to see me. I looked around quickly, taking in the bodega, and out the windows, a small view of Queens. If I could have transported back to Miami with a blink, I would have. But the bodega didn't have an entrance point, and besides, not everything could be solved with magic.

"Um. The museum was okay. Thanks for the directions."

"Whatever," Ari said.

"Is something wrong?" I asked, knowing that the answer was obviously yes. It felt like everything was going wrong. Why wouldn't things crash and burn with my new friend? Lately, it felt like I was stuck running on a hamster wheel of doom.

"Hanging out with friends, were you? I mean, you just moved here and you have friends already. That's, like, super social of you." Ari leaned on the counter, her eyes boring into mine.

"Did I mess up or something?"

Ari laughed, and it was a cold sound, colder than ice cream.

"Oh no. Never. You and your kind are never wrong. Are they, *Calliope*?"

What was going on? What did she mean by "my kind"?

"Ari, I don't know what you're talking abou—"

She laughed again. "Come on now. Friends don't keep secrets, do they? My aunt told me all about you."

"Your aunt?"

"Never mind," Ari said. "Just stay clear of me," she said, slamming her hands on the counter.

I took a step back. Goose bumps covered my arms, but it wasn't muse magic. Why was Ari being so mean?

Maybe I was going about this the wrong way. I pictured her joking with me again, both of us friends again, hoping the muse magic would fix things.

"Stop it. Stop what you're doing. I don't like it," she said. I cleared the pictures from my head at once. Ari stepped around the counter and came to stand by me. She stood very close to me, in fact. "I. Know. What. You. Are," she said, punctuating each word with a little jab of her finger to my shoulder. "None of you can keep me from what I have to do. *She* couldn't stop me, and neither can you. Stay away from me, or you'll be sorry."

My mouth went dry, and my brain was in a fog. Did Ari know I was a muse? But how?

"Ari, I—"

"You and your friends need to leave me alone!" she shouted, then tugged off her apron and ran out of the bodega.

I could only stare after her.

My instincts were telling me to think this through. Ari had said, "I know what you are." That didn't necessarily mean she knew about the muses. Maybe she had misunderstood something I'd said. Maybe Maris had shown her my terrible poem, and she thought I was going to sabotage the Student Showcase. It seemed to mean a lot to her.

She'd said, "*She* couldn't stop me, and neither can you." Who was *she*? Another student at the Corona Arts Academy?

My head was swimming. Mami always told me, "When you're unsure of what to do, take a big breath and give yourself the gift of time."

So that's what I was going to do. Give myself time to think this one through before jumping to any conclusions. Whatever Ari was up against, the muses definitely didn't have anything to do with it. She was safe from us, at least.

But were *we* safe from *her*?

Chapter 10
A MUSTERING OF MUSES

That night, after dinner, I called Mami.

As soon as she heard my voice she said, "Something's wrong," doing that mom-intuition thing she did so well.

"No. It's all good." My voice caught a little. "Maybe I'm just homesick."

"Oh, mi vida. That's natural. But New York can be home for you, too. Talk to your papi. He'll understand."

Except this thing with Ari and with the spiders was not something Papi or Mami could understand. Very few people in the world could, in fact. But I knew three other girls who would totally get it.

"Muse Squad, we need to talk. Let's meet in the museum," I whispered into the bracelet later that night after everyone had fallen asleep. I hoped Thalia, Nia, and Mela would show up.

Back home, I'd slide under my bed and pop up at head-quarters. Now all I had was this noisy pin-pan-pun. It was a tight squeeze under there, and my nose was half an inch from a rusty spring. I closed my eyes, counted to ten, and when I opened them again I appeared to be on a different bed, surrounded by smooth wooden walls. Across from me were two more beds, and a little farther away, a small ladder led up to a dark opening.

Had the magic misfired somehow? Where was I?

I clambered out of the bed and climbed up the ladder. Outside, it was dark, but I spotted emergency lights in the ceiling, and a flickering red Exit sign in the distance. Definitely the museum, then. But *where* in the museum was I?

The ladder had led me up to the deck of a ship, with bright white canvas sails and everything! The ship was in the center of a large room, and I could just make out a sign that said "The Science of Navigation" on the far wall.

Thanks, Clio! I thought. I couldn't have picked a cooler entrance point myself! I was about to talk into my bracelet again, to see if the others had arrived, when I heard someone rustling nearby.

"Aye, aye, Captain Callie!" said Thalia, standing at the ship's helm. Nia had her hands on the wheel and was twisting it left and right. For the first time since I'd met her, she wasn't wearing a science T-shirt. Instead, her shirt read THIRD STREET GYMNASTICS. Meanwhile, Mela was sitting on some coiled rope, headphones over her ears as usual, flipping through an old playbill someone had discarded on the ship.

"I can't believe how awesome your entrance point is," Nia said, noticing me at last. "Did I ever mention I love ships? My mom was in the navy, and she used to take me to see the tall ships when I was little. I *love* tall ships like this. Are we mustering? We're totally mustering, aren't we?"

"Mustarding? Like the condiment?" Thalia asked. Her face looked horrified. "I hate mustard." She squished her features together and stuck out her tongue.

"No. *Mustering*. A gathering of sailors. We are totally mustering." Then Nia grew serious. "So what's up? Spiders again?"

Mela looked around frantically for a moment. "Please don't even mention them," she said, shivering all over.

"Not exactly," I said. "It's this girl at Corona Arts Academy. Her name is Ari, and this afternoon she told me, 'I know what you are.' Like that. And she called me Calliope. I never told her my name was Calliope, you guys."

"That doesn't mean—" Mela began.

"She *knew* I was trying to use my magic on her. It's like she could feel it."

Everyone was silent after that.

Thalia's brow was furrowed in thought, while Nia chewed on a thumbnail. Mela's eyes were glistening.

"We've battled worse," Thalia said. "Some random girl isn't going to be a problem."

Nia nodded, tapping her chin as she spoke. "We need to investigate. Find out what she wants. Is she magical herself? Maybe she's a gorgon in disguise."

"Gorgon?" I asked.

"Mythical monsters. Turn people into stone, like Medusa. She had snakes for hair, you know. Other gorgons eat people whole, like Lamia. She was half snake. Snakes all over the place! No spiders, though," Nia explained.

Mela sniffed from where she sat on the coiled rope. She'd been very quiet.

"Are you okay?" I asked her. More than any of us, Mela wore her heart on her sleeve.

"Ari sounds scared. *Of us*. Why would she be scared of us?" she asked, her voice small.

Once again, we were all quiet. A few minutes ticked by as we all thought this through. My mom would be proud.

"We aren't scary," Thalia said at last.

"Yeah, we are actually. We are super scary," Mela responded. "Think of what we can do, what we can convince others to do. If I knew some strange kids had powers like that, and I didn't know who they were, or if they could be trusted, I'd be scared as well."

"Mela is right. If Ari is scared, we need to find out why. Maybe she needs our help," Thalia added. "Even if she is a gorgon."

We heard a creaking sound off to the right, and the four of us whipped around to watch as the rope ladder that led up to the ship's deck rubbed against the top rail. A pale hand appeared on the ledge, then another. And that's when I saw them.

Two wrists full of friendship bracelets.

How much did Ari hear? I wondered.

I rushed over to help Ari onto the ship. Her wide eyes met mine. Ari looked nervous.

"Callie, I, um, a-apologize for yesterday. I got some advice from my aunt. And I've thought things over. I think you and the others might be able to help me."

"Our help?" I asked, feeling like a whole swarm of butterflies was making a home in my stomach.

"Yeah. I've got a big problem. Let's just say I need some inspiration, okay?"

"So you know who we are," I said quietly.

Ari nodded. "Muses. And if you give me a moment to explain, I'll tell you who I am, too."

She waited, fidgeting with her bracelets. Her dark eyes shone. Whatever Ari was dealing with, I could tell that it was a huge deal.

"Please, Callie," Ari whispered.

I didn't have to think about it much more. "Of course. Yeah," I said, and waved the others forward.

The rest of the muses approached slowly. Ari shook hands with Nia first, then Mela, and finally Thalia. Then Ari sat on a barrel and rubbed her hands on her black jeans over and over again.

"You okay?" I asked.

She flexed her hands. "Your magic tickles."

"You can feel our magic?" Mela asked.

"I'm a little sensitive to it."

"Okay. Spill it," Nia said.

Ari stopped rubbing her hands on her jeans. "Ari is just my nickname. I'm Arachne. Nice to meet you all."

I sat on the deck of the ship with a thump. Arachne? The girl Clio told me about? The one who had entered a competition with Athena and had been turned into a spider for disrespecting the goddess? I'd seen Athena's tapestry at the V and A, had held it in my hands! It was beautiful. And to think that Ari had woven one that was even better!

"Rings a bell," Thalia said, her finger on her chin.

"It should," added Mela. Then she turned to Ari. "Do you mean to say you are *the* Arachne?"

Ari nodded. "The very one. Like I said, nice to meet you."

Clio had said that Arachne had been turned into a spider, but she looked pretty human to me. "How come you're a . . . um, a person?" I asked. "And not a spider?"

Thalia snapped her fingers. "Oh! You're *that* Arachne! The weaver! That's brilliant. And weird. Why are you here?"

"More like, *how* are you here?" Nia asked finally.

"Why don't you start from the beginning," I said.

We all sat down in a tight circle at the ship's bow. I could hear Ari's breathing, tight and fast, and Nia clicking on her app, measuring the stars at this moment.

"You know the story, then. Athena challenged me to a weaving competition, and my people selected my tapestry, yet Athena declared herself the winner anyway. When I stood up for myself, she turned me into a spider. I was twelve when that happened. Been a spider for a couple thousand years, and now I'm twelve again."

"That's a lot to handle," Mela said, her eyes all watery.

"Now I have a second chance."

"How'd that even happen?" Nia asked. "The gods don't change their minds. Ever."

"I don't know for sure. One minute I'm just me, weaving a web, thinking about the fat flies I'm going to catch for lunch—"

Thalia made a gagging sound.

"Shh," Mela reprimanded her. "Go on, Ari."

"Thanks. The next minute—well, it felt like a minute. But it was thousands of years later—I was my old self again. A kid standing in the middle of a bodega in New York City, wondering what was going on." Ari paused, and the rest of us waited carefully for her to begin again. I had about a million questions, and I would bet the others did, too. But those could wait until Ari told us her—

"YOU SENT ALL THOSE SPIDERS TO COME

AFTER US, DIDN'T YOU?" Thalia interrupted loudly, putting two and two together at last.

Ari scrunched up her nose and held up her hands. "Oops?"

"*Oops?* You should know I'm very, very cross with you about that," Thalia added.

Ari sighed. "Listen. I'm sorry. I'm obviously not a spider anymore, and frankly, I'd rather not remember any of that. But I still know how to talk to them and get them to do things for me if I ask nicely. I didn't send any *venomous* ones, and you're very welcome about that."

"But why did you do it?" I was feeling a tight ball of anger forming in my chest. My brother had almost crashed our van. Not to mention the people running away from spiders in the Hall of Science. They could have been hurt.

"I didn't know what side you were on."

"Side?" I asked.

"Mine or Athena's. You can bet she's not happy that I'm back," Ari said. "And my aunt said not to trust anybody. She's the one who told me you'd be meeting here tonight, and the reason I was able to get in the museum after hours. My aunt is . . . resourceful."

"If you're the real Arachne, then how can your aunt be here in New York, too?" Mela asked.

"Not my real aunt, obviously," Ari said. "My real aunts have been dead for thousands of years. She's adopted me as her niece."

That made me think of Tia Annie, of course. She'd only been gone for a few years, not thousands. But I bet it still hurt Ari to think of her family, long gone.

Nia cut in. "Who's your aunt? You aren't telling us everything, and I don't think we should help if—"

"You don't *need* to know everything," Ari said, crossing her arms.

"And we don't *need* to hear you out," I said. "Come on, everyone. Let's go." I got to my feet. Nia and Thalia were up on theirs right away, too.

"Stop," Ari said. "You know what it's like. You're all bound to secrets, like I am. There are certain . . . conditions on my return to human form. Keeping secrets is one of them."

Thalia sat down again. "What?" she said when we gaped at her. "I completely get it. Do you know how hard it is to keep this muse stuff from my mum?"

"Yeah, we have an idea," I said, sitting down. Nia leaned against the ship's railing and said nothing.

Ari glanced at Mela, who nodded at her encouragingly. Ari sighed. "My aunt, well, you'll have to ask her yourself if you want to know more about her. Anyway, she explained everything when I appeared in her bodega. She'd been waiting for me, she said, for 'Just the right time.' I guess it was the right time, because here I am. As for the spider attacks, I'm sorry about that. My aunt thought Athena might use the muses to stop me. I didn't know *who* the muses were. I just figured I'd scare them—um, you—off. I panicked, okay?"

"Why would we try to stop you? Muses *inspire* people. Not the other way around," Mela said.

"Do you normally inspire people to go head-to-head against a goddess? Because that's what we're talking about here," Ari explained.

She was right. Muses were all about encouraging others to tap into their best selves, but had they ever gotten involved in battles between gods and humans? I couldn't be sure, but there was probably a rule about that somewhere.

"No," Mela said. "But we help those whose gifts make the world a better place. Perhaps that's you, Ari."

Ari answered quietly, "I just know I want to prove myself, that's all. Like I said, I'm sorry about the spiders. Are we cool now?"

"Maybe," Nia said. "Why do you need our help?"

Sitting up a little straighter, Ari pushed her sleeves back to her elbows, revealing about a hundred friendship bracelets. "I mean to set the record straight. My tapestry is the winning tapestry. Just because Athena is a goddess doesn't mean she's right all the time."

"It sort of does," Thalia added.

"*No.* It doesn't. It's not just or fair. And if the gods aren't just or fair, what hope does anyone have?" She paused, running her hands through her long black hair. "Listen, my aunt explained that I can only stay in my human form if I can prove that I bested Athena in that competition, and I mean to do just that at the Corona Arts Student Showcase. Let real artists decide the winner this time."

"Our campmates, you mean?" I asked.

"Yeah. You and Maris, and all the other kids. They'll tell the truth."

"What about the donors no longer supporting Corona Arts?" I asked.

Ari frowned. "There probably won't be a Corona Arts summer camp next year if we don't impress the donors. My tapestry will wow them. It's a win-win. You'll see. And if I lose, then I'll go back to making webs and eating bugs." Ari shivered all over and her eyes shimmered with tears. "If I win, though, I'll be a person for good, and I'll get to live my life, and the gods will have learned a lesson."

Mela suddenly launched herself at Ari and hugged her hard. "Yes, we'll help," she said, her voice muffled against Ari's hoodie.

"Hold up. Don't speak for all of us, Mel," Nia said. "This is huge. You're asking us to go up against Athena."

"No, I'm asking you to help *me* do that. You can stay neutral."

"It doesn't work like that," I said. "We're kids, but in some ways, we're goddesses, like her."

"Then maybe you have a lesson to learn as well."

I felt Mela's hand on my wrist. She wasn't using her

magic, but there was something in her eyes that told me how important this moment was. "She's not wrong," Mela whispered.

"Okay. What do you need us to do?" I asked.

Ari smiled a little. "I need help finding my tapestry. Athena tore it into four pieces. It's the best work I ever did, and I need it back."

"But how will we find it?" Thalia asked.

The answer was on my lips before I could even think about whether I should say it.

"The Gray Sisters. They know everything. They'll know where the tapestry pieces are."

"That's genius," Nia said. "They can let us know about the tapestry, and the other thing, too."

"What thing?" Ari asked. Boy, she didn't miss a beat.

"Muse stuff. Classified," Thalia said.

I breathed a sigh of relief that Thalia's loose lips hadn't given away our mission regarding the tenth muse. We were already breaking about a million rules, I was sure.

"So you'll help me?"

We all looked at Ari for a moment without saying a word. Then I felt the others, one by one, turning to look at me, like I held the answer.

I took a deep breath. "We'll see what the Gray Sisters say."

Ari's shoulders drooped a little. I could tell Mela was disappointed that I wasn't agreeing to anything just yet, but Nia and Thalia both nodded at me. Is this what it meant to be a leader? Not pleasing everyone all the time?

Because I really didn't like the feeling.

"What are we waiting for then?" Ari said, getting on her feet. "Let's find these sisters you keep talking about."

"It's late. We'll have to go tomorrow afternoon," I said. "That's when the Gray Sisters will be . . . where they usually hang out." I'd almost said the Queens Botanical Garden but held my tongue instead. What if Ari decided to go find the Gray Sisters herself? I didn't know yet if I fully trusted her.

Nia whispered in my ear, "Should we tell her about the one tooth and the one eyeball thing before we get there?"

My stomach churned at the thought of who we would be meeting.

I made a gagging sound instead of answering her. Whatever these Gray Sisters were, or however they looked, we were in for a very interesting time.

Chapter 11
EXQUISITE CORPSES

"Day two of art camp!" Laura said as she put some scrambled eggs on a plate for me the next morning. Rafaelito was in his high chair, drinking from a bottle of milk.

"Making friends?" Papi asked as he stirred sugar into his coffee.

"Sort of." I didn't think Maris actually wanted to be my friend after my limerick yesterday. I promised myself I'd make it up to her. And as for Ari, well, we *definitely* had to talk.

Laura smiled. "Atta girl," she said. "Have a great day," she added before leaving to get the baby dressed for day care.

"Do you think you can get to Corona Arts on your own?" Papi asked. "I have to be at the work site early today."

"Oh," I said, trying to keep the disappointment out

of my voice. Papi kissed me on the cheek as he gathered his keys. "Papi, maybe tomorrow you and I can go grab some—" I started to say, but he was halfway out the door, slamming it closed before I could finish my sentence. I'd hoped that maybe we could get breakfast tacos, just the two of us. Back when he lived in Miami, we would go on Papi-Callie adventures together sometimes. To the park, or the beach—just the two of us. It had been so long since then. My eyes stung at the memory.

"See ya, Laura. Bye, Rafaelito," I said, peeking into the baby's room, where Laura was struggling to snap a onesie in place around my baby brother's thighs.

Laura seemed to pick up on my mood. "He works hard to provide for everybody, Callie. Don't be too upset with him."

I shook my head. "I'm not. See you this afternoon," I said, though my throat burned like I was going to cry.

"Big camp fun!" Laura cheered, but I only waved good-bye and went out the door.

The walk to Corona Arts helped clear my head, and I was glad to see the papier-mâché bulls standing guard at the entrance of the school. I was even happier to see Ari there, knitting the finishing touches on a sweater the bull on the right was wearing. That's when I noticed it—the lampposts in front of the school were wrapped in colorful yarn, too, as was the base of the fire hydrant. It was summer and boiling hot in the city, but every inanimate object in view was wearing a sweater.

"It's called yarn bombing," Ari said as I walked up slowly to her.

"You did *all this*?"

"I make things when I'm stressed out."

"I get it," I said. I'd be stressed out, too, if I'd been turned into a spider, then back into a human, and had to face off with the goddess Athena. In fact, "stressed" didn't even cover it. I'd be a melted Callie-puddle of anxiety.

Ari twisted bright yellow yarn between her fingers as she spoke. Out of the corner of my eye, it looked like she was weaving a bit of sunshine.

"Stop staring at me, Callie. Seriously, just go find Maris. I've got more yarn bombing to do."

"Okay," I said. "See you later, for the, um, thing we're doing."

Ari gave me a thumbs-up without looking at me, her eyes back on her knitting.

I'd hardly slept, thinking about our visit to the Gray Sisters. Hopefully Clio was right about their soft spot for kids, because we had a couple of big questions to ask them.

I made my way back to the poetry classroom. Maris and Mr. Theo were busy making a poem together.

"Sit with us," Mr. Theo said. Today, he was wearing a

plain blue baseball cap. "We're writing an *exquisite corpse* poem!"

Honestly, he sounded way too excited about writing a poem about a dead body.

I must have made a face, because Mr. Theo quickly added, "It's not what you think, Callie. It's a collaborative poem. One we make together."

"Plus it's a game," Maris added. "None of us know what lines the others are writing, so the poems can sound completely absurd, or totally beautiful, when you put the lines together."

Mr. Theo smiled, and handed me a piece of paper and a pen. "Here are the rules. Write one line that uses the following parts of speech in this exact order: adjective, noun, verb, adjective, noun."

I got to work, but my eyes kept sliding off my page. I noticed how Maris's left leg bounced, making the table we shared shake a little. She had a pencil *and* a marker jammed into her hair bun today. It looked like she had antennae. Mr. Theo had written about ten lines and was on to line number eleven.

Concentrating, I wrote my line, put down my pen, and waited.

Mr. Theo cleared his throat, and Maris stopped writing. "Ready?" he asked.

Mr. Theo shared his line first: "*Chirpy cockatiels bite unsuspecting humans.*"

Maris smoothed her page and read in a slow, clear voice: "*Shimmery sunsets stave off sad sentiments.*"

"Nice use of alliteration, Maris!" Mr. Theo said.

He and Maris turned to look at me. I knew they were thinking of my poem from the day before. Maris had a single eyebrow lifted. Mr. Theo just looked a bit constipated.

"Um. Okay. Here goes," I said, then read my line: "*New campmate apologizes. Super sorry.*"

I didn't think I got the parts of speech right, but I guess it didn't matter because suddenly, Maris was smiling, and Mr. Theo was clapping.

"Best exquisite corpse ever," Mr. Theo announced.

We did a few more rounds of the exquisite corpse game, with lines that included more cockatiels from Mr. Theo, lots more alliteration by Maris, and some stuff about my mom's café con leche and arroz con pollo (because I was really homesick).

After lunch, Mr. Theo assigned us concrete poems, where the shape of the poem matched the words. Maris went to work right away on a poem about Lebanon, where her parents were from. Line by line, the country's shape appeared.

Meanwhile, I was stuck on my poem. Like, neck-deep in quicksand stuck. I might have sighed loudly a few times. Maris glared at me at first, but after my fifth audible groan, she put down her pen.

"Honestly. Just try," she said.

"I *am* trying. This is hard." I usually didn't get so frustrated about writing projects. I earned good grades in language arts class all the time, and for a while there in fifth grade, I kept a diary every day. But my mind was on other things, like the tenth muse, and the spiders, and the possibility that I wouldn't sleep all summer thanks to Rafaelito's crying.

Maris rolled her pen between her hands for a moment, thinking. "Fine. Just think of something blue, that doesn't belong to you, and can be held in one hand," she said.

"Specific much?"

"Specificity helps. Trust me," Maris said.

An image popped into my head at once—Maya had a snow globe on a blue base. Inside, the earth was suspended in water. When you turned the snow globe upside down, silver glitter swirled around the tiny planet. Maya loved that thing. Her abuelita had bought it for her years ago, when she was little.

"Got it," I said.

Maris smiled. "Now think about the person who owns that thing, and what they mean to you. Write about them, and the object, in the shape of whatever that small, blue thing is."

"Oh," I said softly. Then, "Oh!" loudly as the words came to mind.

Maris dusted her hands, like she'd just finished a big job. "Just a little poetry magic, that's all." Then she went back to her own poem.

"Thanks, Maris," I said, and started scribbling away. Just as I was getting to the line about Maya's scientist dreams, Maris suddenly shouted, "Calliope!"

"Callie," I said. Why did people insist on doing that?

Maris laughed. "No, I mean, Calliope, Muse of the epic poem!"

I froze. First Ari knew who I was, now Maris? Clio was going to be so mad.

"Listen, Maris. This is really important. You have to—"

"Muse of poetry! No wonder we were so inspired today!" she said.

"Well, this is absolutely delightful!" Mr. Theo put in.

I needed to come at this from a different angle. Maybe logic would help. "Okay. So you know. But you can't say any—"

Maris gave me a high five. "It's so cool that your parents named you after one of the muses. *So cool.* Or maybe they just named you after one of those circus pipe organs. Aren't they called calliopes, too, Mr. Theo?"

"Ah, well. Let's go with the muse instead. Right, Callie? After your work today, I'd say you were perfectly named," Mr. Theo said.

I felt dizzy with relief. They didn't know my secret after all.

We worked until lunch, then Maris and I watched the salsa dancers in the courtyard as we munched on sandwiches. "Wanna go get some frappuccinos after camp?" Maris asked.

I was surprised to find that I did. I really, really wanted to hang out with Maris. Except I had to find Ari, gather the other muses, and go find the Gray Sisters.

"Can't today. Next time?"

Maris frowned a little and ate the rest of her lunch in silence. I was pretty sure she thought I'd just brushed her off. We spent the afternoon watching a documentary about slam poets. The bell rang just as the film ended. Maris packed her things, said, "Bye, Callie," and walked out of the room.

"Bye," I said. Somehow, I'd managed to hurt Maris's feelings two days in a row. I felt like the world's worst campmate.

Chapter 12
THE GRAY SISTERS

Ari was outside the poetry classroom, waiting for me.

"So where are they? The other muses?" she asked.

"We're meeting back at headquarters," I said. "Come on."

Ari followed me down the stairs, through the school foyer, and out the front doors. The papier-mâché bulls were completely dressed in yarn sweaters. They even had on matching beanies. "You did all this in *one* day?" I asked.

"Not my best work," Ari said, her nose scrunching up as we passed the colorful statues.

We walked quietly to the Hall of Science. I had about a million questions to ask but kept my mouth shut. The rest of the Muse Squad was probably waiting inside the museum.

School buses once again lined the museum driveway, and it looked like all the kids in Queens were jammed into the cafeteria, talking loudly, spilling drinks, laughing, and comparing souvenirs.

Ari looked around, her hands on her hips. "What I could do with a place like this," she said, her eyes spanning the large, open museum. I tried to imagine what she was envisioning—the floor covered in woven rugs, sculptures wearing new yarn outfits, even the rocket outside wrapped in a colorful sweater!

I could picture Ari clearly, surrounded by all that colorful wool. The picture was clear and true in my mind, and I could begin to feel the muse magic around me, the way I always did when I was near someone who was feeling inspired.

"Don't," Ari said with a start. "I don't like it."

"Don't like what?"

"Magic forced on me. I'm not asking for your help, so don't give it." Then she marched away from me, as if she knew exactly where to find the other muses.

I let her go and watched her walk away and enter the museum. Is that what I was doing whenever I used my magic? *Forcing it* on someone? My stomach felt like it was sinking in on itself, and so I sprinted after Ari to shake the sensation.

As we made our way to my entrance point I saw the other muses before Ari did. They were on the deck of the ship, waving at us. Thalia had found a pirate's hat and she had put it on her head, the giant red feather on top bobbing up and down as she waved.

"Ahoy there, mateys!" she shouted, just as Nia plucked the hat off Thalia's head.

Ari smiled. "They're fun to hang around with, huh?" she said a little wistfully.

"Yeah. Tons," I said. It had probably been a long time since Ari had had real friends, and the thought of it made me sad. "Ready?" I asked.

I felt Ari's hand slip into mine for just a moment, squeezing my fingers then letting go. "As I'll ever be," she said.

Clio had said we would find the Gray Sisters at the Queens Botanical Garden, and she was right. They were exactly where she said they would be—in the arboretum, sitting close together on a stone bench. I'd remembered to stop and get churros first, since Clio had suggested that, too.

Except Thalia had already eaten two of them.

"Sorry," she whispered. "It's well past dinnertime back home. I'm starved."

Nia and Mela sent a harsh "shh" in her direction.

"What are we waiting for anyway?" Ari asked.

The five of us were hiding behind topiaries shaped like chess pieces. I was crouched behind a pawn. So was Thalia. Nia and Mela were smashed together behind a bishop, and Ari was peering at the Gray Sisters from between the legs of a leafy horse with a knight on top.

"I don't know, actually," I said. The truth was, I didn't have a clue about how to approach them. Casually? (Hey, there, Gray Sisters, what's up?) Formally? (Your ancient Graynesses, we need your assistance.) How *did* one approach eternal, all-knowing beings?

"Oh, this is ridiculous," Ari hissed, and I watched in horror as she stepped out from behind the bishop topiary. "Yo, ladies," she said loudly.

That's when the Gray Sisters looked up. I say "looked," but the three of them were wearing very dark glasses, and I knew that there was, somehow, only one eyeball staring in our direction behind the lenses.

I cleared my throat, stepping out from behind the pawn, and gesturing to the others to join me. "Um, Sisters. G-Gray Sisters. We need your help."

The sister on the left elbowed the one in the middle. "I told you today would be interesting."

The middle sister said, "Bah!" to that and elbowed the one on the right, who had been sleeping and now startled awake.

"Are you the all-knowing Gray Sisters?" I asked. I had to make sure. What if we'd just stumbled upon three random retirees in the park?

At my question, the sisters began to laugh, and that's when I noticed that only one of them had teeth. Or rather, a tooth. Then they removed their glasses, and where their

eyes should have been were dark holes. Wasn't there supposed to be an eye somewhere?

Mela whimpered beside me. Thalia muttered something
about peeing her pants a little. Nia shoved me forward a
step.

"So, it—it is y-you. Good. That's good," I stumbled.
"We have a question to ask, since you're all-knowing and
all that. We're muses, by the way. Not all of us. Not her," I
said, pointing at Ari. "But the rest of us are and we thought
that maybe you could—"

"Stop talking," the Gray Sister in the center said. She
spit a little bit when she spoke. "If you want our help,
you'll need to do us a favor, dear girl."

"Yes, Calliope, Muse of the epic poem," the sister on
the right said. "How is your little brother, by the way? He's
got a tooth coming in, poor dear." She pointed at the tooth
in her mouth. "If he grows an extra one, feel free to bring
it to us."

The sister on the left piped up then. "Churros! I smell
them!" Extending her hand, the sister curled her fingers in
a "gimme" gesture.

Thalia handed over the oily bag that held what was left
of the churros. The sister on the left took it and divided the
treats among her sisters. In horror, we watched as, one by
one, they took turns sharing the tooth in order to munch
on the churros.

"I can't deal with this," Ari mumbled, and started pacing behind me.

"You said you needed help?" I asked after the last bite of churros was gone.

The three sisters grew serious. "Indeed," the center sister said. "Our eye is missing. Without it, we cannot see very far in any direction. Not the past."

"Not the present," added the left sister.

"Not the future," said the one on the right.

"And so any questions you may want to ask will not be answered. Not until we get the eye back," the center sister finished.

"Where is your eye?" Nia asked.

"An owl took it," the three sisters said at once.

Ari stopped pacing. "An owl?" she asked.

"Yes," they said, spit flying out of their mouths.

"Did you see where it went?" Mela asked.

The Gray Sisters pointed off to the right. "The Queens Zoo," the one on the right said.

"Bring us our eye, and we'll answer your question," the sister on the left said.

"And get us more churros!" the center sister added.

Chapter 13
OWL TROUBLE

We left the Gray Sisters sitting on the stone bench, muttering to one another. The afternoon sky was still bright as we followed a wooded path to the Queens Zoo, which occupied the same park space as the Botanical Garden and the Hall of Science. With so much green everywhere it didn't feel like we were in New York at all.

At the zoo's gates, we fished around in our pockets for money to get in, but we were short.

"What'll we do now?" Ari asked. "Sneak in?"

"I'd rather not get arrested in a foreign country," Thalia said.

"Hello? We are muses. Or have you all forgotten?" Nia asked, pulling her phone out and opening her muse app. "The stars are in a lucky alignment today. Who wants a crack at him?" she asked, gesturing at the man behind the ticket counter.

Ari scowled, and I could almost imagine what she was thinking—that we had powers we were abusing.

"Do you want help getting your tapestry back or not?" I asked her.

"I didn't say anything," Ari said with a shrug.

"No, but you were thinking it." I turned to Thalia. "Bring the funny."

Thalia clapped her hands and bounced over to the ticket counter. Before we knew it, she had the man laughing so hard he was crying and waving us all through the gates. I heard a thump as we passed him and saw that he was laughing so hard he'd fallen off his stool.

"You overdid it," I said.

"No such thing," Thalia sang back, skipping ahead.

We followed a winding path past enclosures with alligators, bears, and pumas. We walked by kids and their parents, ice-cream stands, and soda machines. All the while, we searched the trees for signs of an owl with an eyeball.

We stopped once we got to the massive aviary.

"If there's an owl to be found, it's in there," I said. There was a huge dome covering the aviary. It was made of wire mesh and steel.

"It's a geodesic dome," Nia said, her eyes wide as she

took it in. "First displayed at the World's Fair in 1964, like the rocket at the Hall of Science was. In fact, World's Fairs are—"

"I didn't realize muses were such nerds," Ari said with a sigh.

"Why are we helping her again?" Nia asked.

"Hush, both of you," I said. I'd heard a soft hooting amid the squawks that filled the air. We stepped inside the aviary. It was two stories tall, with lots of trees, and all kinds of birds perched here and there.

"I sort of hate this," Mela said. The rest of the Muse Squad nodded. Last year, we'd fought birds who were sirens in disguise. Feathers *still* made me nervous.

Then I heard it again. A soft *woo-hoo, woo-hoo*, coming from an oak tree. Slowly, I led our group forward until we were in the tree's shade. I looked up into the branches, squinting my eyes in the shadows.

"There!" Mela shouted, but she was too loud. The owl she'd spotted lifted its enormous wings and sailed silently over our heads, but not before we all saw it—in its beak was an eyeball, the pupil dark and darting around.

"I'm going to puke," Nia said with a gag.

"No! No puking. We need to get that eye!" I shouted as we ran after the owl. It stopped on a stand just a few feet away and dropped the eyeball into a bowl full of seeds.

"I'll throw something at it," Thalia was saying, holding her shoe with the smiley face over her head. She paused, waiting for us to tell her not to, which is what we usually did whenever Thalia came up with a plan. (Let's be honest, they were usually really bonkers ideas.)

But Mela, Nia, and I just looked at each other, nodded, and gave her a thumbs-up.

Thalia stopped and stared at us. "Seriously? I mean, this never happens. I'm genuinely chuffed you like my idea," she went on.

"Just do it!" Mela shouted, and Thalia chucked her shoe straight at the owl on its perch.

The bird screeched, spread its wings, and flapped a few times.

Then it dive-bombed us.

"Run!" I shouted.

"The eye!" Nia said, running back to the perch and the seed bowl. She wrapped her hands around the eyeball and shoved it down her shirt. "Gross, gross, gross," she screamed as she ran.

I felt a sharp talon scrape my shoulder and felt feathers grazing my face. Beside me, Mela was swinging her shiny, mirrored headphones at the owl, while Thalia was aiming her other shoe at its head. As for Ari, she was far away, watching it all go down with her arms crossed against her chest.

Suddenly, I heard Ari shout, "Stop it now! You aren't fooling anyone."

Had Ari suddenly lost it, talking to out-of-control birds

as if they could understand her?

The owl flapped its wings and hovered in the air for a moment, leaving off its attack. Then it seemed to spin into itself, becoming a whirl of feathers that grew and grew until it wasn't an owl anymore.

"I'd say I did a marvelous job of fooling them, actually." It was a woman in brown pants and a golden sweater that glimmered in the afternoon light. There were golden sandals on her feet, and her eyes, topped by dark eyebrows, were golden, too. Her skin was the color of the sun, and her hair hung in dark curls all the way down her back.

My heart hammered in my chest. Beside me, I watched as Mela's knees buckled, and she grabbed hold of my sleeve to steady herself.

"I feel funny," Nia said.

"Me, too. But not ha-ha funny," Thalia added.

The golden woman spoke at last. "It's good to see you again, Arachne. Though I've really been enjoying my retirement from human business the last few ages, and now that's all been interrupted." Her voice boomed, and I could swear that all of Queens had heard her. I looked out past the mesh walls of the aviary, but the people I saw here and there seemed to be going about their business.

"It's *not* good to see you again, Athena," Ari said.

Now it was my knees' turn to buckle. Athena? *The* Athena? Had Thalia just thrown a shoe at Athena? Goddess of wisdom, daughter of Zeus, and all that?

"Always the lack of respect." Athena tsked.

"Fine. It's *still* not good to see you again, O Dread Goddess Athena," Ari said, bowing dramatically.

"Better. Only marginally so," Athena said, her nostrils flaring a little. She waited before speaking again. I chanced a look at Nia, who was holding the bottom of her shirt tight against her body, guarding the eyeball inside. Thalia was still holding her shoe, her white socks filthy from the aviary's floor. Mela held on to my sleeve for dear life.

But Ari was standing before Athena, her arms still crossed, her chin in the air. I suppose I understood. She'd already spent centuries as a spider. What was the worst Athena could do to her?

"You'd be surprised what is the worst I can do, Calliope," Athena said. I was 100 percent sure she'd read my mind. That shook me. I had so many questions. This was *Athena*, for crying out loud. She mentioned that she'd been dragged out of retirement. Did that mean that all the gods were back to work? Clio had said that they'd mainly stayed out of the human world for centuries, but was that about to change? Before I could ask a question, though, Athena had one for me. "Have you had any interesting dreams lately?"

I shook my head. I hadn't dreamed much at all, not since coming to New York. But dreaming made me think of Tia Annie—how she used to visit me in dreams and tell me things I needed to know.

"Pity," Athena said, her voice still booming. "There are answers in your dreams. Perhaps one will come to you soon."

"Answers?" I started to ask, drawn toward her. What did that even mean?

"I'm sorry, am I interrupting something?" Ari asked, taking a step forward.

Athena turned her face to Ari. "Go on, Arachne. I'm listening."

"I'm challenging you to a do-over. My old tapestry against yours," Ari said. "But you already knew that."

Athena laughed, and though it should have sounded beautiful, it was also the scariest thing I'd ever heard.

"I did, of course. And you may have your do-over. At the Student Showcase, as you hoped. The terms are fair. And if I win, you go back to being your lovely, spidery self, and never challenge me again."

I watched as, for the first time since Athena appeared, Ari shook a little. "Fine," she said, her voice catching. "And if I win?"

Athena smiled. She looked at all of us, one by one, before turning her gaze back on Ari. "You get to be human. Permanently. Do what you will with your mortal life."

Ari nodded, letting out a long breath. "Deal," she said.

When Athena looked at us again, her face had softened a bit. Mainly, she looked disappointed, as if we'd switched teams on her. Maybe we had.

"Be careful, little sisters. You've decided to go on a quest. I love questing heroes. They keep me entertained. But you are poorly matched against me."

"What quest?" I asked quietly, afraid to raise my voice.

Athena smiled, flashing very bright, white teeth in our direction. "You'll see," she said, and then, before we knew what had happened, we were once again looking at an owl.

We all looked at the silent owl, which had started to preen its feathers as if we weren't there.

"Do we just . . . go?" Mela asked, her eyes never leaving the owl.

"Not before I get my shoe back," Thalia said, picking up the one she'd thrown.

Ari shooed away the owl, and it flapped off with a screech. "Athena's not even here anymore. That's just a regular old owl again."

Meanwhile, Nia was fishing the eyeball out from under her shirt. She held it up, and the pupil swiftly faced her. "Gah!" she shouted, dropping the eye onto the ground. It made a *splat* sound when it fell, and the rest of us screamed when we heard it.

"Pick it up, pick it up," Mela was whispering.

Trembling, I grabbed the gooey eyeball, cringing the whole time. "Let's go," I said, and led the others out of the aviary and the zoo, and back to the Gray Sisters.

Chapter 14
A GAME OF CHESS

We found the Gray Sisters on the chess board, pushing around the huge topiaries as they played a game. They huffed as they hauled the potted plants here and there, shouting out things like "Bishop to knight four!"

"How are they doing that if they can't see?" Mela whispered.

"They memorized the board. There are chess champs that can do it—play whole games blindfolded!" Nia said.

Thalia whistled in awe, and one of the sisters stopped, cocking her head to the side, listening. "You've returned, muses and friend. Have you brought us what we lost?" The other sisters stopped pushing topiaries and faced us.

"Yes," I said, holding the eyeball in the palm of my hand. "You must have known it was Athena who had your eye. Why didn't you tell us?" I demanded.

"You didn't ask," the three said at the same time.

I sighed. "Will you help us now?"

The Gray Sisters hobbled over, six hands reaching out to the eye. They squabbled a bit as to who would get to wear it first, but the tallest of the sisters won out. She slammed the eyeball into her empty socket, blinked a few times, then looked at me with a watery expression.

"There you are," she said, and extended a hand.

I shook it and introduced myself. "Callie Martinez-Silva. Nice to meet you."

"Horror," the sister said.

"Pardon?" Thalia asked.

"Horror. It's my name. And these are my sisters, Dread and Alarm," Horror said. Her sisters reached out to shake hands with everyone.

Mela tried to be polite. "Your names are very, um, they are quite—"

"Dreadful."

"Horrible."

"Alarming," the sisters said in turn.

"Why do I find this so amusing?" Thalia commented, laughing.

Now it was Dread's turn to wear the eye, and they managed the exchange without too much trouble this time. It seemed they had a silent rotation they kept to, and whenever they made the switch I looked away. My stomach just couldn't take it.

"So will you help us?" Nia asked.

"Certainly," Alarm said. "You may ask one question."

"Just one?" I asked.

"Just one," the sisters said together.

One? After all the trouble we'd gone to? We had more than one question!

"Easy," Nia said. "We ask about the tenth muse. That's our mission."

Mela shook her head. "Athena said she's looking forward to our quest. Shouldn't we focus on that?"

Thalia laughed. "Sure she is. More like she's looking forward to turning us all into insects."

"Arachnids," Mela corrected.

Thalia pointed her finger at Mela's face. "Listen, I'm not getting permanently transformed into a *whatever* for her sake," she said, shifting her finger toward Ari.

Nia slid over to stand by Thalia, while Mela linked Ari's arm with hers.

"Two against two," Ari said. "You're the tie-breaker, Callie."

"Why me?" I asked. This wasn't fair. All this time, I'd been the one making all the hard choices. I thought of Clio in her office, calling meetings, figuring out how the muses could be helpful, prioritizing our missions. Is that what this was the beginning of? All that responsibility?

I looked at the Gray Sisters, who had stopped fussing with their eye to stare at me intently. They knew everything—why I was a muse in the first place, whether Ari would be successful in her quest, who the tenth muse was, what Tia Annie had asked of the gods on Mount Olympus, all of it. Suddenly, I felt like this was a game of chess. If I could make the right move, or better yet, if I could ask the perfect question, it would be a key that answered everything at once. I thought of the rules.

A muse always trusts her instincts. Rule number one.

A muse is no better, or worse, than the heroes she inspires. Rule number eight.

Ari was clutching Mela's arm tightly, chewing her bottom lip. Her colorful bracelets caught my eye. She had on so many, the designs and patterns so intricate it was hard to believe a person could make such things. Her work was *inspired*, and I wondered if there had been a muse at her side that day when she faced off against Athena the first time. Athena had thought she was better than Ari, even when everyone else thought differently. If Athena were a muse, she'd be breaking a pretty big rule.

But she wasn't a muse. She wasn't a minor goddess.

She was Athena. She was a very big, very scary, very powerful deal.

Nia was calling my name. "Callie. Make a choice."

"It's hard, okay?" I shot back.

"I know." Nia took a deep breath. "But I'm on your side, no matter what. We're a team, right?" The others nodded.

Closing my eyes tight as though I was making a wish, I

blurted out the question that needed to be asked. Maybe it wasn't the perfect one, but it felt like the *right* one.

"Where can we find Ari's tapestry?"

Behind me, I heard Nia sigh, and Thalia make a little squeaking sound. But they were soon at my side, along with Mela and Ari.

Dread was the first to speak. "The tapestry about which you inquire was torn by the goddess into four pieces. You may find the first in Greenwich Village, in a bookshop called Vision Books."

Ari stepped forward. "You mean here in New York? A piece of my tapestry has been here all along?"

Horror giggled and adjusted the tooth with her tongue. "No, not all along. That's merely where it is now. Athena has set you on a quest, after all."

"A quest, a quest, I love a quest!" Alarm said, clapping her hands like a little girl. "All the best stories are quest stories. First, you have a problem that needs to be solved. In this case, you seek justice," she said, winking at Ari. As she did, the goopy eye leaked a bit.

"Then," continued Horror, "the quester gets some help." She pointed a long, gnarled finger at us.

"The monsters are next! The monsters are next!" Dread sang, skipping around a pawn topiary.

Alarm handed over the eyeball, swapping it with her sister for the tooth. "If you defeat the monsters, you get what you sought!"

"Sometimes," Horror clarified.

"Yes, only sometimes," Dread added. "And some-times . . ." She stopped and dragged her finger across her throat.

Alarm cackled. "It's a fun time either way!"

By that point, Mela had been swaying on her feet, and Thalia caught her before she hit the ground. "Monsters?" she asked weakly.

"Probably," the three sisters said at once. "That's usually how it goes with quests."

"It's a trap," Thalia said. "A rather unfunny one."

"Callie made the call," Nia said. "Trap or not, we have a new mission."

Thank you, I said silently to Nia, who only pressed her lips together in a look that said "You'd better be right."

"What about the other three pieces?" I asked.

Horror lifted a single gnarled finger. "One question. One. And you've asked it already." Then the Gray Sisters gathered their purses, as well as three walking canes they'd stashed behind the stone bench.

"We should be off," Alarm said.

"Our favorite show is on tonight. *Zombie Beach*!" Dread added.

"Lovely to meet you, dears!" Horror called back to us as the three of them walked away.

We watched as they followed the path that led out of the botanical garden, when suddenly they froze and turned to face us. Then, speaking in unison, they said, "It's not a trap, by the way. Athena has designed a real quest. But it doesn't mean it's going to be easy, so keep your heads about you, and thanks for the eye."

Then they went off for real, leaving the five of us standing there, wondering what in the world we were about to face.

Chapter 15
TINY SNACKS

"Let's go!" Ari shouted enthusiastically as soon as the Gray Sisters were out of sight.

The rest of us paused. We needed a plan. We needed to stop and think. Didn't we? The sun was low in the sky, and my stomach grumbled. It was five o'clock, and Papi and Laura were probably wondering where I was by now.

"We can go find the first piece of the tapestry tomorrow. After camp, okay?" I suggested.

Ari folded her arms. "Not okay. My life is on the line here."

"I agree with Ari," Mela said.

"And I want to go home," Thalia added.

Here we were again, splitting into sides. I was tired of it.

"Well, I'm not going to be the deciding vote this time. Nia, tell us what to do."

Nia rolled her eyes. She glanced at the time on her phone. "Fine. It's the middle of the night in London and New Delhi, and my dad thinks I'm at the library back home. Do you have an excuse, Callie?"

I thought of Laura, who was probably just getting home with Rafaelito, and wondering where I was. This was more important, wasn't it? "I'll figure something out," I said.

"Then we'll go to the bookstore," Nia said. "We'll get the first piece of the tapestry, then we all go home. Understood?" She'd leveled the question at Ari, who nodded, then smiled brightly.

"Wait till you see it," Ari said, leading us out of the garden. "The tapestry, I mean. It was my best work."

I hoped Ari was right. I'd already seen Athena's tapestry, and it was amazing. It had made me feel the things that were represented in the pictures. There was magic in it, I was sure. Would Ari's make me feel the same way?

I glanced at my phone to check the time. Five o'clock. Papi was going to ground me for an eternity. Nervous, I gave him a call. The phone rang three times before he picked up.

"¿Oigo?"

"Hi, Papi. Listen, I'm still at camp with Ari. We're working on a project."

In the background, I could hear men hollering directions and the squealing of machines.

"Okay, mi'jita. I'll text Laura. Get home by seven."

"I will. Love you."

"Love you, too."

Then we hung up. My entire face felt hot. I hated lying, and I especially hated lying to my parents. I watched as Ari and Mela chatted, their steps in sync, their long dark hair swinging back and forth at the same time. Mela had said that Ari's mission was the most important thing we'd done, and Mela was almost always right. But I just didn't see it. Out there, somewhere, was a tenth muse, someone who was like us, and we couldn't find her. *That* was our assignment. Not Ari and Athena's ages-old beef with each other.

But Mela had trusted her instincts on this one, and I trusted Mela. Nia and Thalia, too. Like Nia had said, we were a team. We had one another's backs.

Ari led us to the 111th Street station, and we took the 7 train and then the D to Washington Square. Huge skyscrapers rose up in the distance, but in Greenwich Village, there were pretty three-story buildings of red brick, with flower boxes in the windows, and front stoops with flowerpots, and college kids with their backpacks, hurrying here and there.

This was the New York I saw in movies, where people fell in love and kissed on the stoops. I thought of Corona, which looked so different, but felt like home.

Ari had brought us here almost without thinking. She certainly didn't even glance at a subway map. She just knew where we were going. I couldn't imagine it. The city was so big!

Finally, we were standing outside Vision Books. The exterior was painted bright red, and in the curved, leaded window sat rows of books, facing out.

"Do we just ask where they keep the pieces of ancient tapestry, or what?" Thalia wondered.

"Powers, remember?" Nia said. "We have them. Let's use them."

Inside, there was a young white woman behind the counter wearing an NYU sweater. There was a huge textbook open in front of her, and pages of notes. She was biting a pencil between her teeth, and in her hand she held another, which she was using to scratch her eyebrow as she read. The store was tiny, and she was the only other person in there. She glanced up at us, said "Hey," then turned back to her work.

"I've got this," Nia whispered. We watched as Nia approached the counter, startling the girl. She had on a name tag that read AUDREY.

"Can I help you?"

Nia peered at the textbook. "Chemistry?"

Audrey groaned. "Yes. This summer class is kicking my butt."

"May I?" Nia asked, and Audrey turned the textbook around for her to see.

"What are you, like fifteen or something?"

Nia slowly turned the page. "Twelve." Then she brightened up. "See here? This is how you split the ions. On your homework, you forgot to do that."

Audrey glanced at her work, then groaned again.

I watched as Nia rubbed her hands together and chewed on her cheek. That was her kódikas. It was subtle, unlike Mela's hand waving or Thalia's laughing out loud.

"Wait, wait, wait," Audrey started to say, scrabbling for the pencil in her hair. "Complex ions . . . ," she started to mutter.

"Mind if we look around the store?" Nia asked, and Audrey only nodded, waving us all off as she completed problem after problem in her textbook.

Thalia high-fived Nia, then we got to work. One by one, we tugged books off the shelf, hoping that a piece of tapestry might come fluttering out from between the pages. Mela rifled through the drawers behind the counter. Audrey didn't even notice, she was so focused on her chemistry homework. Ari had made sure to lock the door and turn the Open sign over to Closed.

We had worked through the books in the travel section, the fiction section, the poetry section, the history section, picture books, and middle grade books when I heard Thalia say, "Oh! Obviously!" and we all stopped searching.

"The mythology section, of course," Thalia said. We ran over and started opening up books—coffee table books, picture books, pop-up books—all about the different myths of the world.

I heard someone suck in her breath. It was Ari. Her hand rested on the spine of a book entitled *Arachne's Revenge*. The book was glowing under her touch, as if someone were shining a spotlight on it from somewhere.

"It's humming," Ari said. We all reached out to touch the book—she was right.

"Okay then. We've found it. Go on," I nudged. I wanted to send a little muse courage her way, but I resisted—I knew Ari didn't like it. These days, it was like I could always feel my magic, rumbling just under the surface of my skin, but caged up. Or leashed somehow. It was hard to explain. When I let it go, I could feel the magic all over, making my skin tingle like it always did.

"On three," Ari said. "One, two, three." She pulled the book out and turned the pages. But there was nothing there. The book, in fact, was blank.

"What the—" Nia started to say, when the entire shelf holding the mythology books slid off to the right, as if it were on wheels. Behind the shelf was a set of damp stone steps leading down into a dark hold.

"Nuh-uh," Thalia said, taking a step backward.

"*Now* it's a quest," Mela whispered.

"Monsters, remember?" Ari said. "The Gray Sisters were pretty sure about that particular point."

"Trap," Thalia whispered back.

"The Gray Sisters said it wasn't a trap," I said.

"And we trust them why?" Thalia insisted.

"We've come this far," Nia said. She shoved the book into her purse.

I took out my phone, hit the flashlight feature, and aimed the light down the steps. The walls were made of stone, too, and I could hear dripping water echoing below. "Come on," I said, taking the first step forward.

The stairs went on for a long time. I counted thirteen steps before we hit the bottom. It was so dark that our phones only lit up the gloom a few feet ahead of us.

My phone rang then, and we all yelped.

"Hello?"

It was Laura. "Hey. Your dad called, said you were busy?"

"Sorry. Camp stuff," I said.

"I decided to take a walk with Rafaelito and we passed by Corona Arts. It's all closed up for the day. Are you in there?"

"Um. No? No. We went to Ari's house to work on the project."

Ari snatched my phone away from me.

"Hi, Mrs. Silva! Yep. Yep. She's with me. Big project. I'll walk her home when we're done. Okay, bye!"

Ari handed my phone back. "Thanks," I said. "I'm not good at that kind of stuff."

Shrugging, Ari said, "Well, I am." But she didn't seem too proud about it.

A few minutes later, the tunnel we'd been walking through forked in front of us.

"This is the worst," Nia said, throwing up her hands.

"Left or right?" Mela asked.

"Both? But I don't want to split up," I said. Who knew where the tunnels led, or how far we'd already gone? I turned around, and the light from the bookstore was just a speck in the distance now. Plus, I'd also just straight-up lied to Laura.

I decided I did not like quests. I really didn't.

Before we could make up our minds about whether to go left, right, or split up, though, the lights on our phones went out at once.

"Too bright," growled a deep voice just ahead of us.

All five of us screamed as loudly as we could and started running back where we came from. I could feel whatever it was breathing hotly just at my neck. "Stop running, tiny snacks," it was saying.

"We aren't your snacks!" Thalia shouted back.

The door to the bookstore got closer and closer as we ran to it.

"Almost there!" I heard Mela, who was in the lead, shouting.

"TINY SNACKS!" the creature growled.

Just as we were about to reach the door, we watched in horror as it slid shut.

We huddled on the steps, turning slowly to face the thing that was pursuing us. One by one, we lit our phones again, pointing them at the creature.

It was a man. A giant man, who had to bend over to walk through the tunnel. He was barefoot, but he wore shredded jeans and a green T-shirt that read GO JETS! He was completely bald, and his skin was very pale, and there, on his forehead, just above his nose, was a solitary, yellow, enormous eye.

"Cyclops," Ari whispered.

The cyclops was holding a crust-covered fork in one hand and a gleaming knife in the other. Around his neck was a long napkin, and he was drooling as he stared at us.

My knees shook, as did my hands. Could I inspire him to just *not* eat us? Could mythical monsters even be inspired? It hadn't worked last year with the sirens, but I had to try. Just as I started releasing my magic, I watched as a single, smiley-faced shoe bonked the cyclops on the head.

The cyclops roared.

"Timing," Nia said to Thalia, who held up her other shoe in her hand.

"Well, what were you lot planning to do?" she responded.

Ari surged forward then, thrust her hands out, fingers splayed, and stared down the cyclops.

"Give me my tapestry or else," she said, her voice low and dangerous sounding.

That's when I noticed it. The napkin around the cyclops's neck wasn't just a napkin. It was a piece of tapestry! Even in the gloom, its colors were bright, and I could just make out a piece of the intricate scene—a man sniffing a flower, his eyes closed in delight.

"Or else what, tiny snack?" the cyclops said, a drop of drool landing on the tapestry.

Ari made a strangled sound, lifted her hands, and suddenly millions of spiders started crawling out from the cracks in the walls. They skittered over the cyclops's legs, up his jeans, over his T-shirt, and crept into the corners of his mouth and all over his eye until he couldn't see a thing.

The cyclops roared, grabbing at the spiders with his big hands. But they skittered away from his fingers, blocking us from his view.

Ari jumped up and snatched the tapestry from around the cyclops's neck. When she did, the door behind us slid open again. We ran through it and back into the light, shutting out the sound of the cyclops roaring, "My tiny snacks! Where did you go?"

Bending down, I clutched my knees and tried to catch my breath. The others were doing the same. As for Audrey, she was still working on her chemistry homework, utterly unaware of what was happening just a few feet behind her.

"Monsters under the shops in Manhattan," Nia mused. "Unbelievable."

Mela was crying and Thalia was laughing, both from nerves.

As for Ari, she was holding her piece of tapestry gingerly in the palms of her hands. "It's been so long," she was saying, sniffling. Carefully, she folded the cloth, which was about the size of a baby blanket, and tucked it into the waistband of her jeans.

"One down," I said.

"Three to go," Nia added.

"But where's the next one?" Mela asked.

"It's a quest, right?" Thalia said. "That means you tackle one thing at a time, and the answer reveals itself to you after each portion of the quest is completed. Like in the Narnia books, when Eustace and Jill go to Cair Paravel and—"

Mela moaned. "I beg of you, Thalia. Now is not the time for your Narnia obsession."

Suddenly, Ari gasped. "She's right! Each part of a quest leads you to the next clue. The book, Nia! You have it?"

Nia zipped her purse open, rummaged through it for a minute, tossing receipts, two packs of gum, and a phone charger onto the sidewalk before pulling out the book titled *Arachne's Revenge*. It wasn't glowing anymore—it just looked like an old, battered book.

"But the pages were blank, remember?" Nia said, handing the book over to me.

I opened it carefully and held my breath, thinking of an episode of *Zombie Beach* where a monster jumped out of a book.

The first page was blank. I turned it, and there, in glittering gold letters, it read:

The second piece awaits you in the small boot. Bring your appetites.

"This doesn't make sense," I said, and flipped through the rest of the pages in case there was an answer key in there, too.

"It's a clue," Nia said.

Ari straightened. "At least we have this much," she said. "Thanks, everyone. Let's get you back to Queens."

We followed Ari out of the store, flipping the Closed sign back to Open as we went. Thalia had on only one shoe, but nobody around us seemed to notice. The sun was down now, and the trains were packed, and it took a long time to get back to Corona. We were silent the whole way home, each of us thinking about what we'd just gone through, trying to figure out the riddle and wondering what was ahead.

Three more pieces of tapestry to go.

A cyclops?

Almost becoming "tiny snacks" for a monster under a bookstore?

Why did I have a feeling *that* had been the easy part?

Chapter 16
A PICNIC NEAR THE SHORE

We all parted ways in front of the Hall of Science. Nia managed to give one of the security guards an idea about a new camera system for the museum and, distracted, he let the others inside after hours, back to their entrance points, which would take Nia, Thalia, and Mela home.

Then Ari and I walked to Papi and Laura's place.

"You okay?" I asked. Ari had been stroking the piece of tapestry the whole time, lost in thought.

"Better than I've been in ages," she said. "I know we'll figure out the next step. We have to. Thank you, Callie, for using your one question to the Gray Sisters on me. I don't think I'll ever be able to make it up to you."

"It's what we do. We help others." Behind me, the windows of my dad's house were glowing softly. We watched as the curtains parted, and Papi's face appeared. He looked at us both with a frown, then pointed at his watch.

"Busted," Ari said.

"Totally. I'd better go."

"See you at camp, poet. Think 'small boots'!" she called, then walked away.

I unlocked the front door and climbed the steps to the apartment. I could smell what was left of dinner in the air—fish and maduros—and I could hear Laura running the vacuum cleaner. Rafaelito, for once, wasn't crying.

Before I could get my hand on the knob, Papi opened the door. He was holding his wristwatch, dangling it in front of my face.

"What time is it, Callie?"

"Eight fifteen," I said. I could feel my voice quiver. I hated getting in trouble with Papi. He always sounded so . . . disappointed in me.

"And you were supposed to be home when?"

"Seven. I'm sorry, Papi. We lost track of time."

Inside, Papi sat on the couch, and patted the seat next to him so that I would sit, too. He ran his large hand over his face and sighed. "It's a big city. Bigger than you're used to. It makes me nervous when you don't come home on time," he said softly.

The vacuum switched off. "It makes us both nervous," Laura called from the other room before turning the vacuum back on again.

"I'm sorry," I said. I hated not being able to tell him the

truth. But, like Mami, if Papi knew about the muses, he'd want me to quit. He'd think it was too dangerous.

"I know you're sorry," Papi said. "And I want you to know I'm not angry."

"You aren't?"

"¿Bravo? No. But disappointed? Sí. Un poco."

There it was.

"You're a good kid, and I'm a lucky dad."

I hugged him, and he squeezed me back. "We're cool, then?" I asked, my words muffled against his shoulder.

"Always, Callie," he said. When he let me go, he reached out his hand, palm up. "Your teléfono, por favor."

"What?!"

"Your phone. I'm taking your phone for the foreseeable future. It's your castigo."

"Castigo? You're punishing me? I thought we were cool?" I asked, getting to my feet. "I wasn't *that* late!"

"You were late enough. Teléfono, por favor." Papi's hand hovered in the air.

I let out a sound like "Ugh," pulled my phone from my pocket, and handed it to Papi.

"Next time, get home when I ask you to. Laura has your dinner waiting." Then Papi rose and went off to take a shower.

I stomped into the kitchen. Laura was pulling my plate out of the microwave. She set it on a placemat that had the New York skyline drawn on it, then she filled a glass with orange juice and set it down for me. "Eat up," she said.

"Thanks, Laura." My stepmom was an excellent cook, and I ate quickly. I was definitely upset about losing my phone, but I still had my bracelet and could get in touch with the Muse Squad that way if I had to. As for Ari, I knew where to find her.

"So what are you and Ari working on?" Laura asked, pulling up a chair to sit with me as I ate.

I hadn't come up with that part of my excuse, so I told her a half-truth. "We're putting together a puzzle. It's for the Student Showcase." A quest was sort of like a puzzle, wasn't it?

"Oh," Laura said, her eyes narrowing a little. Then her look softened again, and she patted my hand. "I hope you're having fun here, Callie. Your father has really missed you and your brothers. Me, too."

I didn't say what was in my heart: I wondered if what she said was true. Papi and Laura had gotten married and moved far away, and we didn't hear from them as often as Mario, Fernando, and I would have liked. I didn't doubt that Papi loved us. Of course he did. But did he miss us? *Really* miss us? When he had a new wife and a new baby, a new job and a new city? Was he maybe too busy to miss us?

I cleaned off my plate, rinsed and dried it, and helped Laura wipe down the table. She sang softly while she cleaned, a real Snow White, and I said so. Laura laughed.

"I like things orderly. Always have," she said. "Am I a pain about it? I don't mean to be," she added.

"Not really," I said, laughing. "I hope I'm not too much of a slob for you."

"We're cool," Laura said, and held her fist up for a bump.

I gave her a fist bump back, but added, "That's what Papi said, and he still took my phone." I didn't want to make Laura feel bad, though, so I asked, "Want to watch TV?"

"Definitely." Laura made popcorn, and I picked a show. We settled on the latest episode of *Zombie Beach*. I watched under a blanket, cuddling one of Rafaelito's stuffed animals—a zebra—and tried not to close my eyes during the scary parts.

But somehow, halfway through the episode, my head grew heavy, and before I knew it, I wasn't in the apartment with Laura, Papi, and Rafaelito.

I was somewhere else, on a familiar shore, watching as a boat with a small woman in the prow floated toward me in the distance.

"Tia Annie," I shouted, waving my hands over my head. I was back there again, in my dream but also with Tia Annie, in the same place where I'd spoken with her last year. Behind me, a green field rolled on and on. Before me, a large body of water rippled and glimmered, as distant searchlights swept the sky.

The lights were the source of muse magic, and Tia Annie was the guardian of this place, of the lights.

"Callie-Mallie," Tia Annie said, bringing the boat to the shore.

I chewed on my bottom lip, reaching out my hand to help my aunt out of the boat. I must have grown a bit since I saw her last, because Tia Annie and I were almost the same height. Her dark blond hair was up in a ponytail, and she was wearing a white dress with a red shawl around her shoulders.

Athena had told me there would be answers in my dreams. Was this it? Would I wake up and know more than I did before I fell asleep?

"I'm dreaming, right?"

"Yes, of course," Tia Annie said, laughing.

"Well, you're interrupting a good episode of *Zombie Beach*."

"I'm not the one who fell asleep."

Now I laughed. "Good point. Busy day, that's all."

"I know," Tia Annie said, growing serious. She reached into the boat and pulled out a blanket and a basket. "Picnic?"

The weather was warm, and the grass was soft and dry. Tia Annie's blanket was rolled up tight, and she unfurled it with a snap. But it wasn't just a blanket. It was a tapestry!

"Is that Ari's tapestry?" I asked. I'd seen only a bit of the piece we'd gotten from the cyclops.

"It's only a copy, of course," Tia Annie said. She smoothed it out on the grass, settled the basket in the center, and pulled out small sandwiches, two thermoses, and some chocolate-chip cookies, setting the food on pretty blue plates. She dusted her hands of crumbs, then gazed at her work for a moment. "I wanted you to see it, Callie. The whole tapestry. Just so you know what you're getting into," Tia Annie said, then took a bite out of her sandwich.

I reached over and pulled one corner of the tapestry tight. This was the piece we'd found in the cyclops's den under the bookstore. The portrait of a man smelling a flower without a care in the world. Behind him, a dark sky was caught mid-lightning strike. Farther in the background were houses on fire, and tiny people running about with buckets full of water, trying to put the fire out.

I crawled over the blanket to another corner. This section was woven all in blue, as if the figures were underwater, and upon that was embroidered another man. His fingers were webbed, and his teeth were sharp, like a shark's. There was an octopus wrapped around one of his legs, and an eel biting one of his toes. In the background, a ship was half submerged in the water, its mast cracked in half. The man with webbed hands and sharp teeth smiled goofily, as if he couldn't be bothered with what was happening behind him.

"Go on," Tia Annie said, munching on her sandwich.

She scooted over so I could examine the section she'd been sitting on.

The third picture showed yet another man. This one was sitting in a field. The grass had been woven so carefully that I could see every single blade, and on many of the blades, there were drops of dew. This man had a jug in his hand, and he drank from it sloppily. Red wine spilled everywhere. He had one eye closed and one opened, and his hair was a mess, like he hadn't combed it in forever. Off to his right, a woman struggled as she pulled on the reins of a horse, startled by a snake on the path. The horse's nostrils were flared, and its front hooves kicked in the air as it bucked. The woman's mouth was open in a scream, but the drinking man was oblivious to it.

I was sitting on the fourth and final panel, so I stood up to take a good look. It was a portrait of a woman. She was beautiful. Her hair was golden and done up in an intricate braid. She looked really familiar. Just like the first two pictures, something else was going on behind her. Ari had embroidered thousands, and I mean *thousands*, of tiny people, all of them dying. I saw spears, and swords, and horses turned over. It was a war. Meanwhile, the woman, whose face took up most of the frame, smiled on, as if nothing was happening behind her.

"Athena," I whispered. "That's Athena."

"Hmm. Yes," Tia Annie said, her mouth full.

Taking a deep breath, I tried to name the others. "Poseidon, in the water? And who's the guy drinking like he's never heard of good manners?"

"Dionysus. God of wine." Tia Annie lifted her juice box in a toast.

"Got it. That leaves this guy." I looked over the final panel again. The dark, ominous sky was lit up by jagged strikes of lightning. The fire licking the tops of the houses looked almost real. I let my hand hover over the flames. I could imagine the heat of it. The lightning was the clue.

"Zeus," I said. "God of—"

"Sky. Thunder. Lightning."

"The big chief," I added.

"Now you see why Athena was angry about this tapestry."

I walked around the tapestry, taking it all in again. The pictures were so vivid, it felt like I was looking through a window. "I do," I said. Ari had made the gods look so foolish. Worse—she'd made them look heartless.

I sat back down on the tapestry. So this was what we were looking for. Ari hoped to piece it all together again and challenge Athena with it once more.

"Arachne has been trying to make her point for thousands of years," Tia Annie said, unwrapping a sandwich for me.

"Her point?"

"That the gods, like humans, are imperfect."

"But nobody worships the gods anymore. Not really," I said, remembering what Clio told me last year about the gods, how they'd given up on humans, mainly. Except for the muses, of course. We'd stuck around. Inspiration is always needed.

Tia Annie handed me a juice box. "The gods are mostly retired, as you know. Not Athena, though. She's always been the overachiever on Mount Olympus. In charge of too much. Wisdom. Courage. Justice. Strategy, et cetera. She hasn't retired so much as . . . gone on a lengthy semi-vacation. She checks in on humans quite a bit. Which makes her invested, so to speak. Athena won't back down easily."

"You don't think we should help Ari?"

"I didn't say that, Callie. I think what happened to Arachne was unjust. Injustice should be corrected." Tia Annie took hold of my hands. "But be careful, mi niña. You can't bring a war to Athena. You won't win."

"Athena called it a quest," I said.

Tia Annie was thoughtful for a moment. "Did she? Well, that changes things. That's better, in fact. A quest you can complete. A quest you can *finish*." Her eyes lit up with possibility.

We ate some more, and I dimly remembered that I'd just had dinner with Laura back in Queens. Where I was still sleeping on the couch.

It was all very confusing.

But Tia Annie nudged me with her foot, and that felt very real, too.

"The sandwiches were good," I said, finishing the last bite.

"It's the ambrosia spread," Tia Annie said.

"The what?"

"Food of the gods. Ambrosia."

"Tastes like honey mustard," I said.

She smacked her lips and said, "I suppose it does."

I helped Tia Annie put things away in her basket, then rolled up the copy of Ari's tapestry. "Can I ask you a question?"

"Of course."

"Did I make the right choice with the Gray Sisters? Asking about Ari's tapestry and not the tenth muse? Do you know anything about the tenth muse, by the way, 'cause that would be awesome if you did."

Tia Annie laughed. "Bueno, that's two questions." She looked down at her hands. "There have always been nine, never ten."

"That's what Clio said."

"Clio is wise."

I thought for a moment. "Tia Annie, if there *are* ten of us now, why would the gods care?"

Tia Annie leaned back on the grass as she spoke. "The gods may be retired, Callie, but they aren't dead. And it doesn't mean the affairs of humans don't matter to them. They just aren't *working*, so to speak. The Gray Sisters hang out in Queens all day, talk to people, play chess. Sometimes, Athena attends college lectures by classics professors. Poseidon has annual passes to all the best water parks. They blend in. They have fun. But sometimes, like in Ari's case, they get involved again."

I thought that over for a bit. I mean, it made sense. The muses were still around. Why would the gods want to be stuck on Mount Olympus all the time?

"Ari, I understand," I said. "She wants to challenge Athena for the second time. Seems like a big deal. But would the gods actually care if there were nine muses, or ten, or twenty?"

Tia Annie rolled over onto her side, cradling her head in the crook of her arm. She looked like she used to back when she was alive, when she would sit on the rug with me to play board games or Barbies. My heart felt like someone was squeezing it just looking at her. "The muses were created by the gods to help humanity be the best they can be. They decided upon nine. That's it. Their decisions don't usually change. Which is why Ari's mission is so important. When the time comes, you'll know who the tenth muse is, and you'll welcome her, the same way the muses have always welcomed new members. But there will be only nine in the end. I'm sure of it."

I shut my eyes tight and asked another question.

"Tia Annie, are we in danger? Is someone going to d-die?"

My aunt sat up and hugged me. "I don't think that's it. But be safe, okay?"

I'd been secretly hoping that we would find the tenth muse and that it would just be . . . fine. We would be ten from then on. Tia Annie crushed that hope. But at least she didn't say any one of us was about to kick the muse bucket. There was that.

"All right," I said, and gave Tia Annie a big squeeze before letting go. "What about the Gray Sisters? Did I ask them the right question?"

"Absolutely. Think of Arachne's problem as a sort of keystone. It holds all the other questions up."

"I don't get it."

"Everything up until now led to that moment, that question, and your decision to help Arachne. And only you can help her, Callie. In the end, everything will be up to you." Tia Annie put her things back into the little boat, and I knew that our time together was over. In the distance I could hear it, the closing notes of the *Zombie Beach* theme song as the credits scrolled by on the screen.

"If I ask you to explain that, you aren't gonna, are you?"

Tia Annie shook her head.

"Okay. Can I ask one more thing, real quick?"

"You're going to wake up any minute, Callie-Mallie," Tia Annie said.

"Real quick! Why did you go to Mount Olympus? What did you ask the gods?"

"Too many questions. Again," Tia Annie said.

Before she could answer me, I opened my eyes.

Laura was there, nudging me awake.

"You missed the end, muñeca," she was saying.

My eyes were stinging with tears. It wasn't fair! I had been so close!

"Hey, you okay?" Laura asked.

I rubbed my eyes, pretended the tears were just from sleep or something. "I'm fine. Tired. Going to bed now." Laura nodded as if she understood, which she couldn't, of course.

She kissed my cheek and said, "Buenas noches," then turned off the TV and went to check on Rafaelito in his crib.

"Good night," I said quietly. Rubbing my face with my hands, I thought about how the last two days had turned out.

1. Ari had revealed herself to be Arachne. *The* Arachne.
2. We'd met the Gray Sisters, rescued their eyeball from an owl—an owl that turned out to be Athena, *the* Athena, who set us on a quest.
3. Then I got punished for coming home late.
4. Then Tia Annie came to me in a dream and told me that only I could help Arachne defeat Athena. That it was all up to me.

You know when you have to pick up your room, and it's been too messy for too long, so you don't even know where to start? This is what that felt like, but a million times more overwhelming.

I felt super sleepy then. *I can deal with this later,* I reminded myself. *Right now, I just need to go to sleep.*

Which is what I did, without dreaming a thing.

Chapter 17
POETRY-PALOOZA

Every day, Ari asked me if I'd figured out the next part of the quest. "Sorry, no," I'd say, and Ari would stomp the ground in frustration. She hadn't come up with anything, either. I'd see her at work with the textile arts group, and she'd wave at me, her brow wrinkled, and get back to work. I'd tried to figure it out, even searching "small boot" on the internet, but nothing came up besides podiatrist sites and shoe stores.

A week after we'd gotten the first piece of the tapestry from the cyclops, Ari met me by the front doors at camp. "Any luck today?" she asked.

I shook my head. "I'm coming up empty." Kids streamed past us carrying costumes. One girl balanced three tiaras on her head. Another held a bunch of parasols.

"Look around, Callie. The Student Showcase is at the

end of the summer! I need all the pieces of the tapestry back in time to mend it." She placed a finger on her chin as she thought. "We *have* to figure this out."

"I know," I said.

"That clue we found . . . ," Ari began to say when suddenly, Maris was at my side, hair in a bun, pen sticking out of it, as usual.

"We should get started on our Student Showcase Poetry-palooza today," Maris said in a serious tone, like she'd just reminded me to get a flu shot.

"The poetry-pa-whatta?" I asked.

"Our entry for the showcase," Maris said.

I gave her a blank look.

"We discussed it yesterday, Callie. Weren't you paying attention?" Maris said, looking as if I'd run over her pet dog or something.

"Right, right. I forgot," I said, trying to recover.

"It's fine," she said. "Listen, I wanted to talk to you both about something I'm planning for tomorrow."

Ari shook her head. "We were having a conversation, Maris."

"Oh," she said, her face suddenly very sad.

"Meet you upstairs?" I suggested.

"Okay," Maris said. "Parting is such sweet sorrow, et cetera, et cetera." She pulled a book of poetry out of her bag and read it as she walked.

"She's like a cartoon character," Ari said, laughing.

"Don't make fun."

"Come on. She totally is. With the poetry-this, and poetry-that," Ari said, waving her hands around like she was conducting music.

I could feel my temper rising. I hadn't thought of it until now, but Maris reminded me a lot of my sister, Maya. They were both a little off-center, extremely into the things they were passionate about, and always getting teased by people who just didn't get it.

"Why are you being like this?" I asked Ari.

"What? Are you two besties now?" Ari set her hands on her hips. "Maybe your bestie can figure out what 'small boot' means so that we can get on with it."

I spotted Maris in the distance, weaving around other kids with ease, even though she was staring at a page.

"You know what? I bet she *can* help," I said. "If you get any ideas, you know where to find me." I left Ari standing outside the camp doors, looking a little surprised, as if I'd just dumped cold water on her head.

Back in the poetry room, Mr. Theo had covered every wall with colorful butcher paper. "Public poetry," he announced. "In the tradition of masters like Tu Fu and Li Po, China's most important classical poets, we will be papering all of Corona Arts with public poems!" He had a paintbrush behind each ear, and a grin that lit up the room. I couldn't help but be a little excited.

"Original poems? Or previously published ones?" Maris asked very seriously.

"Both!" Mr. Theo said. "Which means you need to find your favorite poems to share, plus write a few of your own."

We got to work. I chose a large piece of blue butcher paper, a pot of purple paint, and a fresh paintbrush. I started by painting a border.

Maris set up her paper beside me, so that we were standing side by side as we painted. "So what were you and Ari talking about this morning? It looked serious," she said.

I stopped mid-brushstroke. "Oh. Nothing, really."

"I knew it," Maris said without looking up from her paper. She was writing out Emily Dickinson's "I'm Nobody" poem with the kind of seriousness most people saved for funerals.

"Knew what?" I asked with a sinking feeling.

"It's okay if you were talking about me," Maris said, dotting an *i* with a frowny face.

"We weren't," I lied.

"Sure," Maris said.

"What is it you wanted to tell us? Something about tomorrow?" I asked, hoping it would make Maris feel better. She was probably planning some poetry reading or something.

"Oh. Nothing," Maris said, echoing me. Her lips were

a straight line, and I could see that she was grinding her teeth.

We were quiet for a while until Mr. Theo turned the radio on, and then we painted in silence to the sounds of an easy listening station. "How long have you known Ari?" I asked after some time had passed, and Maris seemed less angry.

"Let me think," Maris said. "You know her aunt owns the Queen of Corona bodega, right? The shop opened right before Thanksgiving. I remember because they raffled off a turkey, which my mom won, but then we returned it because it wasn't organic."

"Maris, she didn't!" I said.

Maris nodded and rolled her eyes.

Thanksgiving, I thought. Right before then, in fact. I'd just learned I was a muse at that time last year. It was probably a coincidence. It had to be. Because if it wasn't, that might mean that Ari's fate was tied to mine in some way. That my becoming a muse and Ari getting her human form back were linked somehow.

And that was way too much pressure.

"What's she like? Ari's aunt, I mean."

"Nice, I guess," Maris said.

"Gorgeous," Mr. Theo said dreamily, then wandered around the room to look at the poems.

"What in the worl—" I started to remark.

Maris nodded. "Yep. Ari's aunt has that effect on most grown-ups. Half of Queens is in love with her."

"And the other half?" I asked.

"They haven't met her yet," Maris said with a giggle and a shrug.

We painted six signs by the end of the day. It wasn't enough to "paper the walls of Corona Arts," as Mr. Theo suggested, but it was a good start.

"Maybe this year the poets will have something memorable to present at the Student Showcase," Maris said as we stood back to admire our work. The poems were colorful and inspiring, too. I especially liked the concrete poem Maris had painted. It was about her love of pizza but was in the shape of Italy.

"I'm suddenly craving a pineapple pizza like you wouldn't believe," I said.

"Ew. Pineapple is the worst," Maris said. "Have you had a slice of real New York pizza yet?"

I shook my head.

"That's just criminal," Maris said. "Have your dad take you to Little Italy at once."

"Okay," I laughed. After that, Maris kept right on talking as we worked. I learned that she ate peanut butter sandwiches almost every day, with the occasional serving of macaroni and cheese in a faded Wonder Woman thermos. She also happened to own over two hundred *Wonder Woman* comics, and she planned to give herself the middle name Diana, after her favorite superhero, when she turned eighteen. She'd been to Lebanon to see her grandparents twice and was hoping to visit again soon.

The bell rang for lunch so Maris and I gathered our things. She hurried out, saying something about returning a book at the library before eating.

"Help me roll up the dried ones?" Mr. Theo asked.

We went around the room, taking down the poems that were safe to roll up, making new wall space for tomorrow's poems. As I worked, I thought about the clue. *Small boots, small boots,* I said to myself.

"What's that, Callie?" Mr. Theo asked.

"Oh, sorry. I didn't know I was thinking out loud. Just a riddle I heard about 'small boots.'"

Mr. Theo thought for a moment. "Well, I don't know about that, but here's a big boot!" he said with a chuckle, pointing at Maris's pizza poem.

That's right! Italy was shaped like a boot! So a small boot could mean . . .

"Little Italy!" I shouted.

Mr. Theo clutched his chest, startled. "Um. Okay there, Callie?"

I jumped up and down. I'd figured it out! With Mr. Theo's and Maris's help, of course, even if they couldn't know it.

The second piece of tapestry was in Little Italy. It had to be. And I couldn't wait to tell everyone.

Mr. Theo went to his desk drawer and pulled out a sandwich with a wrapper on it that read "The Queen of Corona." He was humming happily to himself as he walked out of the room, cradling the sandwich.

With Mr. Theo gone, I took the opportunity to call the rest of the Muse Squad. I glanced at the clock on the wall. It was noon in New York, which meant it was eleven in the morning in Chicago, where Nia was, five in the afternoon in London, Thalia's home, and after nine o'clock at night in New Delhi, where Mela lived. Being a muse meant knowing your time zones pretty well, I'd learned.

"Mela, Thalia, Nia, anybody out there? I figured out the clue!" I shouted into my bracelet.

"Shh," Mela answered first. "I'm watching a play with my mum and Nani. I'll catch up with you soon."

"Shush!" Thalia said.

"Excuse me?" Mela and I both answered at the same time.

"Sorry. I'm at the library and they've got a C. S. Lewis exhibit on. I've died and gone to Narnia heaven. Gotta go," Thalia said, signing off.

Well, Thalia was busy, and Mela was, too. As for Nia . . .

"Here!" Nia called, out of breath. "I . . . was . . . practicing . . . backflips. . . ."

"Like, real backflips? In the air?" I asked, confused.

"Yeah," Nia huffed. "I made the gymnastics team last

week. Practice . . . ends in . . . a bit. We can talk then?"

"Okay," I said. They were busy, though I'd hoped they'd be a bit more enthusiastic about me figuring out the next part of the quest. All I could do was wait, I supposed. My eyes rested on Maris's poems on the wall. She was so good at coming up with poetry ideas. They just seemed to pop into her head. That was another way Maris reminded me of Maya, and her love of all things scientific. Maya was always dreaming up experiments. *That* made me think of my best friend, Raquel, who loved performing. Then I thought of Mela, who loved the theater and went to plays all the time. Nia had just made the gymnastics team, meanwhile I couldn't even touch my toes without bending at the knees. And Thalia was having a blast volunteering at the library.

They all had their passions, the things they loved to do outside of muse stuff.

But what did *I* love to do?

I could see them now—Raquel onstage, Mela directing plays, Thalia heading the British Library, Nia in the Olympics, Maris reading her poetry to big crowds, and Maya, of course, coming up with solutions to climate change.

What was *my* future going to be like? Thinking about it was like opening your eyes in a dark room and not being able to see beyond the tip of your nose.

Mr. Theo wandered in again, the sandwich wrapper crumpled in his hand. He stood a few feet from the wastebasket and tossed the ball in the air.

"Nothing but net," he said when the garbage fell into the basket. Then he noticed me. "Oh, hey there, Callie. Don't skip lunch, now. Poets have to eat."

"I won't," I said. Mr. Theo nodded, then left the room once more.

Suddenly, I had another idea. Mr. Theo's sandwich had reminded me.

Whoever Ari's aunt was, she couldn't just be any old human. Ari had told us herself that her aunt was the one who had suggested that Athena could use us against her. And whoever she was, she was very beautiful, if Mr. Theo's dreamy face meant anything.

Ari had said we would have to ask her aunt ourselves if we wanted to know anything about her.

Everyone else was busy doing cool things, and I had time to kill.

I guess it was time I got to know the Queen of Corona.

Chapter 18
THE QUEEN OF CORONA

The Queen of Corona was slammed when I got there.
The bell over the door rang again and again as kids from
Corona Arts and other nearby day camps, or kids who
got to hang out at home all day in the summer, filled the
shop. I checked the ice-cream counter, but Ari wasn't
there.

Perhaps her mysterious aunt would know where she
was.

I walked over to a store employee wearing a polo shirt
and a name tag that read JULIO.

"Excuse me," I said.

He held a can of tomato sauce in each hand. "How can
I help you?"

"Where can I find Ari's aunt?" I asked.

Julio pointed toward the registers with his chin. There

was a woman behind the counter, chatting with customers as she scanned and bagged their items. One by one, I watched as the people in line turned and left, clutching their brown bags, wearing huge smiles on their faces.

I grabbed a pack of gum and stood in line. It moved quickly enough, and I could hear Ari's aunt's voice as I got closer to the counter. She spoke quietly, but sort of musically. And everyone she talked with ended up laughing at some point. She told each person to "have a marvelous day," or "un día maravilloso," or she said something in a language I didn't understand, making me wonder how many she spoke.

When it was my turn, I put the pack of gum on the counter.

"Hi," I said. Ari's aunt was, as expected, very beautiful, and people in the store couldn't quite keep from getting fixed to the spot where they stood whenever they looked at her. She was Black and her skin seemed to glow from the inside out. She had long brown hair with streaks of gold in it. Though she wasn't very tall, whenever she spoke to someone, they seemed a little shy around her, as if they were talking to a giant. Round cheeks filled out her face, and when she looked down at me, she gasped.

"Calliope. What an honor. Come, darling, we really should chat."

"H-how do you know who I am?" I asked anxiously, but Ari's aunt just gave me a wink. She waved at Julio, who came skipping over to manage the register. "Follow me," she said.

Ari's aunt led me through the store to the back, where a little blue curtain hid a small, dark hall and a series of doors. She unlocked one with a key that dangled from a rubber bracelet she was wearing.

"Entrez," she said, presenting her *enormous* and totally glam office.

Every inch of the walls, and the ceiling, too, was covered in what looked like pink silk. There was white shag carpeting under our feet. A crystal chandelier dangled above a glass desk. A pair of glossy black bookshelves, crammed with books in pink covers, flanked a fireplace. I hadn't been to any bodega back-room offices before this, but did any of them have a rope swing hanging from one corner of the room, with three fuzzy pink beanbags underneath? I doubted it! Red roses sat in vases on small tables throughout the space, and the whole place smelled like . . .

Honey mustard?

I snapped my fingers. "Ambrosia! This place smells like ambrosia. That means you must be a—"

"Go on, guess which one," Ari's aunt said. She put her hands on her hips and raised her chin, batting her long lashes at me. She was wearing skinny jeans and a T-shirt with a picture of Venus Williams on it, mid-swing. "It's a clue," she added in that musical voice of hers, and pointed at her shirt.

"Venus Williams?" I'm sorry to say it took a minute for my brain to catch up to everything. Maybe I was just dazzled by the room, and by Ari's aunt.

"She's my namesake, of course," Ari's aunt said.

Finally, my thoughts fell into place. "Venus. The Roman name for the goddess—"

"Aphrodite!" she said, flinging her arms up in a "ta-da" gesture.

"*You're* Ari's aunt?"

Aphrodite walked over to one of the beanbags and plopped down on it, then she beckoned me to join her. "Not really. But I agreed to accompany her on her quest. Not help. Can't do that. But every kid needs a parent of some kind, right? And a warm place to stay. Someone to give them their vitamins and read them bedtime stories. I like it," she said, shrugging.

I hadn't given it much thought. Ari's real parents, the ones she'd had when she was twelve the first time, were long gone, weren't they? I suddenly imagined how lonely Ari must feel. Sure, Aphrodite seemed sweet, but I bet Ari missed her family.

"I try at least," Aphrodite added with a sad look. I was pretty sure she'd read my mind just then.

Clio usually complained that I didn't know enough mythology, but I *did* know about Aphrodite. Mario and Fernando had to do a project on her once and they made a poster about some of the most famous myths about her.

And the stories? They usually weren't very complimentary. Usually, they were about how *pretty* Aphrodite was, and how some humans didn't think she was pretty *enough*, which meant they'd get punished, often really brutally. Of all the gods, Aphrodite always came off as the . . . pettiest one.

Now she was looking at me, one eyebrow arched really high.

The mind-reading thing. Right.

"Sorry," I said. "It's just that the stories—"

Aphrodite laughed. "I know the stories. But consider me reformed. I'm a better Aphrodite than I was before," she said, and twirled a lock of hair around her finger. "Right?"

I stood there, silent as a lawn ornament, terrified that at any moment she was going to turn me into one.

"Please do feel free to agree with me at this point, Callie," Aphrodite said through a tight smile.

"Yes, yes," I said quickly, my heart slamming in my chest. When I calmed down, I carefully added, "So you're not angry with Ari? For challenging Athena? And for the stories she wove into her tapestry?"

Aphrodite waved her hand in the air. "That old feud? Ari wasn't wrong, you know." Aphrodite looked at her long nails, and it felt like she was avoiding my eyes. "We gods of Olympus were . . . careless about the people we were meant to love. It's why they stopped worshiping us in the end. We weren't always helpful." She brightened up.

"But you muses. Oh my, you are incredibly helpful. You're model goddesses! And I'm glad you're helping Ari. I hope she beats Athena this time."

"You do?"

Aphrodite had a glimmer in her eye. "Most certainly. Athena is always going on about how smart she is, how wise she is, and she teases me for being girly, and in love with love. She thinks I'm dumb, but you don't get to run the most profitable bodega in the tri-state area being stupid!"

"Congratulations."

"Thank you."

We were both quiet for a second. There was a silver clock on Aphrodite's desk, and I stole a glance at it. Three o'clock. The day was slipping away, and this time, I had to be home before dark.

"So you can't help Ari with the quest?" I asked, and Aphrodite shook her head very solemnly.

"I'm sorry that I can't. But *you* must. You absolutely must. You and the other muses."

"Why? How did we get caught up in this anyway?"

Aphrodite hummed to herself a moment as she thought. "Fate? Duty. Ari needs you."

"She doesn't want us to use magic on her. She says she hates it," I argued.

"Of course she hates it. Olympian magic turned her into a spider, after all. But I didn't mean you should use magic on Ari. She's inspired enough. Talented enough. She needs friends, is all. She needs people who can help her see the paths before her clearly in order to pick the right ones. Helping Ari is the key to everything," Aphrodite said, laying a cool hand on my cheek. I felt warm all over.

"That's what Tia Annie said. Something like that, anyway," I whispered.

"Ah, Annie Martinez. My favorite muse of all. Don't tell the others, but I also like you very much."

My stomach did a flip. I could see why grown-ups went all loopy around Aphrodite. It wasn't her beauty, not really. It was more about the look in her eyes. It felt like she cared about me. And I guess that's what love is, in the end. Caring about someone and having them care back.

But I wasn't a grown-up and I wasn't loopy for Aphrodite.

"Can I tell you something?" I asked her.

Aphrodite took my hands and, okay, maybe I did swoon a bit then. "Ask me anything," she said. Then she grinned, adding, "I'm so good at this mom thing, aren't I? I should absolutely ground you or make you chicken soup or something."

"No, just an answer is good," I said. "Um. What the other muses and I are doing? It's not what we're *supposed* to be doing. We have a whole different mission. And I think we're going to get into big trouble if we help Ari."

Aphrodite's lovely eyebrows knitted together. I observed

them for a second. Not a hair out of place. She clucked her tongue twice, perked up, and said, "You have just one mission."

Now I was confused. "No. We have two. Ari and Athena's quest on one hand," I said, raising my left hand, "and finding the tenth muse on the other," I finished, bringing my right hand up. I lifted them up and down in turn, as if weighing them.

Aphrodite stilled my hands with her own. "They are one and the same. One mission completes the other."

"But how?"

"Like I said, Callie, the muses must help Ari. The tenth muse is helping, too. You just haven't noticed yet."

"She really is here? In Queens?"

"The muse finder clock is never wrong, peaches." Aphrodite released my hands. "There," she said, smiling at me.

I didn't smile back.

Then Aphrodite patted me on the head. "Off you go."

"I feel like I need more information," I said. "Queens is a big place, after all. How is the tenth muse helping us? Does she know she's a muse? Muse of what, for that matter?" That's when I felt my feet start slipping, leading me toward the door without me moving them. It was like trying to walk on a soapy floor!

"You get what you get, and you don't get upset," Aphrodite sang.

I grabbed on to a beanbag chair, but felt it sliding along

with me. "Stop! Please! Can I at least tell Clio and the others?"

My feet stopped slipping at once.

"I don't think so. This bit of info is just for you, pumpkin. In order to solve this mystery, there's something you, and only you, can figure out," she said. She smiled again, and I could have sworn I saw a twinkle.

"It's just that the muses are a team. We work *together*. And anyway, Clio said that our mission is to find the tenth muse. Not to help Ari."

"Then I command you to help my niece." She released my hands and pointed at herself. "One of the major gods in the pantheon here, and I'm pulling rank." Aphrodite squeezed my cheek super hard, and I bit back a yelp.

"Okay. Um. Thanks," I said. I suppose I should have felt some relief at this. Aphrodite herself had now told us that helping Ari was a priority, officially. But I couldn't help feeling as if I were letting Clio and the other grown-up muses down, even if I was trying to protect them by keeping our new mission a secret. Aphrodite started leading me to the door, but I had another question to ask.

"Is it true," I asked, my feet already shuffling out from under me again, "that there can only be nine muses? Why not ten?"

"Nine it is, cupcake. That's how it's always been," Aphrodite said, laying her hands on my shoulders and pushing me out.

"Not helpful," I grunted, trying to keep my feet from moving. But it was no use. When a goddess wants to shove you out the door, she shoves you out the door.

"Sayonara, young goddess. Dasvidaniya. Ma el-salama," she said, goodbye-ing me in lots of languages until I crossed the threshold of her office and felt the door slam behind me.

"Ugh," I said, sick and tired of half-answers. First Tia Annie, now Aphrodite, of all people—er, goddesses.

"How did you like her?" I heard, and looked up. There was Ari, fanning herself with a piece of junk mail.

"Loved her. Doesn't everybody?" I said.

"They do. It's exhausting," Ari said, and we both laughed.

I observed Ari for a moment. I should still be mad at her for how she'd made fun of Maris. But part of me felt bad for Ari, too. Not just the whole multiple-lifetimes-as-a-spider part, but the bit about not having a family anymore. That seemed worse than being a spider. "So, you in the mood for pizza for dinner?" I asked.

"What do you mean?"

"The bookstore clue. I figured it out. Small boot. Little Italy," I said.

Ari smacked herself on the forehead. "Of course! I'd forgotten that Italy was boot-shaped," she said with a frown. "You know, when I was first learning geography, we all thought the earth was flat. I still have a lot of modern-day catching up to do. But you? You're a goddess, Callie!" Ari shouted, and jumped up and down.

I shrugged. "I know."

Then Ari grew serious. "I thought you got in trouble for coming home late last time. What about your dad?"

"I'll figure it out," I said, hoping we had enough time to get to Little Italy and be back before my curfew. "Meet at my place in fifteen minutes?"

"Done," Ari said. "Tell the others."

"Of course." I lifted my bracelet to call the Muse Squad into action when, suddenly, it started to heat up. Clio was calling a meeting.

"What's happening?"

"Muses are mustering. All of them this time. I don't have a phone, so I'll try to meet you outside the museum when we're done. But don't go without us. Promise me, Ari. We don't know what Athena has planned for you."

Letting others take charge wasn't easy for Ari. I could tell. "Okay," she said at last, holding her pinkie finger up. "Promise."

We shook pinkies, then I dashed out of the bodega, back to the Hall of Science, where Clio and the other muses waited for me to tell them what I'd learned about the tenth muse.

I had learned something. That Ari's trouble with Athena, and the mystery of the tenth muse, were somehow linked. And that the tenth muse was already helping us.

Except there were two big problems.

I didn't have a clue who the tenth muse was, or how she was helping us with anything!

And according to Aphrodite, I couldn't tell anybody a single thing.

Chapter 19
HALF-TRUTHS AND MINI-GOLF

The muses weren't inside the Great Hall. The place was swarming with kids jumping on the beanbags and playing with interactive light displays projected onto the walls.

"Hello?" I called into my bracelet. "Anybody here?"

It took a second before Nia responded, "We're playing mini-golf! Come on out!"

This was new.

I made my way to the entrance to Rocket Park, the Hall of Science's mini-golf area. A sign read "Closed for Refurbishment." The mini-golf park was deserted. I walked outside anyway, leaving the chaos in the museum behind me. The door closed, and the sounds of kids playing died down.

"Hello?" I called again.

That's when I saw Mela's head pop out from behind a tree trunk.

"Over here! We're already on the fifth hole." She held a golf club in her hands like a sword. "And I'm winning."

The course was bright and colorful. Blue shapes made up each hole, with globes painted to look like planets embedded into the ground, creating the hazards that made getting the golf ball into the hole tricky. I found the other eight muses gathered around the fifth hole, with Paola lining up her shot.

"Uno, dos, y tres," she said, the bells on her waist jingling. The ball shot out before her, landing in the hole with a plunk.

The muses cheered, and I joined in.

"Here at last," Clio said.

"Where have you been?" Nia asked softly.

"Later," I told her.

"Let's take a bit of a break," Clio announced, and led us all to a grassy knoll off of the sixth hole. It was shady and green. Tomiko and Elnaz sat cross-legged on the grass. Clio sat, too, at the highest point of the knoll. Paola settled onto a bench at the edge of the grass, and Etoro sat in her wheelchair beside that. Thalia, Nia, Mela, and I spread out on our stomachs, hands resting on our chins.

"Can all meetings be like this?" Mela asked dreamily.

"Next time, I'll bring a picnic lunch," Thalia added.

"It's the only unoccupied space in this museum at the

moment," Clio said, with a bit of a frown. I could tell she was missing the V and A, with its dark nooks and crannies and tons of places to hide. "Let's begin with updates on our Fated Ones. Elnaz?"

We watched as Elnaz told everyone about the young man she was helping in Zimbabwe. He was extraordinarily intelligent, had fallen in love with a cello player, and now Elnaz was helping him learn to appreciate classical music for their first date.

"Playing Cupid?" Etoro asked with a smile on her face.

Elnaz shrugged, blushing a little. "The cello player will be good for him, I think."

I looked at the rest of the Muse Squad and, one by one, they rolled their eyes. We had our own problems to deal with, but they had nothing to do with dates, or crushes, or anybody falling in love.

Tomiko told us about a Russian ballet dancer she was helping to choreograph a ballet for dancers who were differently abled, and Etoro described the efforts of a high school principal in New Zealand who was building an environmentally friendly school, after which Paola told us all about a teenager in Bolivia who had created a sanctuary for endangered salamanders in his backyard!

"Maya's at Space Camp," I added, "being her usual genius self."

The muses cheered. Last year, the muses inspired Maya to be her best self. She's a Fated One, a person with the potential to change the world for good, and we'd fought evil sirens to protect her. If anyone deserved to go to Space Camp, it was her.

Once all the Fated One reports were done, the older muses turned to look at us, stretched out on the grass.

"Oh no," Thalia whispered.

Mela buried her face in her arms.

Clio narrowed her eyes at us. "To the business at hand. The tenth muse," she said.

I could feel the others shifting their attention to me.

I sat up and took my time brushing grass off my thighs. When I spoke, I didn't quite meet anybody's eyes. "So we went to see the Gray Sisters."

"They were totally gross, as advertised," Thalia added.

"Um. And they asked us to find their eye, which had been taken by an owl," I explained slowly. "We had to go to the zoo to get the eye from the owl. Which we did."

"Did I mention this whole thing was gross?" Thalia interrupted again.

"And we took it back to the Gray Sisters," I continued.

"Nia actually dropped the eye. It went *splat*, people. Splat! Honestly. So gross," went Thalia again.

I rested my hand on top of Thalia's and gave her a little squeeze. She always joked more when she was nervous, and I could tell that at this point, she was freaking out. Because I was about to either 1) lie to the other muses or 2) tell them the truth.

Both options were terrifying.

"Go on," Clio urged, looking a little green at the turn my story was taking.

"Then we asked the Gray Sisters for help," I said, pausing.

"*And?*" Clio asked impatiently.

"And they helped," I said. Mela made a little whimpering noise beside me.

Silence followed. Tomiko and Elnaz started talking quietly with one another. I caught Etoro giving Paola a very pointed look.

"Now what?" Nia asked beneath her breath. I shrugged.

Clio let the quiet linger for a moment before asking the inevitable. "They helped how, Callie?"

"By giving us a clue. We need to go see about that tonight, actually. A clue that will help us find what we're looking for," I said rapidly.

Clio shook her head. "I see what's happening here," she said.

"You do?" I asked. My brain felt like scrambled eggs as I tried to come up with excuses that would keep us out of trouble.

"I do. You four want some independence. It's understandable, really. You're twelve. It's the natural way of things. As the first junior muses ever, we must—"

"Muse Squad!" Thalia chimed in.

"—we must accommodate your development as people,"

Clio finished. "Go find your clue tonight. But I expect a report soon."

I clamped my hand over Thalia's mouth before she could correct Clio again.

"Will do!" I said, saluting awkwardly.

"Oh my goodness, the cringe is upon me," Nia muttered, but I could tell she was relieved, too. We'd gotten away with it—without having to actually lie!

Sort of.

I mean, I said the Gray Sisters had helped, and they had, just not with the thing we were supposed to be getting help on.

Clio grew serious again. "I wish to impress upon you four the importance of your task. The future of the muses might depend on it. Humans need us, and if we were to disappear from the world, simply because we couldn't figure out this mystery, it would be a tragedy and a disgrace to the memory of those muses who came before us." Clio's eyes fell on me, and my head filled with thoughts of Tia Annie.

I missed her so much. My eyes stung, and I blinked back ridiculous tears.

The meeting ended with Clio passing around the usual plate full of brownies. Nia, Thalia, Mela, and I stuck around for a bit.

"I can't believe that worked," Mela said as soon as the grown-up muses were back inside the museum.

Nia added, "Me neither."

I was very quiet, thinking over what Clio had said. The fate of the muses might rest on finding the tenth. We might be helping Ari, but what about all the future Fated Ones who might never get help because we failed in our mission?

"Has anybody figured out the 'small boot' thing?" Thalia was asking.

Mela spoke up. "There's a western wear store in New Jersey that sells child-sized cowboy boots. I looked it up online. And I think that—"

"Little Italy," I interrupted. "It means Little Italy. It's where we have to go to find the next piece of the tapestry. I'm positive."

"Are you sure?" Mela asked, frowning. I could tell she had been excited about the possibility of visiting a western wear store.

I explained how I'd figured it out, then I told them about Aphrodite and how she'd officially commanded us to help Ari.

"*The* Aphrodite?" Nia responded.

"The one and only."

"Honestly, you have all the luck," Thalia said.

"That's Captain Callie for you," Mela added.

I swallowed a big lump in my throat at that. Why did they insist on putting me in charge? I didn't want it. Except . . .

I was the only one who dreamed of Tia Annie, who

sometimes told me things others didn't know.

And I was the only one whose magic had changed, even though they didn't know it yet.

But I didn't feel special. I felt like I needed help all the time.

We heard someone making a "Psst" sound, and we turned our heads to see Ari peering at us through a chain-link fence that bordered the golf course. "You ready to roll?" she asked.

"Ready as we'll ever be!" Nia called back. "Meet us out front!"

Ari gave us a thumbs-up, and the rest of us went back into the museum only to run into Etoro, who was sitting in the foyer, observing a summer camp group getting ready to board their bus.

We stopped short.

Without looking at us, Etoro lifted an arm and called us to her.

"Busted," Nia muttered.

"Hi, Etoro," Thalia said. "Fancy an afternoon in New York then?"

Etoro nodded. "I love this city. And what of the four of you? Off to find your clue? Going to locate the tenth muse for us? It's quite the mystery, isn't it?"

The four of us nodded. I could actually hear my heart beating.

I started to speak, anxious to say something that would

let us get away, but was cut short by Etoro. "You should know that I am very proud of you all. I wasn't sure at first that it was a good idea having such young muses take on the work that we do. But it wasn't for me to decide, was it? The workings of the universe have always been mysterious, but it seems to me that they are even more so lately. Four muses who are all but children. A tenth muse. Mysterious."

We waited a little fearfully, not knowing what she would say next.

"Do you know what you need?" she asked at last.

We shook our heads.

"A nice meal. Lots of rest. Young things like yourselves are growing still, don't forget. Full bellies mean happy hearts," she said, patting her stomach.

"Italian food would be the ticket!" Thalia said, and I could have kicked her.

Etoro made a happy, humming sound. "Indeed. A nice baked ziti for growing girls."

"Will do," Nia said.

"On it," I added.

"Done and done," Mela said.

Then we left the museum, breathing hard, and ran straight into Ari.

"Are you all okay?" she asked. "You look a bit freaked out."

"All good," I said. "Subway?"

Ari smiled. "Absolutely."

I turned around as we walked away and noticed Etoro sitting in the foyer, looking out the glass window at us.

I reminded myself that we had Aphrodite's permission.

I'd told Clio and the others the truth. Sort of. And they would be safe from Athena's anger.

So why did I feel like a world-class jerk?

Chapter 20
SSSSSSSPAGHETTI

"I need to be home by seven," I said out loud. Again. "And it's five o'clock already. *Five*."

"We know," Ari said. "And we can *totally* have you home by then."

"That's *totally* not a promise you can make."

Ari shrugged. "Just a feeling, I guess. Trust me?"

I didn't say anything, just turned my head to watch Queens zoom by until the train headed underground as it rumbled into Manhattan. How could I answer her? I didn't really trust Ari entirely. It felt like I hardly knew her.

And yet I'd already borrowed Ari's phone to text Papi and Laura, letting them know I was working on the project again with Ari.

Laura had texted back with a thumbs-up emoji.

Papi had merely written, Be home by 7. Hello to Ari.

The train we rode on was packed full of people heading home from work. We were standing in a huddle around a single pole. At every stop, a fresh press of bodies surged around us. I could smell someone's coffee breath and came up with Callie's Muse Rule #629: A muse should avoid the subway at rush hour at all costs.

The ride took longer than I had hoped, and I kept looking at my watch every few minutes.

"Quit it," Nia said, when she saw me looking for the millionth time. "You're making me nervous."

"Well, I'm already nervous. Not only am I probably not going to get back home on time, but the last piece of tapestry was guarded by a cyclops."

"I was there, remember?" Nia said.

"And quests, like video games, have a tendency to increase in difficulty."

"You don't play video games," Nia said, a smirk on her face.

"But my annoying twin brothers do. I'm an expert by association."

Mela was staring at a subway map, her shiny headphones over her ears. "How many more stops?" she asked loudly over her music.

"Nearly there," Ari answered. "Almost at Canal Street."

The train finally squealed to a stop, and the five of us hopped out, climbed the stairs up to the surface, and emerged in the middle of a really busy section of New York.

We all stood there, mouths open, taking it in. The sidewalks were full of people speed-walking and brushing past us. Shop owners called out to one another from doorways. Restaurant hosts held up menus to passersby. People hailed cabs from street corners. The sky was packed with rooflines. They didn't call them skyscrapers for nothing!

"Wow. Makes London look a bit quiet," Thalia said.

"Feels a little like home," Nia said. "But different. It's hard to explain."

I thought of my neighborhood back in Miami, of the terra-cotta roof tiles, and the bay glimmering in the distance between buildings. "This is nothing like home," I said.

"Same," Mela whispered.

"Hard same," Ari said, and I found myself wondering what home was to Ari. It wasn't just a place, but a time, a long, long-ago time, one she probably remembered in an ancient language.

"Move it or lose it, little sisters," a man shouted at us as he pushed a cart full of purses for sale up the sidewalk.

"We'd better get going," I said, nodding at Ari, who started up the street toward Little Italy.

"Prepare yourselves for the tourist trap," Ari said, and she was right. There were souvenir shops everywhere, and

Italian restaurants lined both sides of the street, one after the other, each with red-and-white-checkered tablecloths, fat menus, and the delicious smell of cheese and garlic in the air. Family groups were taking pictures under a large metal sign that spanned the street and read "Welcome to Little Italy."

"So where do we start?" Mela asked, looking up and down the street.

"Over there!" Thalia said, and she was off down the block, the rest of us sprinting after her. Ferrante's Pizzeria was one of the smallest restaurants in Little Italy as far as I could tell. The sign was hand-painted in green and in the shape of a boot.

"Tiny place," Ari observed.

"One might even call it 'small,'" Thalia added, pointing at the boot-shaped sign.

When I looked at the sign closely, I noticed that the letters were actually designed to look like snakes, complete with glittery scales and tiny forked tongues.

We peered into the windows. The tables were empty, but a few waiters seemed to be standing around.

"Door's locked," Mela said, wiggling the handle.

Nia knocked on the window to get the waiters' attention. They didn't seem to hear it.

That's when Ari pulled a needle from her pocket. "Easy peasy," she whispered to herself as she slid the needle into the lock on the door.

"Breaking and entering now, are we?" Nia asked, but Ari kept at it, pretending not to hear her.

"Hey, you kids, step away from there," a white man across the street yelled. He was holding a wet paintbrush and was wearing overalls covered in blue splatters. "I know lock-pickers when I see 'em!" He started to cross the road toward us when suddenly he started laughing, covering his mouth as he giggled.

Beside me, Thalia was giggling, too. "Hurry up, Ari," she said between breaths. "This guy doesn't joke much. Making him laugh is hard work." Thalia clutched her sides as she focused her magic on the painter.

Ari kept at it, muttering about old locks. Inside, the waiters were very still.

That's when we heard another voice call out. "You think you're a funny guy, eh, chuckling in the middle of the road like a dummy. Move it," yelled a second white man from inside his cab. It was true, the laughing painter really was blocking traffic. The cabdriver was wearing a Mets ball cap and a Mets T-shirt. A tiny baseball bat on a chain dangled from his rearview mirror.

"*You* move it," the painter called back, then blew a big raspberry in the direction of the cabdriver, which made him laugh even harder.

The cabdriver started to get out of his car, a murderous look on his face, when he suddenly started crying. I could see Mela's fingers moving from the corner of my eye.

The taxi driver sobbed and sobbed. The man in the road laughed and laughed.

"You two are crazy, you know that?" shouted a waitress from the restaurant across the street. Then she noticed us. "And what are you kids up to, anyway?"

Just like that, the waitress stopped to examine the flickering neon Open sign at the door to her restaurant.

"Was that you, Nia?" I asked, and Nia only nodded, chewing on the inside of her cheek and concentrating on the woman, who was now unplugging the sign and detaching it from the wall.

Ari was still working the lock. "Everyone on the street is going to go bananas before we get in here," she said. "There!" The front door creaked open, and Ari tucked away her knitting needle.

The others entered the restaurant, and I took a minute to make things right with everybody outside. I got to work dreaming up the pictures in my head of the laughing man suddenly getting a great idea for a mural he could paint, and the cabdriver quitting his crying and daydreaming about playing baseball. They settled down immediately. As for the woman fixing the sign, well, it needed fixing, I guess, so I left her to it.

"Is all right with the world?" Ari asked when I joined them inside. "Because it isn't in here."

Ari pointed at the four waiters standing around, holding thin menus fanned out in their hands. They wore black pants, white shirts, and black ties. Nothing unique there. But there was something not quite right about them.

"Hey," Ari said. "Can we get a table?"

The waiters didn't seem to hear her. They just stood there, blank looks on their faces.

Nia and I walked up to the closest one. She snapped her fingers in front of his eyes. He didn't blink.

"Callie," Mela called from beside another waiter. "I don't think they're . . ."

"Real," Thalia finished, walking up to one of the waiters and placing her finger squarely on his cheek. She sucked in a loud breath. "I know what these are! I've seen them at Madame Tussaud's back home. They're made of wax!"

"Hey. Muses. Take a look at this," Ari said. She'd plucked a menu out of the hand of one of the wax figures. I reached out and took one, too.

MENU
ANTIPASTO
FROZEN-IN-TIME CROQUETTES
TUSCAN WAX SALAD
BRUSH-WITH-DEATH BRUSCHETTA

PASTA
FOUR-WAX MAN-A-COTTI
PENNE ALLA STILLNESS
SSSSSSSPAGHETTI

PIZZA
WHEN THE MOON HITS YOUR EYE, LIKE A BIG PIZZA PIE, YOU'RE NOT-A-MOVING

"None of this sounds very appetizing," Mela said, carefully putting the menu back into the waiter's hand.

"I don't understand," Ari said.

"Oh, look, this one had a dessert menu," Thalia said, holding a single sheet of paper. We huddled close to take a look. It had only one item on it.

DESSERT
THREE-LAYER TAPESTRY CAKE—"COME ON BACK AND MAKE IT YOURSELF!"

None of us said a word. In fact, I was pretty sure all of us were holding our breath. I scanned the restaurant and noticed a light coming from a door in the back. "That must be the kitchen," I whispered.

"Whoever is back there, they want us to make the first move," Nia said.

"Courage, everyone," Thalia said.

"We *are* goddesses," I said, reminding myself of muse rule number nine.

"And don't forget it," Nia, Thalia, and Mela said in return, very, very quietly.

I led the way, pushing through the swinging double

doors and entering a brightly lit kitchen. A woman wearing a large chef's hat was standing behind a stove, stirring something in a big copper pot. Her skin had a greenish-grayish cast to it, as if she had the flu.

"Come in, girls, come in. Dinner is nearly ready," she said without looking at us.

In the center of the room was a table with five chairs around it. It had five place settings, too, and a tablecloth that wasn't checkered like the ones in the dining room.

"My tapestry," Ari whispered, starting toward the table.

Nia pulled her back by the shirt. "It can't be this easy," she said under her breath, and Ari halted.

"What do you want?" I asked the woman in the chef's hat. She stirred her pot calmly, still not looking at us.

"I just want to feed you up," she said in a singsong voice.

"Great," Mela said. "The first monster wanted to eat us. Now this one wants to feed us."

"Probably because she's going to eat us," Thalia said.

That's when I noticed Ari moving toward the table and the tablecloth. Suddenly, a waiter appeared out of the shadows. He was a young man with his hair cropped short and a couple of pimples on his cheeks. He looked pale against his white shirt and black bow tie. And he was shaking.

"C-c-can I of-f-er you this s-seat, m-m-iss?" he said, pulling a chair out for Ari.

Ari glanced back at us, a determined look in her eye.

"Thanks," she told the trembling waiter.

We all followed, letting the waiter arrange us around the table. His hands shook so hard that when he tried to offer us menus, he dropped them. He was sweaty, and I was pretty sure I could hear his teeth chattering. Bending down to retrieve the menus, he stopped right by my ear and whispered, "Don't look at her. If you value your life, don't look at her."

I didn't even have to will my magic to come. It just did, and I sent it with all my might to this waiter, the words "courage" and "help us" pounding in my head along with a picture of him with a look of determination set on his face. Once he stopped trembling, his eyes met mine. The sweat was gone, and when he stood up, I could swear he was taller.

The chef was humming to herself as she ladled soup out of the pot and into five bowls. "I'm so glad you're here," she said, interrupting her song. "I've wanted company for so long. And these waiters can be so stiff."

"Ahhhhh!" the waiter shouted, holding up a plastic tray like a shield and running toward the chef, knocking her off her feet. The chef screamed, and the sound was like the squealing of the subway's wheels on the track, a sound that feels like it creeps into your bones.

Her hat slid off her head, and where her hair should have been were hundreds of tiny, hissing snakes.

"Medusa," Thalia said, breathless.

"Don't look at her!" I shouted, clapping my hands over my eyes.

For once, we all already knew the myth. Anybody who looked Medusa in the eyes was usually turned to stone. But this time, Medusa had turned those waiters to wax.

I peeked, though. We all did. It's impossible not to look at something when someone tells you not to. We watched as the waiter lifted the tray to strike Medusa, saw how he froze in place with one glance of her terrible eyes.

Just like the others.

Medusa started to laugh, low and horrible. "You may be wondering about my new methods. I've been perfecting them over the ages. Wax, you see, is preferable to stone. Stone is forever. But wax? Wax can melt," she said, and cranked up the heat on her stove. I was watching her hands, not her face, but it was difficult, like I wasn't fully in control of my own eyes. We all were struggling.

Just then, Ari pulled the tablecloth off the table like a magician doing that trick where they yank the tablecloth away and leave the plates sitting there, undisturbed. She rolled her tapestry up and shoved it under her shirt.

We all stood up to go.

"Leaving so soon?" Medusa called.

"That's the plan, yeah," I said, backing away. Ari and the muses followed.

Medusa started humming again, and that's when we heard it—a low hissing sound behind us. We turned around and watched in horror as snakes slithered into the kitchen, covering the floor, wrapping themselves around chair legs, and trying to climb the walls. They slid over the waiter, frozen in wax, and nudged their heads against Medusa's ankles, like puppies asking for a belly rub.

"It's a party now!" Medusa said. "Soup for everyone!" She began to lay out more bowls around her, stirring the pot and humming.

"We need backup," Ari said. "These snakes will gobble up my spiders. Callie, do your thing! Make a bunch of heroes to come rescue us! New York is full of heroes! Go on!" She bounced from one foot to the other, clutching the tapestry under her shirt.

"We can't put others in danger," I said. I'd already managed to get the waiter turned to wax. If I'd have known that would happen, I wouldn't have used my magic on him at all. Even so, I could feel the muse magic threatening to come, to reach out to people on the street and get them in here to fight Medusa.

"It has to be us," Nia said, kicking at a snake that was inching toward her foot. All the while, Medusa hummed and cooked, and the snakes hissed and opened their mouths, showing off their fangs.

"Eventually, you'll slip. You'll look. They always do. And then you'll be mine forever. The four little muses and their spidery friend!" Medusa laughed and laughed.

The snakes drew closer, and Nia pulled me toward the table. I took hold of Thalia's hand, and she grabbed Mela, who grabbed Ari. Eventually, we were all sitting on top of the table.

"You could also just leave the tapestry behind, you know. It's my favorite tablecloth. If you do, I promise to let you go. I really do." I could no longer tell what Medusa was doing, because I kept my eyes fixed on my lap. She was right. It was really hard not to look at her, and the longer we were there, the more I wanted to.

I heard a sniffle from Ari, who was holding on to the tapestry in a fierce hug. "It's fine. We can go. I'll leave it here, and, and—"

I knew what she was thinking. If Ari gave up her quest, she'd never be able to prove Athena wrong. She'd return to being a spider forever.

It was unacceptable.

"We'll think of something," I whispered.

"We always do," Nia said.

"I think one of us already has," Thalia said, and we looked up to see Mela, already off the table, heading straight toward Medusa.

"Mela, no!" I cried out, and launched myself off the table, too.

But snakes soon rose up around me, curling up like cobras and spitting at me. Medusa snapped her fingers, and the snakes parted for Mela, leaving a path straight to where Medusa waited.

"Yes, child. Come to me. Oh, tragic one, so sad all the time," Medusa said. "I'm sad, too. This snake thing is a curse for me, as well. But you'll keep me company—perfect, frozen company."

I stared at Mela's long braid, afraid to look anywhere else. She was keeping her head down, her eyes off Medusa. I watched as she lifted her shiny headphones off her neck.

"Yes, Medusa. I can feel your sadness. It makes me want to weep," Mela said softly.

"Finally, a soul who understands," Medusa said. "Now, little one, look at me."

"Don't, Mela!" Thalia shouted.

"No!" Nia screamed.

Mela stopped just before Medusa. "No, Medusa. *You* look at *me*." She held up her headphones quickly.

Medusa looked at herself in the mirrored surface of Mela's new headphones. Her eyes went wide and she screamed, then went completely still, turning to wax before us, the serpents that were her hair going silent at last.

One by one, the snakes around us slithered away, back into the nooks and crannies they'd come from. The waiter came to life, and outside, we could hear the other waiters asking each other what had happened.

Thalia was the first to grab Mela and hug her. "You absolute wonder!" she said.

"How did you know what to do?" Nia asked.

Mela laughed. "This is going to sound like the most Clio thing any one of us has ever said out loud, but you all really should read more. It's in all the stories about Medusa. She and her reflection don't mix well."

Soon we were all hugging her, and Mela started crying out of relief, which made us cry a little bit, too.

"Thank you," Ari said, still clutching the tapestry.

Mela gripped Ari's shoulders. "We weren't giving up on you. We won't ever," she said fiercely.

I tiptoed over to Medusa, waxy now and very still.

"What are you doing?" Nia asked, panic in her voice.

"The next clue. The one that will help us find piece number three," I said. "It has to be here somewhere."

We started looking around the restaurant, searching in menus, inside the cash register, under tables, opening boxes of pasta, and rummaging through the pantry.

"Nothing," Thalia announced.

It had to be somewhere, I thought. I peered down at Medusa and saw a slip of paper peeking out from a pocket in her apron. I slowly reached down. My hand trembled the whole time, and all I could picture were horror movies where the dead villain comes back to life for one more jump scare.

Her pockets were covered in what I *really* hoped was just red sauce. I tugged at the folded piece of paper. "Hey, everybody!" I called.

The others gathered around as I slowly unfolded the page.

"This has to be it," Ari whispered.

I opened the sheet and it was . . .

Blank.

I stomped my foot in disappointment. Our quest would be over really quickly if we didn't find the next clue soon. On the far wall of the kitchen, a clock in the shape of a cat ticked away, its tail a pendulum swinging back and forth.

Six fifteen.

I was never going to make it home on time.

"No way," Nia said, and blew out a breath. We all turned toward her just as she peered into the pot Medusa had been stirring. Gathering around, we all saw it, the soup Medusa had been cooking. It was alphabet soup, and the noodles spelled out a message:

> A *place under the earth*
> *Named after the sea*
> *Is where you'll find*
> *The tapestry*

Nia started rattling off sea names. "Caspian, Black, Red, Aegean, East China, Jasmin, Arabian, Caribbean, Philippine, Coral—"

"Stop!" Thalia cried. "You're doing my head in."

"How can the sea be under the earth?" Mela asked. The steam from the alphabet soup fogged up her headphones.

Ari shook her head. "No, not a sea, specifically. It's a place under the earth *named after* the sea."

"I feel like Nia could go on naming seas all night," I said.

"Not *all* night," Nia replied.

"What about the big ones? The Pacific Ocean? The Atlantic Ocean?" Thalia asked.

Mela wiped down her headphones as she talked. "Don't forget the Arctic and the Indian Oceans!"

We heard a rustling in the dining room. We listened as the waiters pulled chairs out to sit and wonder what had happened to them.

"It's time to go," I said. "We can figure this out on the ride home."

Ari found a back door to the restaurant, and we headed out. I took one last look at Medusa. She was very still but fading away. "Look," I whispered, and the others turned.

"She's disappearing," Ari said in wonder.

"I thought she might melt like the Wicked Witch of the West," Nia said.

We all looked at her questioningly.

"What?" Nia said. "The woman was *green*."

The back door opened onto a narrow alley, where we stepped over flattened cardboard boxes and discarded cans on the way to a side street. A rat startled us as it ran close by, and we all screamed.

"Do you think the cyclops disappeared, too?" Mela asked me, once we were out of the alley.

I shrugged. "Maybe. Athena must have brought him here to New York for the quest. Medusa, too."

I thought of the tenth muse, the one Aphrodite said was helping us all along. If I knew who she was, I'd call her right away. But of course, I didn't have any idea who the tenth muse might be, or how she'd already helped us before. We'd have to figure this one out ourselves.

Nia dug out a wrinkled subway map from her back pocket. "Station's this way," she said. We were bumped and jostled as we made our way down the steps to the subway platform. It was rush hour in New York. My watch read six thirty as we boarded the train.

When we finally got outside, it was dusk. My watch read 7:22 p.m.

My curfew?

Completely broken.

Chapter 21

THE GIANT IN THE ROOM

When we got off the subway at the 111th Street station in Corona, my dad was standing there, arms crossed, waiting for me. I'd used Ari's phone to text him the whole ride back, apologizing for being late, telling him we'd had to fetch something for the Student Showcase (again, not technically a lie), and that I'd be home as soon as I could.

But there he was, waiting. With a scowl so deep on his face that I thought it might get stuck that way.

"What do you have to say for yourself, muchachita?" he asked.

"I'm sorry, Papi. Time got away from me."

"And you? Who are all of you?" he asked next, eyeballing the muses.

The muses didn't say anything, so I jumped in. "Friends from camp, Papi."

"You live in Corona?" he asked them.

"Flushing!" Ari answered for them. "And I'll walk them home."

"Sorry, sir," Nia said at last, and shook my dad's hand. "Nia Watson."

Thalia stepped forward next. "Thalia Berry here," she said with a wave.

"Mela Gupta. Pleased to make your acquaintance."

My father uncrossed his arms. "Rafael Silva. Mucho gusto," he said, nodding at them sharply. "Bueno. At least your friends have good manners," he told me. Then, he turned back to Ari and the muses and said, "Go straight home, or I'll call your parents."

Ari led the muses away quickly, and soon they were out of sight.

"Papi, I—"

My father held up a hand. "You're grounded for the rest of the summer. You come home directly after camp each day. Free time for you is family time. Punto. Understand?"

I could feel my cheeks getting hot. Yes, I'd broken curfew, but it was for a good reason. If only I could make Papi understand.

"I'm sorry I wasn't home in time, but it really was for a camp thing."

Papi huffed and started walking. "I don't want to talk about this now," he said.

"Well, I do. I'm not a baby anymore! I'm responsible!"

Now Papi laughed, but it was that fake, sarcastic laugh people sometimes do when what they mean to show is how deeply *not* funny the situation is.

"I *am* responsible. You have no idea how much."

I wanted to tell him everything so badly—about the muses, and Ari, and Athena. About saving Maya last year, which meant helping to maybe save the world someday. About Tia Annie, and how much Mami cried when she left us, and how tough my brothers had to be, how they didn't cry even when they wanted to.

"Callie!" Papi shouted, startling me.

"What?" I asked.

"Have you been listening to a word I've said? And you say you're responsible. Responsible girls listen to their fathers when they're talking with them."

"*At* them, you mean," I mumbled.

"What?"

"Nada, Papi." I was so mad, my vision was blurry. It wasn't fair! Why did Papi invite me to New York anyway? To punish me? To spend the whole day working and never see me at all?

Two blocks from home, Papi stopped at a bench on the edge of a park. In the distance, I spied a small church carnival with a Ferris wheel, food trucks, a stage, and a reggaeton group performing. We could hear the music and the squeals of kids on the rides.

"Come. Sit with your old dad a while," he said. I sat

down. "I know you're growing up. But I don't have to like it. I worry about you and your brothers like you wouldn't believe. From the moment you were born, and I held you, so tiny and pink, I promised that I would never let anything bad happen to you."

"But bad things happen to people all the time," I said.

"It's true. They do. I just worry. Can you understand that?"

I held Papi's hand, felt the calluses there. He used to tell my brothers and me about what it was like growing up in Cuba, how so many of his friends left the island on rickety boats and patched-up rafts, and how he never heard from them again. Sometimes Papi would tear up remembering this friend, or that one. Then he'd tell us about his own trip, the days at sea, the safety of the beach, and the hard work ahead of him, and we were so proud.

I wondered if Papi thought of the open ocean when he worried about us. Or if he remembered the dark shadows that slunk underneath his raft.

If I had known him then, I would have pumped him full of magic and courage.

Then again, perhaps he'd already had enough of his own magic.

"I tell you what. You can have this back." He took my phone out of his pocket. "And I promise to come home early from work all this week. And this weekend, we can do whatever you want to. The city is yours."

I felt better, and not just because my phone was back.

"Okay. Just, let's skip Little Italy. I heard it's a tourist trap."

Papi nodded. Then he kissed the top of my head.

"I love you, mi niña."

"I love you, too, Papi."

We got up from the bench and walked home, hand in hand. Papi wasn't a very tall man, and I'd grown past his shoulder. He always joked, "I'm the giant in the room," and everyone would laugh, but I always believed him.

Chapter 22
WHOSE CAMP? OUR CAMP!

The next day, Papi walked me to Corona Arts. We heard people banging on the pots and pans before we saw them.

There was chanting, too—"Whose camp? OUR CAMP!" shouted again and again.

Then they were in view—dozens of campers marching in front of Corona Arts, holding up signs that read "Save Our Camp," and "We Demand Arts Funding!" and "Mayor, Fund Our Camp!" The ones without signs were banging on pots and pans with wooden spoons.

Papi slowed down and held me back. "I'd heard the camp was in financial trouble," he said.

I nodded. "Ari told me that the private donors who helped fund Corona Arts in the summer were considering pulling their money for next year."

"Ay," Papi said. "That would be a shame." His eyes

darted to a place beyond me. "Mira," he said, pointing to the front doors.

There stood Maris. She was standing on a milk crate and had connected a microphone to an amp. "Testing," she said into the mic, her voice blasting out onto the street. The pots and pans stilled, and the signs dropped a few inches.

Maris smiled. "Thanks for coming out, everyone. This was just phase one of our plan to save Corona Arts!"

Everyone shouted, and the signs went up again. So *this* is what Maris wanted to talk to me and Ari about! She'd planned a whole protest!

"There's a petition going around asking the borough president to speak to the mayor about earmarking more funding for our summer camp. Please sign it! Our message is clear," Maris said. "We love our camp and want it to remain open next summer. Phase two of our plan is the Student Showcase and impressing the private donors. Their help, along with the mayor's funding, would ensure that Corona Arts will not only stay open, but will thrive for years to come! We need to give it all we've got. What do you say, Corona Arts?"

Everyone cheered. I noticed that Maris was wearing two cuffs made of aluminum foil, one on each wrist. She'd drawn a star on each one with a permanent marker.

"Are those supposed to be handcuffs?" Papi said, squinting at Maris.

I laughed. "I'm guessing those are Wonder Woman's bracelets on a budget."

Papi chuckled, too. "Well, if there's a kid with super-powers around here, I'd put money on her," he said.

If only you knew, I thought. I was pretty sure that if Papi found out I was a muse, he'd search out Clio and have several words with her before making me quit.

"Have a good time at school and be home by five today."

"Okay," I said. By now, the crowd of students was heading into the school, most of them on their phones posting pictures of the protest. I caught up with Maris in the stairwell on the way to our poetry class. "Maris!" I shouted. "That was amazing."

She looked down, a rosy glow coloring her cheeks. "Thanks. Somebody had to do something. Hopefully, news of our protest gets back to the mayor. Do you like my sign?" Maris held up what looked like a flattened cardboard box. In simple black crayon, she'd scrawled:

THIS SIGN WOULD LOOK BETTER
IF THE ARTS WERE FUNDED.

It was the ugliest, plainest sign I'd ever seen, but that was the point.

"Genius!" I said.

Maris dropped her voice to a whisper. "I know."

We walked into class, where Mr. Theo was scrolling

through his phone. When he looked up, he beamed and made a trumpeting sound. "Brava, Ms. Emad! You're the talk of the town!" he said, and showed us a local neighborhood app full of pictures of the protest, and lots of comments that read "Good job, kids!"

Maris thanked him, set down her sign, and started gathering paintbrushes and paint for our poems.

"Hey," I said to Maris as I sat down beside her with a fresh section of butcher paper. "I'm sorry Ari and I didn't let you tell us about your plans yesterday."

"Sometimes even cartoon characters have good ideas," she said softly.

My heart dropped. She'd heard Ari, then. "I'm sorry," I whispered.

Maris didn't say anything. She only went back to work quietly, her aluminum foil cuffs crinkling as she painted.

At lunch, the camp director came on the PA system. "I appreciate your enthusiasm this morning, campers," Ms. Neptune said. "But we must ban protests without permits, by order of the 112th Precinct of the New York Police Department."

I heard the moans and complaints of students all through the camp.

Ms. Neptune went on. "However, I have sent a recording of your protest to the borough president's office, as well as the mayor's, and to our donors, who have since expressed the hope that the Student Showcase goes off without a hitch and promised to be there in person this year. So chin up, campers! Let's do our best to save Corona Arts!"

The speaker shut off, and Maris, Mr. Theo, and I sat in silence for a while.

"This neighborhood won't be the same without Corona Arts," Mr. Theo said.

"No, it won't," Ari said, standing in the doorway. As usual, bright threads were stuck in her hair here and there. She came over to Maris, sat down, and pulled out two squares knitted with bright yellow yarn. "For you. Because I'm sorry I pushed you away yesterday. And because you're pretty cool."

Maris picked up one of the yellow squares, unfolding it to reveal a red star stitched into the center. She gasped, tore off her aluminum foil cuffs, and put on the new ones Ari had made. Then she struck a Wonder Woman pose. "What do you think?"

"Amazing!" I said.

"Wonderful!" Ari added. Maris got up to show Mr. Theo. Meanwhile, Ari whispered, "Distract them."

"What?"

"Use your powers. Distract them. We have work to do." Ari brought out her phone and searched for a map of Brooklyn. She tapped a few icons, zoomed in on the page, and said, "There. Atlantic Avenue."

"And?"

"There's an abandoned subway tunnel under Atlantic. *A place under the earth named after the sea*, remember? That has to be it," Ari said. "So, magic time, baby."

"You want to go now?" I asked. The clock in the classroom read two. That only gave me three hours to get home by five, like Papi had said.

Frustration bubbled up in my body. Yes, I wanted to help Ari, especially now that I knew the tenth muse and Ari's quest were linked, but I also didn't want to get in trouble with Papi again. I'd come all this way to spend time with him, Laura, and Rafaelito, but it felt like all I'd done was make everyone upset.

Ari glared at me. "You need to get your priorities straight," she said.

"My priorities?" I whispered back. "You tell me that this quest is a priority. Clio tells me that the tenth muse is a priority. My father says being home on time is a priority."

Ari leaned back into her chair and rolled her eyes. "Only one of those ends with me losing my humanity forever. Gosh. How can you choose between that and being grounded?"

I wanted to scream. Just shove my face into a pillow and shout until I lost my voice.

"You okay?" Mr. Theo asked. Maris looked up at us, too. She lifted her arms up and showed off her Wonder Woman cuffs again.

If I could turn the moment into a comic book page, the words "Get tough, Callie" would be right over Maris's head, inside a white speech bubble. That's what Mario had told me to do, and my brother was right.

I made a choice and imagined Mr. Theo and Maris working on a long poem, one that took up an entire wall, both of them so lost in it that they didn't notice I was gone. The magic tingled, like it always did, and the picture in my head grew clearer and more precise until . . .

"Mr. Theo!" Maris shouted, an idea lighting up her whole face.

"Maris!" Mr. Theo replied.

Then they were off, running for their notebooks, jotting down ideas.

"Thanks," Ari said.

I lifted my bracelet to my mouth and called the others. "Muses, it's time to muster. Meet at the museum ASAP."

Chapter 23
APHRODITE'S GIFTS

By the time Thalia, Nia, and Mela got to the museum, it was already three o'clock. Guilt ate at the corners of my brain, like a little mouse making a home for itself. But I tried to remember that Ari was in immediate danger. Getting into trouble again would be worth it if we saved her.

We narrowly missed bumping into Clio on the way out of the museum. Nia, Mela, Thalia, and I crouched behind a set of vending machines in the café, while Ari pretended to browse the sandwich selections.

"I'm starting to feel really bad about disobeying Clio's orders," Nia said, now that Ari was out of earshot.

Clio paused as she neared the machines, patted her pockets, then went into the café. I could have sworn I heard her stomach growling as she passed us by.

"Me, too," Mela said.

"Me, three," Thalia added. "How are we ever going to find the tenth muse without help from the Gray Sisters?"

"One problem at a time, I guess," I said, but my heart wasn't in it. I hated the idea of disappointing Clio and the other grown-up muses.

We watched as Clio chose a salad and a bottle of water. She sat with her food near a window, picking at limp lettuce with a sad look on her face.

"She looks absolutely gutted," Thalia said. "And it's all our fault. We're supposed to be helping her locate the tenth muse."

I felt a pang in my chest. It was possible that the very existence of the muses was in danger. That's what Clio had said. And here we were . . . hiding behind junk food. Clio sighed over her sad salad, and I nearly bolted out from where we hid, ready to confess everything.

Just then, Ari made her way casually back to us. She made a show of pressing buttons on the machine while whispering, "Your boss isn't looking. Let's go!"

Once the coast was clear, we ran all the way to the subway station, stopping a few yards in front of the metal stairs that would take us to the platform. There was a woman sitting on the lowest step, strumming a golden guitar. She wore a beanie on her head, a leather jacket, and black jeans. At her feet was a guitar case, full of money from people who'd dropped bills and coins inside.

The music she was playing was like nothing I'd ever heard before. Each chord drew a listener, and soon the sidewalk was crowded with people swaying together to the music and blocking our way up the stairs.

"She's amazing," Mela said, tugging off her headphones.

Thalia grabbed hold of Nia's hands, and the two of them spun around twice to the music.

As for Ari, she'd covered her face with her hands and was muttering, "Now what?"

"Excuse me," I said, pushing through the crowd. "Coming through." When I put a foot on the lower step, the woman stopped playing and grabbed my ankle.

"Hey!" I said, looking down at the top of her head.

Then she turned to gaze up at me, and I realized why everyone was so enchanted.

"Aphrodite," I whispered. "What are you doing here?"

She laid the golden guitar in its case, and the people sighed, sad that the music had ended.

Very quietly, so that only I could hear it, she said, "Glad you could come out, too. Shall we?" She put her hand up and wriggled her fingers, inviting me to take it.

"You said you couldn't get involved," I said.

"I shouldn't. But who is going to stop me, honestly?"

I shrugged. If Aphrodite herself wanted to help, then I was all for it.

Nia was at my side at once. "We should go, Callie."

"Didn't your parents tell you about Stranger Danger?" Thalia said under her breath.

"It's fine, everybody. She's going to help us," I said. The others stared at me as though I'd suddenly started speaking a different language. Only Ari shrugged and shook her head. "Okay, let's go," I said to Aphrodite. "Do you have a MetroCard we can all use for the subway?" I asked.

Aphrodite laughed, gripped my hand hard, and yanked me toward her. I grabbed on to Nia and Thalia, who must have taken ahold of Mela, who probably grabbed on to Ari for support. Because before I knew it, my feet had slipped on the metal step, and I fell.

And kept falling.

Dropping through nothing, holding on to Aphrodite's hand.

It took a second, maybe less, but when we stopped, we were standing in an old, dark tunnel, wide enough for a train. The faintest moonlight pierced the manhole cover over our heads. It was damp, and cold, and I thought I heard somebody snoring very far away.

"Is everybody all right?" I asked a little weakly, my stomach queasy from all the falling.

Nia looked up, and we all followed her gaze as she looked at the manhole cover. "Are we underground now? Like *mole people*?"

"More importantly," Mela said, "are we going to encounter any mole people down here?"

"Most importantly," Thalia asked, "who is *she*?"

They all turned to look at Aphrodite, who took a little bow as she waited for introductions.

"Everybody," I said, hoping they would all be cool about this, "this is Ari's aunt. Aphrodite."

Thalia screamed, Mela closed her eyes, and Nia stumbled back a step.

So much for being cool.

"Auntie A, what are you doing here?" Ari asked, coming forward and hugging Aphrodite around the waist.

"I couldn't let you do this one on your own, sweet girl," Aphrodite said.

"We've got this," Ari said, a touch of irritation in her voice.

"Your aunt is beautiful," Thalia whispered. "Like, total celebrity status gorgeous."

Aphrodite smiled and twirled a strand of hair around her finger.

The snoring in the distance stopped, then started again with a mucus-y snort.

"Pretty is not going to help with whatever is making that noise," Nia said under her breath.

"I'm more than a pretty face, young one," Aphrodite said. She snapped her fingers, and suddenly a wooden chest appeared at her feet. "Come closer, darlings. I can't help you fight what's lying in the dark, but nobody said I can't give you gifts. Everyone knows the cool aunt is the one with the best gifts."

"My aunt Ellen always gives me a new toothbrush for Christmas," Thalia said, scrunching up her nose.

Aphrodite beckoned everyone closer. "No toothbrushes here. Behold." She opened up the chest, and a soft, golden light filled the cavernous tunnel. "These are your emblems. Emblems are objects associated with your magic and were gifts from Olympus bestowed upon the muses from time to time. Ancient artists would always depict the muses holding their emblems."

I remembered the statue of Calliope my mom still had on her dresser. She held a scroll and a writing instrument. Is that what Aphrodite was going to give me?

"For you, Thalia, Muse of comedy," Aphrodite said, pulling out an instrument that mostly resembled a horn.

Thalia took the horn in hand. A smiling theater mask was etched into its side.

Aphrodite smiled. "In the ancient days, actors used this item to amplify their voices onstage. You, dear funny one, are loud, but this? This will make your voice so loud that the heavens will hear it."

"Oh no," Nia muttered.

Aphrodite dug into the chest again, and this time she

pulled out a beautiful silver mask, the mouth turned down into a grimace.

"I suppose that's mine," Mela said, looking a little sad about it.

Nodding, Aphrodite settled the mask over Mela's face. "What is tragedy but a reminder that life is short, and that love in all its forms is the best way to make the days long? When you wear this mask and call your magic, you will remind the one who receives it about these truths, and you will help them heal their hurt."

Mela slid the mask onto her head. "Okay," she said quietly.

"My turn?" Nia asked.

Now the chest glowed even more brightly. "Nia. Muse of science, a gift from the heavens for you." Aphrodite reached into the chest and pulled out her hand, balled into a fist. "Take it," she said, and Nia held her hands out. Aphrodite then dropped a glowing ball of light into her cupped palms. It was so bright we couldn't really look at it.

"It is your very own star, Nia. Let it shine in darkness, and all will be well."

Nia blinked at the light in her hands. "Oh my goodness," she whispered.

I cleared my throat. I was next. What would Aphrodite give me? I looked up at the goddess, who was biting her bottom lip.

"Is there something in there for me?" I asked quietly.

Aphrodite shook her head.

My stomach felt as if it had fallen all the way to my feet. It was like never getting picked for the team at recess, but a million times worse. The other muses looked away, holding tightly to their emblems. I thought about the tenth muse, and how there could only be nine of us. Was this a sign?

"Why?" I asked, my voice just a whisper.

Aphrodite laid a hand on my head. "Dear one," she said. "There is an emblem for you, but it is not mine to give. It will come to you only when you most need it, for it is too powerful a thing. Take heart, Callie."

I swallowed thickly, trying to fight back tears. "Okay, I guess," I said.

The others gathered around me and gave me a hug. "Don't be sad," Thalia said.

"It's okay to be sad," Mela put in.

Nia let me hold her star, which was cool, not warm at all. Like holding a marble that you left in the refrigerator. It was hard to look at straight on, but very beautiful. "I'll let you borrow it," she told me with a wink.

"Thanks," I said. Then, turning to Aphrodite, I asked, "What do these emblems do, anyway?"

Aphrodite stood up straight, slamming the chest closed, and it disappeared in a flash of light. "Glad you asked," she said. "Firstly, they are physical reminders of your gifts. But they're more powerful than just that. Up until now, your powers have been, shall we say, human-bound. Beings like me, and like the one snoring away in the distance, have been immune to your efforts."

I thought of how we couldn't fight the sirens last year with our powers. Or the cyclops, or Medusa, for that matter.

"But these emblems help you . . . amplify things. They wouldn't affect me, of course, or my sister Athena. But the other beings, the ones that are not quite gods, yet not quite humans? Well, these items should help with them a great deal."

The snoring stopped all at once, and silence filled the tunnel. Somehow, the silence was louder than the snoring had been.

"That's my cue to go," Aphrodite said. She ruffled Ari's hair. "Love and luck to you all, darlings. Remember your gifts! And don't tell Athena I was here." She put her fingers to her lips in the "shh" sign and disappeared with a small whooshing sound.

"Now what?" Nia whispered.

"Be brave, I guess. What else is there to do?" I said.

Nia lifted the star in her hand high overhead, illuminating the tunnel for miles and miles.

"How is everybody feeling?" I asked.

"Good," Thalia said.

"Ready," Mela added.

"Let's get that tapestry," Nia said.

I looked at Ari, who was breathing hard.

"Come on, hero, you've got work to do," I told her. She put her hand in mine, and together the five of us walked in the light of Nia's star toward the unknown.

Chapter 24
QUESTIONS AND ANSWERS

Gray stones, stacked one on top of the other, lined the walls of the tunnel, which arched overhead. Here and there, as we walked, I noticed staircases leading up to sealed doors. Every once in a while the tunnels shook, as if the ghosts of subway trains were rumbling by.

The snoring had started up again, and it was getting louder by the moment.

"What is this place, anyway?" Mela asked.

Ari answered. "It's the oldest subway tunnel! The rails on the ground aren't live, which is why we can walk on them. Otherwise, we'd be electrocuted!"

Nia kicked some rocks, which bounced against rails that ran along the ground.

Thalia hummed a little tune and twirled her trumpet like a baton. "My mum used to say that there were giants that lived in the London Underground. Maybe that's what we're heading towar—"

We all stopped. The star in Nia's hand had lit up the farthest reaches of the tunnel, and in the distance we could see a glimmering *something*. The snoring was louder than ever.

Nia shaded the starlight a bit. Thalia quit spinning the trumpet. Mela slid on her mask.

We took a few more steps, and there was a flash of light against a large, flat object. Slowly, we made our way forward, the starlight illuminating the shape as we got closer.

"What in the world is that?" Ari whispered.

Four more steps and I noticed the wheels, a massive hunk of metal painted black, a clock, and a bell.

"It's a train!" Mela exclaimed.

"An old-timey one!" Thalia added.

They were right. A steam engine sat there on the tracks, underground. It looked exactly like the kind of train I'd seen in movies set in the past. I rubbed my sleeve against the side of the engine, polishing it in circles until its bright red color appeared.

Nia climbed aboard and started messing with a lever jutting out of the floor. "Take us to the North Pole!" she said, laughing.

Thalia and Mela jumped in next, elbowing one another for a spot at the window.

"What about the snoring?" Ari asked. She was right—it

was loud now. Whoever or whatever was making that noise wasn't far away.

"Sound asleep still," I said. "Come on. A look inside won't hurt. Besides, the train is blocking the tunnel. This might just be a dead end for us." I shuffled in, holding out a hand for Ari. She took it, stepped up, and—

Ooooooooooooooh!

The train whistle blasted, shrill and long, right over our heads. A great big plume of smoke poured out of the train's smokestack, and ahead of us, an iron box full of coal went up in flames. We all screamed, scrambling for the hand-rails. But before any of us could even think of jumping off, the train was rolling forward, gathering speed, and whis-tling every so often. The dark tunnel opened like a mouth ahead of us, and a moist wind whipped our hair back.

I grabbed the lever and pulled it toward me, hoping it was the brake. The train's wheels squealed, but it didn't slow down one bit.

"What are we going to do, Callie?" Mela was shout-ing, but I had no idea. The train rolled on for a while in the dark. Nia's star lit up the tunnel far into the distance. She laid it safely behind a lever, then she examined the compartment we found ourselves in, muttering to herself about fireboxes, and boilers, the properties of steam, and other science-y things that didn't make sense to me.

Eventually, the train began to slow, rolling to a stop. The snoring behind us rumbled on, undisturbed. But now a new sound had joined in. It was a crackling noise, like cellophane being crumpled up, and it grew louder by the second.

We all drew closer to one another, until Mela's shoulder bumped against mine on one side, and Ari's on the other.

"What is it?" I heard Thalia ask. Something was coming toward us, its shape becoming clearer with each snapping step. Was this why Aphrodite had given us emblems?

"I think I see something," Nia said, narrowing her eyes. She picked up her star and held it out so that more of the tunnel was illuminated.

"Oh my gods," Ari gasped. "Do you know what that is?" Ahead, a lion stalked the tracks, back and forth. But it wasn't *just* a lion. This lion had golden wings speckled in blue leopard spots, and it had the head and neck of a man with flaming red hair. He flapped his wings lazily, which is what made the crackling sound, as if his bones were grinding together. The lion stopped several yards from the train, his tail swishing so violently behind him that we could hear it cut through the air.

"Here at last," he said, sitting on the tracks. A bored look crossed his face, and he started to lick his paws.

"That's a sphinx," Mela said with a moan.

"A sphinx?" I asked. "They're the creatures that ask riddles, right?" I remembered reading about them in a textbook back in elementary school.

Ari nodded. "Yep. And they eat you when you get the answer wrong."

"Does this thing go in reverse?" Thalia asked, eyeing the train compartment.

"It's part of the quest," I said. "We have to try." I knew I sounded braver than I actually felt. Ari mouthed the words *thank you* at me, then turned to face the sphinx.

"I'm guessing you have some questions for us," Ari said, putting her hands on her hips. "Let's hear them."

The sphinx stopped licking his paws. "Not for you, bug. For the muses." He coughed once, then again, until he was hacking.

"You okay there, mate?" Thalia asked.

We watched as the sphinx puked up a giant hairball, which plopped wetly on the tracks. "Ah. Much better," he said.

"I'm going to be sick," Nia mumbled.

The big cat slowly made his way closer to the train. He was bigger than a regular lion, with paws the size of watermelons. He sat again and let his tail curl around him. "I have three questions for you."

"Three?" I asked. Didn't the sphinxes in stories just ask one?

The sphinx purred. "Yes. Three. Get them wrong, I beg of you. I'm very hungry."

"And if we get the answers right?" I asked.

"That would be boring. But I'd have to let you through and go catch a rat or something for my dinner instead. Deal?"

"Do we have a choice?" I asked. Even if we did, this was part of the quest. We'd agreed to help Ari, and we couldn't back out now.

The sphinx laughed. "Of course not. Shall we?"

I looked at the others, and they all nodded grimly, ready for anything.

"Go on," I said.

The cat sat down again before speaking. "My first riddle is for Nia, descendent of Urania, Muse of science."

Nia straightened up to listen, clasping her hands behind her back, her posture perfect as usual.

"What can fill up a room but takes no space?" the sphinx asked. "And no helping her!" he warned the rest of us. The sphinx made a funny face, as if even thinking about people cooperating with one another grossed him out.

Nia stood very still and closed her eyes.

"Come on, Nia," Thalia cheered her on.

"You can do it," I said.

"I know she's got this," Mela added.

Nia stomped her left foot in frustration as she thought. She picked up the star and held it in her hand.

"I don't think these are going to help," Mela added, holding up her own emblem.

I nodded. Why had Aphrodite given us these emblems anyway? What use were they in this situation? Anyhow, I didn't even *have* an emblem. If they were any help at all, I'd be out of luck.

Thalia disagreed. "I don't know. Aphrodite said, 'Remember your gifts,' didn't she? It had to mean something."

Suddenly, Nia gasped, looking at the star in her hand, then back up again. "Of course!" she said, delighted. She turned to the sphinx, whose ears had perked up. "The answer is light. Light fills up a room but takes no space!"

The sphinx clapped lazily, his huge paws making a muffled *thwap* sound when he put them together. "The next question is one you will like. It requires a team effort," he said, rolling his eyes. "Mela, Muse of tragedy, and Thalia, Muse of comedy, put your tiny brains together and work this one out: I am a player at work, and a worker at play. Who am I?"

Lying down, the sphinx closed his eyes, as if he expected this to take a while.

Mela groaned, balancing her mask on her fingers. "I hate riddles."

"I sort of like them," Thalia said. "But only when they're in books, and the main character figures them out, and not when we might actually become part of a sphinx's digestive system. Muse Squad–flavored hairballs," she said with a whimper.

The rest of us watched as Mela and Thalia tried to work out the riddle. The sphinx had said we couldn't help, and I tried hard to distract myself so that I wouldn't accidentally use my muse magic. The thing was, it had gotten so easy to use. Just a picture in my head was all it took to inspire someone. I started counting backward from a hundred by sevens.

"You look like you're about to break your brain," Ari whispered.

Seventy-nine, seventy-two, sixty-five . . . "I think I did," I said, then had to start counting all over again.

Mela clapped her hands, and I could tell she'd had an idea. "Thalia, your emblem and mine are both used in the theater, right?"

Thalia nodded. "Yes, that's true. Go on."

"Well, back home in New Delhi, the youth theater that my mum bought me season passes for calls themselves the Garden Players, because they perform in the Garden of the Five Senses each spring. They work very hard . . ."

Thalia's mouth dropped open. "Because they're players at work, and workers at play, and players is another word for . . ."

"Actors!" Thalia and Mela said at once.

The sphinx stood up and lumbered closer to the train until we could hear him breathing. With each riddle answered, he had gotten closer. "Took you long enough," he purred. "Now it's Calliope's turn."

I swallowed loudly. So far, everyone's riddles had something to do with their magic. The clue to the riddle Nia was given was in her emblem. Thalia and Mela, whose magic was inspired by comedy and tragedy, were given a theater riddle. Would my riddle be about poems? *I wish Maris was here,* I thought sadly. She'd know the answer to any poem-inspired riddle.

The sphinx crouched, looking like a cat about to spring. His tail whipped the air above his body. "Ready?"

I nodded.

"What is always in front of you, but can't be seen?"

I tried to concentrate, shutting everyone else out by closing my eyes. But I could hear the sphinx breathing, and somebody fiddling with something metallic on the train, which didn't help me focus at all, so I opened my eyes again.

The answer would be something obvious. What was in front of me now? Air? That *could* work, but what if I was underwater? The answer wouldn't be right then. What about my nose? It was always in front of me and I couldn't see it without a mirror. Except when I crossed my eyes, of course.

I could feel myself getting frustrated, and every little noise around me just sounded louder now. The sphinx started to laugh, low and rumbly, and I wished I could inspire him to go chase his tail for eternity, but my magic didn't work on mythical creatures.

Except that gave me an idea!

The sphinx had said we couldn't help one another with the riddles, but he didn't say we couldn't help ourselves. Slowly, I began to picture myself rising to my feet. I'd open my mouth, and the answer would just fly out. Again and again, I tried to imagine it, but I couldn't. It was like I could have a hand in everyone else's future, but I couldn't see very far into mine.

I growled in frustration. As always, my own destiny felt like a mystery to me. I could just picture everyone else doing the things they loved to do, changing the world, living up to their muse potential. But me? My future felt like a blank piece of paper.

The sphinx startled to chuckle, and I lifted my head at the sound.

"Calliope, full of questions. But she never has any answers," the sphinx teased.

"Don't listen to that dumb cat," Nia said.

"I hope you get another hairball," Thalia shouted.

I got to my feet. "What did you say?" I asked the sphinx, a thought bubbling in my brain.

The sphinx arched its back in a long stretch. "I said, you are full of questions, but have no answers. A bit like me actually. Would you like to trade places?"

The answer to the riddle popped into my brain in bright lights, like fireworks spelling something out in the sky.

"The future!" I shouted. "That's the answer! It's always

before me, but I can't see it."

The others clapped, while Ari shouted, "Let us through!"

Huffing, the sphinx left the tracks without a word, and in one leap bounded up into a little alcove in the ceiling of the tunnel. The train rumbled back to life, and we passed by the sphinx, who peered down at us silently with golden, glowing eyes.

"I thought I liked cats," Mela said sadly.

"You can still like them," Thalia comforted her. "But maybe not that one."

I slumped down to the floor of the compartment. We'd gotten past the sphinx, but we still had no idea where the train was taking us. And while the emblems Aphrodite had given the others were helpful back there, would they be useful up ahead?

Even worse, the sphinx had confirmed something for me—no matter how hard I tried, my future would be impossible to predict.

Chapter 25
A GIANT PARTY

After a while, the train took a sharp left turn, revealing a light up ahead. I didn't know if we were still under New York City, or somewhere under Connecticut, or if we'd somehow rolled into another dimension. All I knew was that where the tunnel had been tight, now it was open, and in the distance were shadowy hills.

We have to be ready for anything, I thought.

Beside me, Nia, Thalia, and Mela had grabbed on to their emblems, shielding Ari behind them. The train slowed down, screeching as it came to a stop. The tunnel's ceiling was now high above us, and we found ourselves in an open place, like a station of some kind. The hills in the distance remained in shadows.

"Okay. Things just got really freaky," Nia said.

"Like they haven't already been?" I asked. Just then, the

train wobbled a little, as if something had pushed it.

"What was that?" Ari asked.

Before any of us could guess, a huge face appeared at one of the train cab's windows. The face was so big that only one eye and half a nose was visible.

"Gah!" Nia exclaimed, and held the star up, as if she was going to throw it at whatever *that* was.

"Giant!" Thalia shouted, clutching her trumpet. "My mum was right!"

"Howdy," the giant said, her voice low and rumbly. She yawned, and her hot breath blasted over us.

"Ew. It smells like stale popcorn," Mela whispered.

"Thanks for the ride," the giant said, then she lumbered away toward the hills, calling out, "Momma! I'm back!"

One of the hills shook, unfolding into another giant, taller than the first. "Harper Ann, you're out past curfew."

Another hill awoke, smaller than the first two. "How was New York City?" he asked. The first giant, Harper Ann, pinched the shorter one's cheeks.

"It was big, Jackson. So big! What a city. I explored all the tunnels. But there's nothing like home," she said. "Those kids brought me back on the train. I slept the whole way. Awful kind of them."

"Can we keep 'em, Momma?" Jackson, the littlest giant, asked.

The largest giant laughed and hugged the one that had been on our train. "I missed you, darling. And what have you got there?" she asked, pointing at Harper Ann's pocket.

Harper Ann dug into her pocket and pulled out the third piece of tapestry. "Momma, this was a gift from Athena herself. I told you New York was full of celebrities, but I didn't expect to meet one of the Olympian gods."

Harper Ann's mother plucked the tapestry from her daughter's fingers. "That's a wonderful gift. We ought to write her a thank-you note."

"What is it, Momma?" Harper Ann asked. "A scarf?"

"Handkerchief," Momma answered, and Harper Ann brought it to her nose and sniffed delicately into it.

Ari was trembling from head to toe. "Yuck! How are we going to get that back, Callie? How?"

"We can't fight them," Mela said. "They seem so nice."

"Maybe we can talk to them," I suggested.

Nia cleared her throat. "Excuse me, giant family? Can we talk?" she shouted.

"Momma, look!" Jackson cried, and came running toward us. He thrust his fingers into the cab, wrapped them around Thalia's waist, and yanked her out, hoisting her above his head.

"No!" we all shouted, tumbling out of the train.

"He'll crush her!" Ari was saying.

"Thalia, your emblem!" I shouted.

Thalia managed to get her arms free from the young giant's grip and lifted her trumpet to her mouth.

"HAAAA HAAAAAAA!" she shouted into his face, using the trumpet to laugh so loudly that dust descended from the ceiling high above us.

Jackson started to chuckle, then guffaw, until his eyes filled with tears and he started to cry and laugh at the same time. I knew the feeling. One time, at dinner, Maya and I started laughing so hard that she fell off her chair, and *that* made *me* laugh so hard I started to cry. Jackson dropped to the ground, letting Thalia tumble out of his hands. Once she was on her feet, she ran back to us, breathless.

Momma's eyes snapped in our direction. She stomped toward us, each step rattling the train. "My little boy is crying! Y'all weren't taught any manners at all, that's clear," she said, pointing a finger at us.

"That's my tapestry!" Ari said, pointing at the cloth Harper Ann was holding up to her nose again. "And now it has boogers in it!"

"Athena's handkerchief was a gift to my daughter. How dare you?" Momma asked, her nostrils flaring as if we'd just insulted her outfit, or the way she decorated her house.

"But I made him happy!" Thalia said. In the distance, Jackson was wailing as he laughed. "Sort of," Thalia added.

"Ma'am?" I asked. "Um, I think there's been a mistake. That is a tapestry, an ancient one—and we need it."

"It was a gift!" Momma roared in our faces. "And I'll not have you ruining Harper Ann's big day. We are having a party, and giants from all over Jefferson County will be here in ten minutes to welcome her. And she *will* show off her gift from Athena, you mark my words. You can either go back the way you came, or you can be appetizers. *Your call.*"

"We're in *Jefferson County*?" Ari whispered. "That's like five hours away from New York City by car!"

"How fast was that train moving?" Nia asked.

"Who cares?" Mela said. "More of their *relatives* are coming!"

Ten minutes. In ten minutes, this place would be full of giants.

And I did not want to become giant party food.

"Thalia, you take the kid. Mela, Momma is all yours. Nia, can you start up the train again? Good. I'll work on Harper Ann," I said.

"What about me?" Ari asked.

"Let's get this party canceled. Seems to me the giants have a bit of an insect problem on their hands."

Ari laughed. "You mean arachnids, but I've got you." She sat crisscross on the floor of the train and closed her eyes. Within seconds, a tiny spider had crawled out from under a floorboard and was climbing up onto Ari's hand. She held it up to her mouth and whispered something to it, and then the spider was off, running as fast as it could to spread the word.

Thalia had crawled onto Jackson's lap. She jumped onto

his shoulder and started talking in his ear and making him laugh so hard that the tears started up again, this time the good, happy kind.

As for Mela, she faced off with Momma, who had lowered herself into a crouch, trying to snatch her if she came too close.

Mela's mask rested on her face. She cocked her head to the side, and suddenly, Mela was no longer . . . Mela. She grew, filling out, until she was as tall as Momma and looked just like a giant, too.

"Papa?" Momma asked. Mela lumbered forward and held Momma in a hug. "Oh, Papa, how I've missed you," Momma said, crying softly. "These humans have come to ruin our Harper Ann's party."

"They haven't," I heard Mela say in the giant's rumbly voice. "They are good, like you. Let 'em go."

"I don't want to," she cried. "And I don't want to let you go again, either."

Mela patted Momma's head tenderly. "Give 'em what they want, honeybee. And you've got to let me go, too. I'm not really here, after all. Be at peace."

"I've missed you, Papa," Momma said softly.

I blinked back tears, reminded of Tia Annie and how she'd told me never to come looking for her again.

Grief. Waves and waves of it, like Clio said. I hated it.

Behind me, Nia clattered around on the train, shining her starlight into the dark places. "I think if I can get the boiler going, we can maybe get this thing to head in reverse. I wonder if starlight is hot enough to—"

Suddenly, the firebox behind me lit up again, and the train whistle blew. I high-fived Nia and jumped down to where Harper Ann stood, clutching the tapestry to her nose.

"That wasn't a gift, Harper Ann," I said gently. "It was a trick. Athena wanted you to have it so that we couldn't get it back."

Harper Ann shook her head. "That's not true. I'm *special*. It's my birthday, you know. This is my birthday gift from Athena." Her eyes were glittering with tears, and her voice cracked as she spoke.

"Happy birthday, Harper Ann. You *are* special. You can be anything you want to be," I said.

"I want to be an architect. That's why I convinced Momma to let me go to New York." Harper Ann blew her nose again, and the tapestry was starting to look a bit damp.

"You want to make . . . buildings?" I asked.

"All kinds!" Harper Ann said. "Skyscrapers, and castles, and rooms without walls, and buildings shaped like food!"

"Then do it!" I said. At this point, every inch of me was tingling with muse magic. I imagined Harper Ann surrounded by blueprints, her big hands doing delicate work with rulers and sharpened pencils, designing the buildings of her dreams. I'd never been able to use it against anyone who wasn't human before. Whenever I'd tried, I'd felt the resistance, like my magic hitting a wall. Now the wall was gone. But I didn't have an emblem like the others. How was I doing it?

Thalia had Jackson laughing hard, while Mela and Momma were holding hands, conversing, and she was smiling through her tears. Mela may have been the Muse of tragedy, but right now, she was helping Momma feel better. The train shook on its wheels, ready to head back to New York City.

And Harper Ann?

Harper Ann was drawing designs into the dust at her feet. They were large, and detailed, and it looked like she was planning a building with three arched entries separated by Greek columns.

"What's that?" I asked.

"A library. It's modeled after the New York Public Library, in fact. Have you ever been?"

I shook my head no.

"Well," Harper Ann continued, "it's a wonder. I want to build a library like that here. You should go see it. Maybe you'll find what you're looking for," she said absently.

I laid my hand on hers. My whole hand was the size of her pinkie fingernail. "What makes you say that?" I asked.

Harper Ann bit her lip in concentration as she drew. "Dunno. Just sprung to mind, that's all."

"Hey, Harper Ann? This right here," I said, pointing at her drawings, "this is what will impress the guests at your birthday party. Not a soggy handkerchief."

She was so caught up in her drawings that Harper Ann only nodded, let the tapestry fall at my feet, and kept working.

I bundled up the wet and sticky tapestry, gagging a bit, and ran to the train. "Come on!" I shouted to the others.

But Momma jerked her head up at the last minute, her eyes narrowing. "Athena's gift!" she shouted, and pushed Mela away. The mask slipped off Mela's face, and she was Mela-sized again, rolling away to avoid getting stepped on by Momma.

"Run!" I shouted, while Nia waved us all on board.

But Momma put her hands on either side of the train, holding it in place. "You return Athena's gift, young ladies!" she hollered at us.

"It's mine!" Ari shouted, and in that moment, about a million spiders poured into the giants' station.

"Our party!" Momma cried at the sight of the spiders. "Ruined by an infestation of bugs!"

"Arachnids!" Thalia shouted through her horn, which made Momma let go of the train.

We lurched backward, hurtling down the tunnel back to New York City. We watched them until the giants were tiny, and then, they were gone.

"I hope they're okay," Mela said, sniffing.

"Me, too," Nia added.

"That was rotten of Athena to use Harper Ann in such a way," Thalia said.

As for Ari, she was holding the third piece of the tapestry with the tips of her fingers. "I can't believe this has giant boogers on it."

I sat in a corner while the train rolled on, thinking about what had just happened. I didn't even have an emblem, and I'd managed to inspire the giant to follow her dreams. And while the other eight muses all still needed a kódikas, the only thing I had to do was *think* my magic to me, use my imagination to picture what I wanted to happen, and there it was.

I watched as Nia, Thalia, Mela, and Ari played hot potato with Nia's star.

I imagined: *scratch*.

Thalia raked her fingers against her knee.

I pictured: *yawn*.

Mela opened her mouth in a huge, sleepy yawn.

By then my hands were trembling a little and my stomach was doing backflips. Had my magic really become *this* easy to use?

I started to envision: *sneeze*, but Ari looked up at me, a frown on her face. Slowly, she shook her head. I'd forgotten that Ari could feel our magic. Ashamed, I drew my knees up to my chest and rested my head on them. I sat that way until we got back to the Atlantic Avenue tunnel, and the manhole where we had first stepped down into it.

"What were you doing back there?" Ari asked me quietly. "You know I don't like it. The last time someone used magic on me . . . well, you know." She shuddered.

"Sorry," I whispered. "I was just . . . testing it. My magic. It's different from what it used to be."

"Different?" Ari asked.

I nodded. "Yes. Easier, too," I confessed.

Ari thought for a moment. "There's something scary about that, you know?"

I did know. What did it mean to be different from the others? Why was I different, anyway?

We got off the train and began the long trek back to the manhole at street level. Ari grumbled about her snotty tapestry the whole way.

"Three down, one to—" Thalia started, then stopped and stared.

"Oh no," Mela and Nia said at the same time.

I looked up and saw what they meant.

There, standing before us, were the last people I thought we'd see—

Clio.

Paola.

Elnaz.

Tomiko.

I looked up at the manhole, its cover off, and saw Etoro in her wheelchair, peering down at us, too.

There they all were—the grown-up muses, with their arms folded, their faces stern, and a look that said, "You are all so very deeply busted."

Chapter 26
BUSTED. AGAIN.

I fully expected one of Clio's scowls, the one that usually came before telling us how we'd disappointed her. I hoped we wouldn't be stripped of our muse powers, which had almost happened last year when we nearly broke the law trying to rescue a killer whale.

What I didn't expect was for Clio and the other muses to stand there, smiling at us and nodding their heads.

"What is happening?" Thalia asked without moving her lips.

"Just go with it," Nia said, similarly stiff.

I put my hand in the air in a weak wave. "Hi, everybody. What are you doing here?"

Then the muses laughed in an "Oh, Callie, you are a *treat*!" kind of way.

Soon they'd circled us. I caught a glimpse of Ari cringing

while she shoved the still-damp section of the tapestry down the back of her pants, making her look like she had the world's biggest butt.

"You really did it! Elnaz and I had our doubts, but you did it!" Tomiko was saying.

Paola was clapping her hands, the bells on her belt jingling happily. Clio was just beaming at us. And overhead, Etoro was smiling so hard she had her hands on her cheeks, as if to keep her smile contained.

Clio approached Ari, extending her hand. "This must be the tenth muse. I am Clio. Muse of history."

"What?" Ari asked, backing away from Clio's hand.

"Each time a muse receives her gifts, she does something very special, like saving a lost child, or rescuing a friend in danger. Something that most people would say is heroic. Tell me, child, how was your gift first revealed?" Clio went on.

"She's nervous, Clio, can't you see?" Elnaz said.

"Pish-posh, she's not nervous! Right?" Thalia interrupted, and pushed Ari forward so that she stumbled into Clio.

"I'm not—I'm not—" Ari started to say.

Clio beamed. "We all felt it—a surge in magic around us tonight, didn't we?" she asked the other muses, who nodded, smiling.

A surge in magic? I knew it had to be the emblems, Aphrodite's gifts, making that happen.

I watched as, slowly, Nia, Thalia, and Mela hid their emblems behind their backs. They realized the same thing I had.

"We'll have to find out what her gift is, no? The tenth muse probably inspires something different. Something special. Technology?" Paola suggested.

"Hey! That's my thing!" Nia put in, holding up her phone with her app on display.

"Ah, sí. How about gardening? The world could use more flores y árboles!" Paola continued.

I felt a hand clutching mine. It was Mela. "Tell them the truth, Callie." I nodded.

"She isn't the tenth muse," I said out loud, but at this point, all the muses were talking at once except for Clio, who had taken a step back and was looking at everyone as if she could see through us. Mela and Thalia had their hands behind their backs, and there was a suspiciously bright light behind Nia.

"Emblems. Who gave them to you?" Clio said, cutting through the noise.

Everyone fell silent. Tomiko's eyes widened. Elnaz's mouth dropped open.

"My aunt brought them," Ari said.

Clio took a step toward Ari, then another. "Who is your aunt?" she asked slowly, as if each word was a sentence.

"Aphrodite. You know. *The* Aphrodite. But she's not my real aunt. She's sort of, like, my guardian."

The grown-up muses could not have looked more stunned if Ari had dumped a bucket of ice down their shirts.

Only the bells of Paola's belt tinkled softly as she moved forward. She took Ari's hands in hers. "Don't be afraid. Tell us. Who are you, niña?"

Ari looked at me, and then at the rest of the Muse Squad. We nodded at her. *Go on,* I thought. *You can trust them.*

"Arachne. You know. *The* Arachne. I'm on a quest to retrieve this." She tugged at the tapestry in her pants, pulling it out and letting it float to the ground. "There are four sections. This is the third. There's one more out there. We just don't know where the last one is."

I cleared my throat. "I think I know," I said, feeling very certain for once. "Harper Ann mentioned the New York Public Library. My gut tells me that's it—that's where the last piece is."

The grown-up muses examined the section of tapestry. "What do you want to do with it once you have all four pieces?" Elnaz asked. She touched the tapestry with the tip of a finger, then snatched her hand back. "And why is it wet?"

"You may want to wash that hand," Thalia said.

"What I *will* do is challenge Athena again. She was wrong. Her tapestry wasn't the best. Mine was. She had no right," Ari said, and as she spoke, her chin lifted, and she stood a bit straighter.

"Athena had every right!" Clio said. "She is the Dread Goddess."

"Dread*ful* goddess, more like," Thalia muttered nearby.

Ari's cheeks were blazing now. "She lied to save face. And she ruined my life." Ari's voice broke a bit, and her eyes were shining. But she didn't cry.

I took a deep breath. "We helped her, Clio. Because Ari is right. What Athena did was unfair."

"Do you realize the danger you are in?" Paola said softly.

I looked at the others, the Muse Squad, my sisters in this adventure. Any one of them could have been cyclops food, squashed by a giant, or turned into wax by Medusa. Not to mention whatever it was that Athena could do to them. Suddenly, I felt incredibly foolish.

"But Aphrodite is on our side!" Nia said. "That has to count for something."

Clio nodded. "It does. It means the Olympians are torn on the issue of Athena's contest with Arachne." Looking thoughtful, she walked off a way into the shadows.

"Are we in trouble?" Thalia asked the others.

"Of course you are!" Etoro called from the street level. "You had a mission, did you not?"

"We had to make a choice," I said. "The Gray Sisters would only answer one question. Between asking about the tenth muse or Ari's tapestry, we went with the tapestry locations." I wanted to tell them what Aphrodite had revealed to me—that Athena's quest and the mystery of the tenth muse were linked somehow. That if we solved one, we would solve the other. But Aphrodite said that this was a secret I had to keep.

Elnaz groaned. "We thought you'd found the tenth muse. We were so excited." She sounded so bummed out that my heart gave a little lurch for her.

I glanced at my watch. It was four thirty. I looked around for a second, taking in the part of Brooklyn we were in. There wasn't enough time to get home before my five o'clock curfew. My phone! I yanked it out of my pocket. I had ten unread messages from Papi and Laura, which I didn't feel brave enough to open.

"Can we keep arguing on the way back to Queens? My dad is going to ground me until I am old enough to vote," I said.

Clio laid a hand on my shoulder. "Callie, if I'd known, I could have held time back for you a little while."

I hadn't thought of that. I'd been so afraid of Clio's disapproval that I didn't stop to think if she'd actually help us.

"I was afraid of what Athena would do to you if you and the others knew, Clio."

"Ay," Paola said, shaking her head sadly.

"There are nine of us for a reason," Clio said.

Nine. But soon there would be ten, and one of us would have to go. Or worse, be *made* to go, probably during a dangerous mission. I shivered all over.

We made our way to the ladder, climbing up in silence, and joining Etoro there in the middle of the street. Cars honked and cabbies yelled at us as we scrambled onto the sidewalk. Clio made sure to slip the manhole cover back, and it slotted into place with a clang.

"How did you know where we were?" Nia asked.

"Clio has her ways," Tomiko said.

"I should have been watching you all this time, frankly," Clio said. "But I trusted that you were sticking to the mission."

Clio had *trusted* us. And we'd let her down. I suddenly wished Harper Ann's momma would come snatch me. I'd gladly go to a party for giants if it meant I didn't have to face my guilt.

Clio hailed a pair of cabs for us. The older muses piled into one, while Clio rode in the other with us, squeezed tight into the back seat, all the way back to Queens.

Clio convinced the cabbie to let her sit up front, and he asked where we were going. I watched Clio tug on her earring. Without another word, he fiddled with the radio until he was listening to a station that broadcast the news. She had used her kódikas, and the cabdriver was now completely focused on the radio, ignoring us altogether.

Clio turned in her seat to face us. There was a plexiglass plate with a small opening separating us from her, but we could hear her all right. "Listen, all of you. Leave the rest of your . . . quest . . . to me. Things can be achieved via diplomacy that—"

"You mean you can get Athena to admit that she was wrong?" Ari asked. She had folded the tapestry and it sat on her lap. I could see vibrant colors, and silver thread twining its way through the fabric. After so many years, it was still delicate and beautiful.

Clio shook her head. "I doubt that. But the Dread Goddess might be convinced to let you keep your human form, especially now that her sister, Aphrodite, is involved. The two of them have always bickered, but they love each other in the end."

"No deal," Ari said. "She needs to take back what she said about me and my weaving."

Clio pursed her lips. "Be reasonable, child."

"I may be a kid, but I'm older than you," Ari said, crossing her arms and staring out the window. "I don't need your help anyway."

"Except you do," Mela said softly. "The quest has gotten harder, not easier."

"We've almost died like three times," Thalia said.

Nia shifted in her seat. "I'm not afraid," she said, sitting taller. It was too bad her parents could never know she was a muse. My guess was they'd be so proud.

Clio turned up the volume on the radio. When she turned toward us again, she looked sad, like she wasn't happy about what she was about to say.

"I have to forbid the participation of the junior muses in your quest for now, Arachne. It's not safe," Clio said.

"They don't get a say in this?" Ari asked.

"No," Clio said.

We were quiet again as the cab rolled through the city. Ari had crossed her arms and rested her head on her lap, the tapestry underneath her. I stared at the back of Clio's head, her white hair in a tight, smooth bun.

She could forbid us if she wanted to, but I had other orders.

The final section of the tapestry was at the New York Public Library. I could feel it in my bones. But just because I knew where the tapestry was didn't mean it would be easy to retrieve. The other tasks had taken all of us to get through, so we needed to stick together.

Maybe Clio was right. Maybe diplomacy was the answer.

"Here we are," Clio said, stopping at the end of my block. I glanced at my watch. It was a quarter after five. "Good luck, Callie."

I waved goodbye to the Muse Squad and to Ari and made my way up the street. I spotted him three houses down. Papi. He was standing on the lawn, with my suitcase beside him.

"Papi, I—" I started to say.

"If you don't want to be here, then you can go back

home to Miami for the rest of the summer. I won't keep you against your will," he said.

"It's not that!" I said.

"Then explain."

"I can't," I cried.

Papi's eyes stared into mine. How could I make sure he knew that I wasn't breaking rules to get away from him? That I wanted to be in New York this summer with him, and Laura, and Rafaelito?

"I'm sorry, Papi," I said, and wrapped my arms around his waist.

But Papi peeled my arms off him. "Sometimes, kiddo, sorry doesn't cut it. You have a choice to make."

Then he left me there, standing in the yard, with my suitcase. I lifted it. He'd packed it all up for me.

Somehow, I had to make things right. With Papi. With Ari. With Clio.

With everyone.

Chapter 27
TIA ANNIE'S SECRET

"Papi, just listen," I said, hauling my suitcase back up the stairs to the apartment.

"No more talking. Not unless you plan on telling me the truth about where you've been going after camp and where you went this afternoon," Papi said.

He pushed open the door to our apartment. Laura was sitting on the sofa, bouncing Rafaelito in her arms.

"Oh, Callie," she said when our eyes met. Papi sat beside her. They both looked at me, waiting.

I could just go home, I guess. But where would that leave Papi and me? Would he even want me to come to New York again? And how would I be able to help Ari from Miami? I had to be honest with Papi. At least, as honest as I could be.

"I've been helping Ari, like I said."

Papi's face was frozen while I spoke, and I couldn't seem to look at him straight on.

"And it really is for the Student Showcase. But the materials she needed are sort of all over the city."

Papi's eyebrows lifted.

"Like Little Italy. Brooklyn. Um, Greenwich Village." I named the places where we'd gotten pieces of the tapestry really quickly. I left out Jefferson County on purpose, since that was *miles* away.

Papi got to his feet, flustered, then sat down again. "You've been *everywhere*," he said.

"I know. I'm sorry. But I knew you wouldn't let me go on my own, and so—"

"Because the city isn't safe!"

"Other kids ride the subway alone, Papi! I've seen them!" And it was true. All over New York, kids got themselves to school on their own. It wasn't like Miami, where you never saw a Cuban kid my age alone on the sidewalk without a grown-up.

"You aren't other kids. You are my daughter. And this is my house, and these are my rules," Papi said. "Okay?"

I didn't answer right away. Was it okay? It really wasn't, actually. The fourth piece of the tapestry was out there. Clio said we couldn't retrieve it.

What choice did I have?

"Okay, Papi."

Papi patted the seat beside him and I sat. He hugged me, but I didn't hug him back. I was mad at him, and at myself. Everything was terrible.

"I was just trying to help a friend," I whispered, and I could feel the tears forming in my eyes and my throat squeezing. "I promise."

"Loyalty is a good quality. But family is family."

Rafaelito squealed then, and Laura passed him over to Papi, who started bouncing the baby until he settled down.

"Can I stay here? In New York for the rest of the summer?"

Papi made a face. "Of course you can. I was just making a point. But I want you to think about how you're going to make this up to the family. I ground you, you leave anyway. I take your phone, it doesn't matter." He was working himself up again, I could tell.

Papi, be calm, I thought without meaning to, and I watched his shoulders relax, watched him take a deep breath. I did it again. *Papi, please trust me.*

"I'll make it up to you and Laura," I said.

"Okay," Papi said quietly.

"I guess I'll go unpack then?"

Papi scratched his chin. "I didn't pack your things," he said. "It's just books in there. No shortage of books in this house. Laura won't stop buying them, and we are running out of bookshelves."

Laura rolled her eyes. "And you should start *reading* them more often. It will do you good," she said. Papi shrugged. She was right. Papi only ever read the newspaper.

"Packing my suitcase full of books *is* pretty dramatic," I agreed, glad in my heart that he hadn't actually packed my suitcase, but still sad about the trick he'd pulled. Mami would have never done something like that. It wasn't easy having parents who were so different. It was confusing. I didn't doubt that they both loved me, but I couldn't help but think that I was two people now. Miami-Callie and New York–Callie, which was hard to keep straight.

I went to my room in the gloomiest mood. Unless Clio's "diplomacy skills" worked, Ari would have to forfeit the contest with Athena and be turned back into a spider forever. Plus, the Muse Squad had completely bailed on their mission to find the tenth muse. Who knew if the older muses would ever give us a chance like that again after we'd let them down so badly?

Then there was the problem of my magic. Ari had called it scary, and I had to agree. Last year, Ms. Rinse, my old science teacher, turned out to be a Lost Muse. She'd gotten power-hungry and had tried to steal all the magic in the world for herself. When we fought, she'd asked me what I would do with that kind of power.

I could do so much.

I thought of Papi, so far away from our little family in

Miami. I thought of Maya and her big dreams of changing the world. I thought of my brothers, and my mom, and the other muses, all of them with their hearts' desires. I thought of Ari.

I could fix it. I could fix all of it.

But was that the right thing to do?

"No more tears," said a voice I recognized.

I turned at once. No longer in my bedroom in Queens, I was sitting on warm grass, with the familiar water and the searchlights in the distance. It was Tia Annie who had spoken.

"I fell asleep?"

Tia Annie said, "You sure did. Must be tired from all that monster-battling you've been doing lately."

I gave Tia Annie a big hug. There was a book in my lap. It wasn't anything special. Just an old, worn book without a title. "What's this?"

Tia Annie smiled. "It tells the stories of every heroic act ever done."

"How is that possible?" I asked.

Tia Annie smiled. "Oh, Callie. Do you believe in magic or not?"

I felt the weight of the book. I'd flipped through it a few times, and I never seemed to see the same pages twice. It really did feel like the pages were infinite, but the size of the book never changed. "Who wrote all these pages?" I asked.

Tia Annie took the book gently out of my hands. "I wrote some of them myself," she said, chuckling softly as she turned page after page. "Other muses throughout time have written the others."

"Will I have to do that? Because that sounds like homework," I said.

"Maybe," Tia Annie answered. "The book has other properties, too."

"Like what?"

I watched as she passed her hand lightly over the cover, and for a moment, she seemed lost in thought. "This book will never be finished. Whoever is in possession of it gets to continue the story. And there's power in a story. When you are the storyteller, you control the story, it doesn't control you."

"I don't get it," I said. "When you used the book, how did you 'control the story'?"

"I thought you'd ask that. It's time you knew certain things. Once I received this book and understood its power, I used it to change the story." Tia Annie flipped through the pages, stopping when she found what she'd been looking for. "Here," she said, handing me the book. "Go ahead and read."

I carefully held it in both hands and started to read.

Except, once I started, it wasn't like reading at all.

It was like I was *there*, in the book, surrounded by it.

In the distance was Tia Annie. She was wearing jeans and a heavy down-filled jacket, and her hair was tied up in a ponytail. Sweat dripped off her forehead as she climbed a set of stone steps that went on and on. Beyond her was the bluest sky I'd ever seen. Mountain peaks rested against the sky in the distance, like a painting. I could hear Tia Annie panting as she climbed. When she finally stopped, she had arrived at a temple, gleaming and white in the afternoon sun. I could see the book tucked under her arm.

Tia Annie entered the temple, which was empty except for bright lights floating in the air all around her. They shimmered when she approached, and many voices spoke at once.

"Ann, Muse of the epic poem, Maker of Heroes, what is your request?"

I watched as Tia Annie jutted her chin, clutching the book tightly to her. "I have come to Mount Olympus to ask for an exchange. My life for another's."

The lights twinkled, humming as if in conversation. When they spoke, they said, "Arachne is not deserving. That was decided long ago."

Tia Annie closed her eyes. "I have the book. I am the storyteller, and I tell you that she is deserving, and she always was. I'll trade my place in the Elysian Fields for her life on earth. I'll guard the searchlights for eternity."

The lights hummed again, rumbling now, like race cars at a starting line.

"She must complete a quest, then," the voices said.

"She will need help. And you know I am ill. Will you help her?" Tia Annie asked.

The lights brightened. "We cannot. But the new story-teller will help her. Arachne may live again, as you've requested. In return, you shall guard the searchlights, where our magic is kept, for all time. First of the muses, Annie Martinez, your story is now complete."

The book closed in my lap with a snap. My heart pounded and I couldn't catch my breath. All this time, I'd thought Tia Annie had gone to Mount Olympus to ask the gods to make me a muse. But she hadn't! She'd gone to bargain for Arachne's life.

"Why?" I asked at last.

"You know why," Tia Annie said.

The thing was, I did. What had happened to Arachne wasn't fair. It was unjust. She'd stood up to Athena, to the gods, and had been punished for being right. For telling the truth.

"And the book. It helped you?" I asked, holding it away from me.

Tia Annie took it with gentle hands. "It gave me power over the stories of heroes. I knew it wasn't right to try to change them all. And the truth is, I don't think that would be allowed. But Arachne's story was different. She was just a kid. She reminded me of you, and your brothers, and what happened to her was so unfair. If having the book meant I could change the end of her story somehow, I knew I had to try."

A thought entered my mind and I choked back a sob. "You could've saved yourself, Tia Annie. You could've," I said, wishing with all my heart that she had marched up to Mount Olympus and asked the gods for a cure so that she could still be with me, and Mami, and my brothers.

"Oh, mi vida," Tia Annie said, and held me in a crushing hug. "You wouldn't have made that choice for yourself either."

I shook my head against her. "I would. I'm not good like you," I cried, thinking of waves pounding on a distant shore.

"You're so much like me," Tia Annie whispered. "I didn't ask the gods to involve you. They selected a helper for Arachne. You're her helper. You are the storyteller. It's your story to complete now."

"Why me?" I asked. I could hear how small my voice was.

Thinking for a moment, Tia Annie gazed out toward the searchlights. "Maybe your big heart? You're fair. You always stand up for the little guy or girl. You're kind. Get tough and get even is not your thing. Even when it's your brothers covering your bed with 'dork' sticky notes."

I could feel myself blushing. Taking compliments wasn't easy.

"When bullies come at you at school, criticizing your family, or your body, or some other dumb thing that bullies, in all of their ignorance, use as weapons, you turn toward those who love you, realizing the bullies don't deserve the time of day." Tia Annie thought some more.

"You can stop now," I said softly.

"Nope," Tia Annie said. "You love big. I mean *big*. But sometimes you have a hard time letting go."

That's when I burst into tears.

"I wasn't ready to let you go, Tia Annie," I said, the words hardly sounding like words, I was sobbing so hard. It felt as if all the tears that had squeaked out of my eyes all year, the ones I kept trying to hold back, were gushing now, and I couldn't stop them.

I felt her arms around me. She didn't say "shush" or "there, there." Tia Annie didn't say anything at all. She was firm and steady. She was an island to hold on to in a stormy sea. And when I was all cried out, only then did she let me go.

"There's nothing wrong with crying," she said. "Stop fighting it." Tia Annie tucked my hair behind my ears. "Your brothers fight it, too, you know, though they shouldn't. The harder you fight, the deeper the pain goes, until you're always sad and can't figure out why."

"I'll always be sad that you're gone," I said.

Tia Annie nodded. "Of course. Big heart, and all. Just acknowledge the sadness from time to time, and you'll be okay."

"So I'm the storyteller," I said after a while. "But why is my magic changing *now*?"

"Everyone needs to take baby steps. From the largest elephant to the tiniest caterpillar. We're all wobbly at first," she said, and poked me in the ribs.

"You mean I really did level up?" I laughed. "Mario and Fernando would be so proud!"

Tia Annie laughed, too. "They still love video games, huh? Yes, you leveled up. Or rather, you earned it. But the boss level is next, mi niña. Don't celebrate just yet."

It was a frightening thought. If this were a video game, the boss level meant facing Athena. Tia Annie gently brushed the knots out of my hair with her fingers, and I grew serious again thinking about everything she'd done to save Arachne. My tia Annie, who had brought up so many heroes, had righted an ancient wrong. And she'd sacrificed an eternity to make it happen.

Now it was my turn.

What would I have to sacrifice to make things right?

"How will I know what to do?" I asked, sniffling.

Tia Annie smoothed my hair. "I was the storyteller. The gods could not deny me, and they knew it. Athena will not be able to deny you, either. But you have to make sure you've made the right request."

"Wait a minute. I just got an idea," I said.

"An epiphany?"

I looked at her blankly.

Tia Annie sniffed her old former-English-teacher sniff. "An epiphany is a moment of sudden insight. A revelation!"

"Well, I've just had one of those," I said. "This book, was it your emblem?"

Smiling, Tia Annie nodded. "Indeed. But it will only come to you when you need it most. That's the way with emblems. Some muses wait a lifetime to receive theirs." She paused, putting the book in my hands again. "The poets of old sang life to the heroes. They made them believe in themselves. You have a hero here who needs you. She needs her story to be told, and only you can tell it. You can't change how a story *begins*, but you can change how it *ends*."

I held the book close to me.

"Your gifts are different, Callie. You've always known this. The gods made them so because of my request, so that you could wield the power of the book. Use it wisely."

I nodded. "I want to help. I want to use my power to help others find theirs." A slight wind kicked up as soon as I said it, forming little waves in the water. The searchlights swept the sky, as they always did. Beyond the water were the Elysian Fields that Tia Annie had mentioned, that place she'd given up forever to help a girl who'd been unjustly punished.

Tia Annie turned her face toward the wind and closed her eyes. "Hmm," she hummed happily. "We don't get a breeze here often."

"Tia Annie, there's one piece of tapestry left. Clio says she's going to try diplomacy. But diplomacy won't work with Athena, will it?"

Tia Annie shook her head. "I don't think so."

"I'm going to get it. The final tapestry piece, I mean."

"Not alone," she warned. "Athena must know you're getting close. She won't hesitate to stop you once and for all. What I started, and you're finishing, will upend the order of things. A god has never apologized to a human or raised a human above themselves. Athena won't let that happen without a fight."

I understood. But now that I knew what Tia Annie had sacrificed, I was more determined than ever to get the job done. "I promise I won't go alone. In fact, I'm never alone," I said, and held on to Tia Annie's hand. "I've got you."

Tia Annie smiled, her eyes going all crinkly. "Not just that, you've got a whole squad."

I laughed. It was true. I had a squad. And I had Papi, and Laura. Mami and Maya. Rafaelito, Fernando, and Mario. And Raquel, too.

I felt like a lucky girl just then, in spite of the scary things ahead.

"Thank you, Tia Annie," I whispered, leaning forward and resting my forehead on hers. "I love you."

"I love you, Callie-Mallie. Now go tell your story."

Chapter 28
PATIENCE AND FORTITUDE

When I woke it was morning, and I was back in my room, lying on the pin-pan-pun. I half expected Tia Annie's book, her emblem, to be in my room. I even looked for it, but it wasn't there. The truth was, sometimes I couldn't tell if my Tia Annie dreams were real, or just dreams. One time last spring, I dreamed she'd joined the circus and learned how to walk on a tightrope.

But this dream felt different, more like the other times she'd met me in my sleep and told me something important. I'd have to hold on to that.

Camp would be starting soon, and I could smell the breakfast that Laura was cooking. I got dressed quickly and went to the kitchen. Papi had already gone for the day, and it was just Laura and Rafaelito. She rushed around, muttering something about an annoying colleague, while

Rafaelito drank from a bottle. I finished off scrambled eggs and a muffin quickly.

"Okay, Laura! I'm off to camp," I said.

"Please be home on time today," she pleaded, which made me feel awful.

"I will," I promised. I wasn't sure if I could keep that promise or not, but I would try. Tia Annie had sacrificed too much, and Ari needed our help.

When I walked into the poetry room, Maris was already there, vibrating with excitement.

"What's up?" I asked. The room had stacks of poems on butcher paper for Poetry-palooza. Maris must have worked all night!

"Mr. Theo is taking us on a field trip as a reward for painting so many poems!" she said happily.

"Don't get so excited," Mr. Theo said. "We're just going to the public library here in Queens."

"But libraries *are* exciting!" Maris said, clapping her hands together. "I mean, I *have* had a library card since birth."

Of course she has, I thought, smiling at her.

But then I had an idea.

It was a brilliant, crazy idea. Harper Ann *had* suggested I visit a very specific library, hadn't she?

"Hey, Mr. Theo," I called out. He was sitting at his desk, filling out some paperwork. He looked up. "What if we go to the New York Public Library instead. The big one? I've never been," I said, adding some terrific puppy dog eyes into the mix.

"You haven't?" Maris exclaimed. "You one hundred percent must visit it!"

I gave Mr. Theo a little boost of muse magic. Just a nudge. It wouldn't take much.

Mr. Theo laughed, giving us a look that said, "I love my job." "Okay, let's go."

We took the 7 train to Fifth Avenue. On the way to the station, I texted everyone:

Going to the library. Who's in?

One by one, the Muse Squad answered.

Nia: On the way!

Thalia: Brilliant!

Mela: See you there.

I couldn't afford to use my bracelet, in case Clio was listening in. Once again, I was breaking the rules, but this time, I knew exactly why I had to. If I was the storyteller, then it was my job to see the story through, whether I had the emblem or not. Clio and the other grown-up muses had been scared for us when they learned that Athena was involved, and I didn't blame them. Clio wanted us to step back because she was terrified of what Athena could do.

But I wasn't afraid anymore. Tia Annie had given up too much for me to let fear win.

I texted Ari, too, but she didn't respond. "Hey," I asked Maris. "Did you see Ari today at camp?"

She shook her head no.

Part of me feared I'd get to the library and find her already there, battling some horrible monster on her own. Would she do that? Leave me and the other muses out of it altogether?

It was a pretty uneventful subway ride, so Maris spent it telling me about how last summer the Student Showcase had to be abruptly canceled when someone pulled the fire alarm.

"Our dramatic recitation of Edgar Allan Poe's *The Raven* was absolutely ruined!" Maris said. I was only half listening, to tell the truth. My mind was racing ahead, wondering where the final piece of the tapestry might be.

"The camp donors will be there this year," I said, trying to keep up my part of the conversation. "Who are they, anyway?"

"No idea," Maris said. "Patrons of the arts, I guess."

"Who'll shut down Corona Arts if they aren't suitably impressed. *So* generous," I said.

"If that happens, I don't know what I'll do in the summer. Which is why Poetry-palooza has to be a hit!"

"It will!" Mr. Theo said encouragingly.

"We worked so hard. And the other campers are working hard, too. Have you seen the sets for *Into the Woods*?"

Maris said, and then she was off, chatting rapidly about what the other artist groups were doing for the showcase. There were musical numbers, one-act plays, interpretive dance routines, and more.

We arrived at the Fifth Avenue station and walked along the busy sidewalk until we were standing directly in front of the library. It was flanked by two enormous statues of lions. They were a familiar sight—one I'd seen in movies a bunch of times. In person they looked even bigger. I almost expected to see them take a breath.

"Did you know that the lions have names? That's Patience," said Mr. Theo, pointing to the marble lion on the south side of the stairs. "And that's Fortitude," he added, indicating the one on the north side.

"Excellent qualities," Maris said.

We walked past them up the stairs. That's when I noticed it—a piece of tapestry peeking out from under Fortitude. I stopped and stared up at the lion, still as can be.

Oh, this was *not* going to be easy, was it?

Mr. Theo led us into the library, pointing out elements of the architecture. He stopped in the center of a massive room lined with huge windows, chandeliers, and rows and rows of dark, gleaming wood tables, each with a green lamp on top.

"This is the Rose Reading Room, kids," he said in a whisper, as if a loud sound might make the whole place vanish. The ceiling was anything but plain, with a sky painted in the center. The clouds seemed to glow, as if a rising sun was just out of view.

Maris dabbed a tear from her eye. "It's beautiful," she whispered. Along the walls were shelves and shelves full of books. "I love us," she said.

"Us?" I asked.

Maris beamed. "Yeah, us. Writers and readers. I wouldn't want to be in any other artist group, would you?" she asked.

All around us, people were reading and writing. They were concentrating. They were creating whole worlds in their heads. For the first time since I'd set foot at Corona Arts, I felt like I got it. Maybe poets really *were* special. Maris may not have been as showy as the theater kids, or paint-splattered like the visual artists. Maybe she couldn't dance or build a massive set. Hers was a quieter kind of gift, but that didn't mean it wasn't a powerful one.

"There's an exhibit I want you both to see in the children's room. It features displays of children's poems from World War II. Once you've spent time there, please select one of the poems on display, and write a new one in response. Imagine that kid from long ago is your pen pal, and your poem is going to time travel," Mr. Theo said. "After you've seen the exhibit, meet back here in the Rose Reading Room, say in . . ." He glanced at his watch. "Forty-five minutes. Good?" We nodded, then Mr. Theo left us, his own notebook tucked under his arm.

"So where should we go? Exhibit first, or wandering first?" Maris asked.

I didn't want to leave the Rose Reading Room just yet. Besides, the other muses hadn't arrived. Tia Annie said I had to finish Ari's story. Maris was good at stories. Maybe she could help.

"Maris, can you help me with a poem?" I asked.

Maris's eyes widened. "Yes!" she said, and we sat together at one of the tables. Maris folded her hands, waiting.

I cleared my throat. "Okay. So let's say I wanted to write a long poem. An epic one. About righting a wrong." I stopped and thought for a second. Maris just looked on, listening carefully. "And I want to write about a person who has to defeat someone very powerful."

"Sounds like a hero myth," Maris said.

"Hero myth?"

Maris nodded. "Mm-hmm. There's a pattern to those kinds of stories," she said. "Heroes are called to action somehow, mostly to correct an injustice. It's usually a challenge, or a loss of some kind, that gets them going. They find a wise person to guide them. Then they go on a quest. They usually have a magical item that helps them defeat their antagonist." She ticked off each element with her fingers.

"This all sounds really familiar," I said.

"'Course it is. *Star Wars*. *The Lord of the Rings*. They

all follow the same pattern."

Maris couldn't know that those movies weren't why I found it all so familiar.

The hero's myth sounded like Arachne's life.

And mine.

"And don't forget Hercules!" Maris said. "He had to defeat twelve monsters in order to fight off Hera."

"Wait, wait, wait. Hercules fought Hera—the queen of the gods?" I asked.

Maris grinned. "Not one-on-one. She sent all these monsters his way, and he beat every last one. He defeated a nine-headed hydra, captured a magical deer! Then there was the boar. And he cleaned some yucky stables!" Maris said. "There was a three-headed dog, I think. And some-thing about some cattle?" She tapped her chin thoughtfully. "Oh! And the lion!"

I sat up at that. "A what?"

"The Nemean lion," Maris said. "That was the first monster he defeated."

The moment she said it, I knew. Those lions outside weren't just statues. The hairs on my arms stood up. The lions were enormous and muscular, and suddenly I felt very small.

"How did Hercules win?" I asked.

"Well, he was strong. Mainly, he just overpowered all the monsters," Maris said, and she flexed her arms with a grin. "Most heroes, though, require help. From friends.

There's more power in numbers than in muscles. And they use their brains most of all."

Out of the corner of my eye, I spotted the Muse Squad making their way into the Rose Reading Room. I jumped up, startling Maris. "Um, thanks. This was super helpful. I think I'll find a spot to write in. But you should go see the exhibits."

Maris looked at me funny, of course. "Oh. Happy to help," she said a bit gloomily. She rose and turned around. "I am excited to read your poem," Maris added. Then she left, and headed deep into the library. She had three pens in her hair today, and they bobbed in her bun as she walked away.

"Hey!" Thalia shouted as soon as she spotted me, earning her a "Shh!" from about twenty different people. She had on a butterfly-shaped backpack, and I could tell that she'd packed her emblem into it. Mela's mask dangled around her neck, along with her headphones. As for Nia, the left pocket of her sweatpants was glowing.

I rushed up to greet them. "Thanks for coming. I know where the tapestry is."

"Where?" Nia asked.

"Underneath one of the lions outside the library," I whispered.

Mela and Thalia both gasped, then said "Awww" at once, clasping their hands under their chins like I'd just said something adorable.

Nia and I just stared at them. "What's wrong with you two?" she asked.

"They haven't read it," Mela said.

"No, clearly," Thalia responded.

"What are you talking about?" I asked.

Mela sighed. "It's a picture book my mother used to read to me. *Katie in London*."

"My mum read it to me, too," Thalia said. "A girl named Katie climbs atop a lion statue in Trafalgar Square. The lion comes to life and gives her and her brother a tour of the city. As a reward, Katie gives her shawl to the lion, so that he has something warm to sleep on."

"It's sweet," Mela said. "You know how I feel about cats. We can't take the sweet lion's blanket!" Mela *did* love cats, but this was taking it too far.

Nia and I were silent for a moment. I clapped my hands and shouted, "Snap out of it! Focus!"

More librarygoers went "Shhh," and I led the Muse Squad out of the Rose Reading Room before we got in bigger trouble.

We looked at the lion through the window in the library's foyer. It was as still as ever, and there was the final tapestry piece, completely stuck under the statue, as if it had always been there.

"Where's Ari, by the way?" Nia asked.

I shrugged. "Don't know. I've been texting her, but she hasn't answered."

"She's definitely around here somewhere," Thalia said, pointing a shaky finger back at the lion.

We watched as thousands of spiders began crawling up the lion's pedestal in straight rows. There was an army of them, squeezing in between the lion and the tapestry. Slowly, the lion started to wobble.

"You think they can just lift it?" Mela asked.

"There's more power in numbers than in muscles," I whispered, repeating what Maris had said earlier.

The lion tilted to the left a little. I saw a flash of dark hair behind it. Ari! She was sneaking around the back of the statue, her hands reaching out for the tapestry. Her fingers grasped the edge of the cloth, pinching hard and pulling.

"Come on, Ari!" Nia whispered.

Ari put her foot up on the pedestal, bracing herself, when suddenly we heard a deep, rumbling roar.

"Let's go!" I shouted, and we poured out of the front doors, toward Ari and the lion.

If you've ever heard a lion roar in real life, then you know it sounds as if it's coming from deep underground. Like the lion has pulled the roar out from some hidden, echoing cavern. It's a majestic sound, but also a really scary one.

And this lion, Fortitude, was roaring as if Hades himself had supplied its voice.

People who had been climbing the stairs to the library stopped and ran, though a few took out their cell phones to record. Ari had her fingers around the tapestry, and her spiders just kept coming, trying to lift the stone lion off its base.

Another roar, and another after that, filled the air. Now Patience, the other lion, was roaring, too. But neither moved. They were still statues.

"Give me my tapestry!" Ari was shouting as she tugged on the cloth, her voice drowned out by the noisy, grumbling lions.

People were gathering at the foot of the stairs.

"We need to get these people out of here," I said.

Beside me, Nia tapped on her phone, read the results of her app, and got to work. Mela's fingers fluttered before her, sending two nearby men into tears. Thalia pulled her trumpet from her backpack. She giggled into it, and suddenly everyone on the stairs was laughing. A moment later, every cell phone in the vicinity started ringing, and people fetched their phones out of pockets and purses and wandered away from the stairs and the stone lions.

For a second, I let myself think we had it under control, but that's when the lions sprang to life, fur, teeth, and all.

Ari jumped back, a set of massive jaws just missing her hands. The spiders scurried away, as both Patience and Fortitude bounded off their pedestals. Fortitude had the tapestry in its mouth now and was whipping it around like a puppy with a new toy.

An angry puppy.

An angry, vicious puppy.

Snarling, Patience bounded over to us. The fur on its back rose. A long line of spit dangled from its lower jaw. Patience was guarding Fortitude as it played with the tapestry.

Of course, we lost our concentration then, and we heard shrieks all around us as people started noticing the lions again. I looked in one of the library windows, and there were loads of people with their noses pressed to the glass, their eyes wide.

How are we going to fix this? I thought desperately.

What had Tia Annie said last night? She'd said I wasn't alone. In fact, she'd said, *You've got a whole squad.*

I lifted my bracelet to my mouth. "Clio, we need help at the New York Public Library."

The others heard me, and soon they were talking into their communication items, too.

Nia cupped the globe on her necklace in her hands, and I could hear her saying, "Mayday, mayday! We've got feline trouble!"

Mela was muttering into her ring, "They're just big cats, right? Somebody bring some catnip!"

Thalia was talking into her ring, too: "All right, you lot. We've battled enough monsters on our own. And now half of New York is watching!"

Fortitude lay down, tired from playing at last. Its front paws held down the tapestry while it gnawed on one end. Patience backed up and cuddled with Fortitude. If they weren't so terrifying, it would have been sort of cute.

Meanwhile, we tried to keep people away from the stairs. They were laughing, or crying, or staring at their cell phones. I inspired twenty-two people to go get an ice-cream cone two blocks away before I started getting dizzy and had to stop. At one point my eyes locked onto Maris, who was standing at the door to the museum, tugging on the collars of two little boys who were just standing there, mouths wide, pointing at the lions.

"Come on, kids. Coloring pages in the children's section. Lots of coloring pages!" I heard her shouting as she yanked the kids back into the library.

There were people at every one of the library's windows, crowding around. I thought: *epiphany*, and suddenly the people jumped out of sight. I was pretty sure they'd be working on poems all afternoon.

A fire truck parked in front of the library, its lights on and sirens blasting. A firefighter spoke through a megaphone: "Step away from the lions. Step away from the lions."

"Over my dead body," Ari muttered.

I was afraid she actually meant that.

That's when we heard the first stirring notes of a flute filling the air. The firefighter with the megaphone started swaying. Elnaz and Tomiko were standing on one of the lions' pedestals, conducting New Yorkers, who began dancing away from the library.

Here and there, people were hugging one another, while couples kissed. I knew Etoro was nearby, and I searched until I found her sitting in the shade of an elm tree.

The shrieking that had been constant slowed down and stopped, until all was quiet except for the grumbling lions. I saw Paola step out of a taxi, her bells ringing, peacefulness following her wherever she went.

"That's everyone but Clio," Nia said.

Thalia pointed at one of the library windows. "There she is." We watched as Clio moved through the rooms. As she passed them, people froze in place. She was holding back time for a little while.

Paola climbed the steps slowly until she reached us. She observed the lions. "What are you going to do now, muchachitas?"

"Over here!" Ari called. She'd gone down the steps to the sidewalk and was standing in front of a hot-dog stand. I like a good hot dog as much as anybody, but her timing was terrible.

"Lunch later!" I shouted at her, not wanting to turn my back on the lions.

Ari stomped her foot and climbed back up the stairs. "Not for me," she said. "For the lions. Do your thing with the hot-dog guy and *get those dogs*."

Thalia was the first to snap to it. She lifted her trumpet to her mouth and asked in the hot-dog vendor's direction, "What did the ketchup say to the hot dog?"

The vendor, a man with a long, red beard and a top-knot, looked up and shrugged.

"'Nice to meat you!' Get it? Nice to *meat* you?"

The hot-dog vendor giggled, snorted, and finally started laughing so hard that he wandered away from his cart, wiping his eyes and muttering, "Meat you . . . meat you . . ."

"Go! Go! Go!" Ari shouted, and the five of us scrambled down the stairs, and together, hoisted the cart up until we were just a few feet away from the lions.

"Get 'em while they're hot!" Nia shouted as we tilted the cart onto its side, spilling hot dogs everywhere.

The lions sniffed the air, their nostrils flaring. Then, they jumped right onto the pile of hot dogs, leaving Ari's tapestry alone at last. It was their first meal ever, and they purred as they ate.

"Aw, hungry kitties," Mela said.

Ari scrambled forward and grabbed the chewed-up tapestry. The moment it was in her possession, the lions stopped eating. They glanced at one another, then climbed back onto their pedestals. In an instant, they were once again stone lions, guarding the New York Public Library, just as they'd done for over a hundred years.

"They really do need a blanket," Thalia said sadly.

By then, the other muses had managed to get rid of nearly everyone who had been watching the chaos unfold. Clio emerged from the library eventually, having unfrozen everyone from time.

"Won't they remember what they saw?" Mela asked Clio when she joined us.

Clio shook her head. "Sometimes, the way time passes can feel like a dream. They'll go home, have foggy thoughts about their funny day, and forget it ever happened."

There was something I had to say. It was something I should have said long ago. "Clio, I'm sorry. But I couldn't do what you asked. Athena isn't going to just change her mind," I said. I realized that it didn't matter if Clio approved or didn't. I turned to look at Ari, who was holding up the final piece of the tapestry to the light. There was a smile on her face, and a look I hadn't seen there before. It was happiness, I realized. I knew we'd made the right choice.

"I think you are right," Clio said softly.

"Come again?" Nia asked.

"Yes, please do repeat that. I think I just had a momentary hallucination," Thalia added.

"You were right to help Ari," Clio said. "A muse always trusts her instincts, and you did. But now it's up to her."

We all watched Ari for a moment—all nine muses.

Ari looked back at us and squared her shoulders. We'd faced a cyclops, a pasta-making Medusa, a family of giants, and two ferocious lions. She smiled at us and mouthed the words *thank you.*

Clio stepped forward, her hand reaching out to Ari when, suddenly, a large owl swooped down from the sky, landing right on top of Fortitude's head.

I knew that owl.

The owl fluffed up its feathers and screeched twice. Then, in a single, swirling gesture, the owl transformed into Athena. She slid down Fortitude's back and came to stand between Ari and the muses.

"Greetings," Athena said, wiping her hands on the blue velvet pants she was wearing. She had on a matching top, the color of the sky, and her hair was in a high ponytail. "Poor lions, they only wanted to play," she said.

"We've completed your quest," Ari said.

Athena shook her finger at her. "No, no, no. We still have the contest to hold. Your tapestry against mine. I have to say, mine is in better shape. But perhaps a bit dusty, isn't that right, Clio?"

Clio's face was very serious. It felt like ages ago that she and I had found Athena's tapestry in Clio's office.

"Yes, Dread Goddess. Your tapestry is safe," Clio said.

"I'm so glad," Athena said, smiling at all of us as if this were just a nice little visit. "We should arrange the terms of the contest."

Ari was clutching her piece of tapestry to herself. The lion had torn it a great deal, and it looked like little more than scraps of fabric. "Name the terms," Ari said.

"Just as before. We will present both tapestries and let the people decide," Athena said.

Ari's bottom lip trembled as she stood there. *Courage*, I thought desperately, but held my magic back. I knew Ari didn't like it when I used my magic on her.

"This time, you'll honor the people's vote?" Ari asked.

"I'll honor the truth, little spinner," Athena said.

Etoro wheeled forward, with Paola right behind her. "That is not an answer."

Athena whirled in Etoro and Paola's direction, anger etched on her face for the first time since she'd arrived. "IT IS THE ANSWER YOU ARE GETTING, MUSES."

The elder muses didn't flinch, even when Athena tried to stare them down.

Eventually, it was Athena who turned away, smiling, as if she'd secretly won a prize. "It's all settled then. See you at the contest!" She waved goodbye and was an owl again, soaring into the sky above New York.

We all breathed a sigh of relief, knowing that the biggest challenge of all was still to come.

Ari versus the Dread Goddess, Athena.

I didn't know if Ari would win. The tapestry in her hands was nearly shredded to bits. How could she beat Athena with *that*?

Somewhere in the distance, a clock chimed the hour. It was only noon. No matter how intimidating Athena's visit had been, today felt like a victory, because Ari had all the pieces of the tapestry at last.

And you know what else? This time, I wouldn't be home late.

Chapter 29
FUTURE-CALLIE'S PROBLEMS

There were two weeks left until the Student Showcase. Ever since the lions at the library, Papi had been coming home early, as promised. We'd spent the afternoons going to the park, or eating at Laura's favorite pizza place in Flushing, or having ice cream at the Queen of Corona. One weekend, Papi took us to see the American Museum of Natural History and the Metropolitan Museum of Art. Laura bought books in the gift shops, and I spent much of the time wondering what my entrance point might be if we moved Muse Headquarters to either location.

"I wish your brothers were here," Papi said in the room full of mummies at the Met. "They'd like this place."

My heart broke a little. Mario and Fernando were still mad at Papi for leaving us. I wasn't mad anymore. Just sad sometimes.

"Maybe next summer? You'll have to get two more pin-pan-puns," I said.

Papi brightened a little. "You want to come back here next summer? ¿De verdad?"

"Yeah, Papi. I'd love that. And I'd love to go back to Corona Arts, too. If it's still open, that is."

He crossed his fingers. "Here's hoping," Papi said, and we left the mummy room hand in hand.

Sometimes my muse bracelet would heat up, and I'd go over to headquarters at the Hall of Science. We were still looking for the tenth muse. For a second, we thought we'd found her when a twenty-three-year-old in Brooklyn saved a man who had fallen onto the subway tracks. But when Clio, posing as a detective, asked her a few questions, she quickly realized that the woman was brave and heroic, but not a muse after all.

We were stumped.

As for Ari, she was worried and anxious about her tapestry, which had been damaged by all the monsters in some way or another. I was nervous for her. She was spending all her time restoring her artwork, skipping camp sessions, and refusing to answer any texts I sent her.

One night, I went looking for her at the bodega. There was Aphrodite, greeting customers and being her usual, fabulous self.

"Hi," I said to her, trying not to be too nervous. It was

hard knowing you were speaking with a goddess, one with incredible powers and a reputation for having a temper. Even though Aphrodite said she'd changed, I was still careful. "Is Ari here? I've been missing her at camp," I said.

Aphrodite's smile turned into a frown. "She's holed up in my apartment, working on that tapestry. I can barely get her to eat dinner most days," she said. "This is why I'm stealing her away for the weekend." Aphrodite opened the palm of her hand and a postcard appeared. It read "Come to Seaside Heights, N.J.!"

"There's a boardwalk, and arcades, and amusement park rides." Aphrodite's voice dropped to a whisper. "This here is called a roller coaster," she said, pointing to one on the postcard. "It's a torture device. It turns you upside down and drops you from great heights. Apparently humans love them," she said with a smile.

I swallowed a laugh. I guess there are certain things the gods just didn't get.

"Looks like fun," I said.

"I hope so." Aphrodite sighed. "I hate seeing Ari so worried. Her tapestry is gorgeous. Almost as breathtaking as I am, honestly. She needs a getaway. And from what I hear, Seaside Heights is a top-notch New Jersey attraction."

This time I did laugh, just a little. But I hid it with a cough. Aphrodite smacked me hard on the back a few times.

"Are you all right?" she asked, concerned.

"Oh, yes. And I think taking Ari on a vacation is a great idea."

"Good to know. I have to get back to work, little muse. Inventory calls!" Aphrodite swept away, picking up items that had been incorrectly shelved as she went.

I was watching her go when I felt a tap on my shoulder.

"Hey." It was Maris. She was holding an ice-cream cone. "Double chocolate mint," she said. "Ice cream always helps when I'm down. Want to go for a walk?"

"Sure," I said. Clio had been true to her word. Nobody at the library that day remembered a thing about the lions, including Maris, who called the trip "a total bust" after she found out the World War II exhibit was closed. I followed Maris out of the bodega and down a shady street. We stopped at a park with a small playground and a baseball diamond. Kids were playing ball, while their friends sat on the bleachers and shouted.

"I don't do sports. Do you?" Maris asked.

"Nope. One time, I broke my arm playing kickball. I meant to kick the ball and ended up standing on it, balancing like a circus performer for a second before falling," I told her.

Maris laughed. "Sorry. It probably wasn't funny."

"Not to me. But my brothers laughed a lot."

"Ouch. Literally." We headed over to a seesaw, sat on either end of it, and started moving up and down.

"Excited about the Student Showcase?" I asked.

Maris nodded. "And nervous. If we don't impress the donors, then I really won't have any place where it feels like I belong, you know?" I didn't say anything, so Maris went on. "I love Corona Arts. I get to write poems all day, and nobody thinks I'm weird for loving that. At school, I'm the only kid who likes poetry. I wish I played sports or could be part of the school play. But the truth is, I love poems. I love how words sound, how they make me feel. The word 'crystal' is my favorite. It's so quiet, like a hush. Or the word 'haunted.' *So spooky.*"

"I guess I don't feel that way about anything. Well, I love people. Certain people," I said. "I wish I had a passion. My best friend back home, she wants to be a performer. And my sister is going to be a scientist. I've got, um, another friend who loves comedy, one who is obsessed with all things NASA, and another one who likes sad plays and country western music. But me? I'm just Callie."

Maris thought for a minute as she went up and down on the seesaw. She was wearing her Wonder Woman cuffs again. She'd been wearing them so often they'd gotten a little dingy. "The way I see it," Maris said at last, "these are problems for Future-Callie."

"Future-Callie?" I asked.

"Yes. You are Now-Callie, not Future-Callie. When Future-Callie becomes Now-Callie, she'll be able to deal with all her problems and realize they aren't actually problems at all. Future-Callie will find her purpose."

"Purpose," I repeated.

Maris nodded. "Your destiny. The thing you're supposed to be someday. It's going to be great, but it's Future-Callie's problem. Now-Callie should just take a deep breath and focus on the showcase."

That night, I lay awake in bed, thinking about the way my summer had turned out. When I came to New York, I thought I knew exactly who I was. Callie Martinez-Silva, Muse of the epic poem, Eater of Arroz con Pollo, Watcher of Television, and Good Friend.

But then I learned about what Tia Annie had done to help save Ari. I'd broken curfew a bunch of times, lying to my dad and Laura. My magic had changed, and I was the storyteller. I had all this power and I didn't exactly know what I was supposed to do with it. All my friends seemed to know who they were, and what they were meant to be.

Me? I didn't have a clue.

I was New York–Callie. Miami-Callie. Now-Callie. Future-Callie. Papi's daughter. Mami's daughter. Fernando and Mario's little sister. Maya and Rafaelito's big sister. The ninth muse.

I was all these things, and yet I still didn't know what my purpose was, or if I had one.

Future-Callie definitely had her work cut out for her.

Chapter 30
SHOWDOWN AT THE STUDENT SHOWCASE

Maris and I finished our poems for Poetry-palooza a week early. We'd painted 107 different poems onto colorful butcher paper. It wasn't enough to wallpaper the school, but it was a lot. I'd learned about sonnets and sestinas, haikus and ghazals. Who knew there were so many kinds of poems?

"*I* knew there were so many different kinds of poems," Maris said one day when I asked just that, as we were hanging up the last of the butcher paper. Next to Emily Dickinson, her other favorite poet was Khalil Gibran, who was Lebanese-American, like Maris. There were fifteen Gibran poems represented in our Poetry-palooza presentation, and fourteen by Dickinson.

"All done," Maris announced, tacking up the last poem near the auditorium. "What should we do now?"

I peeked through the doors and saw Ari hard at work on her tapestry in the back of the auditorium. "Let's help a friend," I said.

The place was dimly lit. Onstage, a few students were quietly singing the opening song of *Into the Woods*. Ari was crouched on the floor, stitching the pieces of the tapestry together with a long needle.

Ari's cheeks were still rosy from her trip to Seaside Heights with her aunt. She'd come back bearing gifts for me and Maris that she'd won in carnival games on the boardwalk. I got a stuffed crab with googly eyes, and she'd brought Maris a blow-up T. rex in a pink dress.

"You wove this?" Maris asked in awe as she studied Ari's tapestry.

Ari looked up and smiled. "Yep. I used a standing loom back when I first made it. I'm just sewing it back together now. It got . . . a little beat up."

"This is amazing," Maris gushed, kneeling down to get a good look at the fabric. "How'd you get it to look so old?"

Smooth as ever, Ari only shrugged. "It's a family technique," she said, leaving it at that.

Maris whistled a long, low note. "Well, if this doesn't impress the donors, nothing will. I hope they don't shut down Corona Arts. Even if there aren't many poets around, it feels like home when I'm here," she said.

My eyes got a little prickly then, which I decided was

okay. I was going to miss Maris when I went back to Miami. I made up Callie's Muse Rule #742 on the spot: A muse never knows where she'll find a friend.

When the summer first started, I could never have imagined befriending an ancient twelve-year-old girl, who could summon spiders and was courageous enough to face a god, or a Wonder Woman–obsessed poet. But I was so glad I did.

"If those donors don't love your tapestry, Ari, I'll eat my left shoe," I said.

"With ketchup?" Maris asked.

"Honey mustard will make it go down easier," Ari said, winking at me. I remembered Aphrodite's office, and the ambrosia she was eating.

"Definitely," I said.

The morning of the Student Showcase was a rainy one. Water ran down in torrents from the sky, and students hustled into Corona Arts Academy as quickly as they could, shielding their props and costumes. It was the first rainy day of the summer. Inside, everyone was running around getting their presentations together. So many students filled the halls carrying props, buckets of paint, costumes, and slabs of plywood, that the teachers had to stand around and direct traffic in case anybody got knocked on the head by a stray canvas or tangled up in a long wig.

Back in the poetry room, Maris, Mr. Theo, and I wrote one last exquisite corpse poem together.

Mr. Theo wrote: *Talented poets impressed whole school.*

I wrote: *Reluctant girl appreciates magnificent poetry!*

Maris read hers out loud. "Good friends are living poems," she said, looking at me with a smile.

"You're not much of a hugger, are you?" I asked, because what I really wanted to do was give Maris the biggest hug.

"Nope."

So I reached out my hand, and we shook on it. "To friends," I said.

"To friends. I'll miss you when you go back to Miami," Maris said.

"I'll miss you, too."

Mr. Theo sniffed and wiped his eyes.

"Come on, you two. The Student Showcase is about to start, and I'm the emcee!" Mr. Theo reached behind his desk and pulled out a blue sequined jacket. "How do I look?"

"Like a star," I said, laughing.

"Poetry in motion," Maris said.

Mr. Theo beamed at us and pulled a bedazzled microphone out of his pocket.

Together, we left the room and headed to the auditorium.

The Muse Squad was already in their seats when we arrived. Maris gave me a questioning look as I walked in. I waved at them and they all waved back.

"These are my friends," I said, and introduced Maris to the others. The grown-up muses were scattered around the auditorium. One by one, they turned around and waved hello. Clio was right in the front row, and beside her were—

"That's impossible," I said, standing up to get a better look.

Mela got to her feet, too. "No way," she said, pulling her headphones off her ears.

"Well, that's a treat," Thalia said.

"What are the Gray Sisters doing here?" Nia asked.

They were sitting down, wearing flower-print dresses, house slippers, and big, dark sunglasses. Each sister carried a shiny black purse on her lap. Clio was trying to talk to them, but they were ignoring her as they bickered over an oily bag full of churros.

Finally, Maris got up to see what we were talking about. "Those ladies up there? I just found out that they're the donors!" She narrowed her eyes and her voice dropped to a whisper. "Why are they wearing sunglasses indoors? Who knows what they're hiding."

It was probably for the best that Maris didn't know about the one eye, one tooth thing. "If the Gray Sisters don't like what they see today, they could yank their funding from the school," I explained to the others.

"And Corona Arts will be no more," Maris said, slumping in her seat.

"We'll see about that, right, squad?" Nia said quietly, cracking her fingers one at a time.

"On it," Thalia said, then left her seat and went to whisper into the ear of each of the muses.

Ari joined us a moment later, and she squeezed into the row, sitting down next to Maris. She looked a little green, as if she'd eaten something funky for lunch.

"Where's your tapestry?" Maris asked her.

"Backstage," Ari said. Then she fell silent, chewing on her thumbnail. Her friendship bracelets seemed to have tripled overnight.

"Did you make all of those . . . recently?" I asked.

"I told you I like to make things when I'm nervous, okay?" she grumbled, and after that I let her be.

A moment later, Mr. Theo took the stage in his glittering blue jacket, holding the bedazzled microphone. "Hello, Corona Arts Summer Camp! Welcome to the Student Showcase. Parents, friends, and family, settle in for an hour of visual and auditory delight!"

The house lights dimmed, and the theater kids took their places. They ran through a few musical numbers, which had everyone on their feet and cheering. *Do they look even better than usual?* I wondered. I scanned the room and spotted Tomiko twirling on her feet. Elnaz was in a different spot in the room, accompanying the musicians with her flute. Nobody seemed to think this was strange, and I guess that made sense. It was an artsy kind of audience, after all.

A soloist sang next. From her seat in the second row, I spotted Paola conducting the music with her fingers, and I could swear I heard her bells ringing.

When the one-act plays started, Mela and Thalia went into full concentration mode. The first play, a sad story about a boy grieving his brother, made everyone cry, including Mela, who was definitely inspiring the actors with her magic.

The second play, about a baker who couldn't get a single cake right, had everyone howling with laughter. Thalia, of course, was laughing right along with them.

The Gray Sisters *had* to be impressed!

Ballet dancers, salsa dancers, and Irish step dancers were next, followed by three violinists, and a live portrait-painting demonstration. Through each act, the muses were hard at work. The air buzzed with muse magic! Finally, after an intermission and another round of dancers, it was Ari's turn.

Mr. Theo called her onstage. My insides started writhing as I watched her go. Somewhere, Athena was waiting.

Gritting her teeth, Ari climbed the steps to the stage. Mr. Theo gestured at someone standing in the wings. A white girl with blond hair, freckles, and thick black glasses emerged from the opposite side of the stage. She was wearing a plaid skirt and a sweatshirt that was too big on her. She moved forward, every careful step echoing loudly in the auditorium, which was quiet except for the occasional voice whispering, "Who is she?"

Mr. Theo raised the glittering microphone to his lips. "We have a new student in camp this week with a spectacular project for the Student Showcase. Please welcome Tina Olimpica!"

Thalia muttered, "Not very subtle with the name thing, is she?"

"Tina and Ari will be staging a little textile arts competition just for us. Presenting . . . the Battle of the Tapestries!" Mr. Theo announced. The curtain rose, revealing both tapestries hanging from the ceiling, the images carefully illuminated by a spotlight from the back of the auditorium.

People gasped, then applauded. I would never get tired of looking at the two tapestries. The effect of both was similar—they appeared to be real, living figures, not just people and creatures woven from wool.

But while both tapestries were beautiful, Ari's was simply more—

"Astonishing," Maris said, rubbing her arms. "Emily Dickinson once said, 'If I read a book and it makes my whole body so cold no fire can warm me, I know that is poetry.' That's how looking at Ari's tapestry makes me feel."

Mr. Theo said, "Let's do an old-fashioned applause contest. But first, we'll have the weavers onstage tell us a little bit about their tapestries."

Athena smiled brightly. Ari's cheeks looked even greener than before.

"Oh no," Nia said. "She looks really nervous up there."

"Callie, I don't feel so good," Maris was suddenly saying beside me, massaging her temples. She moaned as she rubbed her head.

I turned to face her. "Hey, are you okay?" She was breathing hard through her nose and bending forward, as if she'd just run a marathon.

Then, suddenly, Maris popped back up. "Huh. That was weird," she said. "Maybe I'm allergic to the paint on the sets, or . . . ," she started to say, then just muttered to herself.

I set my eyes back on the stage, on Ari, "Tina," and their tapestries.

Horror, Dread, and Alarm sat primly in the front row, clipboards on their laps.

All around the auditorium, the muses sat very still, their eyes trained on the stage.

"Tina Olimpica, please present your tapestry to the audience," Mr. Theo said, handing the microphone to Athena.

Athena curtsied. The students in the audience giggled, and then she frowned. Beside me, Thalia started laughing, and I elbowed her. "That won't help," I said. "Don't make everybody laugh. This needs to be fair and square or Ari will be disqualified." Thalia cleared her throat and tried hard not to smile at Athena's odd behavior.

Athena seemed awkward, because she was. It was as if she wasn't exactly sure how a kid our age was supposed to act, like she was wearing a costume that didn't fit her right. Finally she licked her lips and spoke into the microphone. "My tapestry is a representation of the ways in which human pride can lead to disaster." She looked over at Ari and nodded. "In each panel, a human being has filled themselves up with so much pride, puffed themselves up with so much arrogance, that they lose everything they ever loved—in some cases, even their lives." Again Athena looked at Ari, who stared at her feet, her hands trembling against her tapestry.

Curtsying one more time, Athena handed the mic to Mr. Theo.

"Um, thank you, Tina," Mr. Theo said. "That was . . . intense. Now, Ari, your turn."

Ari stood very still. So still that I worried for a moment that Medusa was back and had turned her to wax.

"Ari?" Mr. Theo asked.

Athena smiled at the audience, stroking her tapestry with her right hand.

Ari stared at all of us, stage-struck.

That's when I heard Maris whispering beside me, "My

tapestry is a representation of . . . come on . . . come on . . ."

Ari cleared her throat. She took a long, long breath that seemed to fill her up. "My tapestry is a representation of—" She stopped, blinking rapidly.

"Come on, come on," Maris was whispering again. She was still rubbing one of her temples and wincing a little.

Onstage, Ari relaxed visibly and pointed to the tapestry. "It's a representation of the ways in which the ancient gods denied love to the humans who worshiped them. It's a lesson for everyone. We are supposed to take care of one another. Love one another. Even when we make mistakes. Even when we are full of pride," she said, stopping to stare at Athena. "Especially then."

The room had gone very quiet. Ari went on. "I'm sorry if I was ever rude to any of you. If I was too proud. I know I have been. I really am sorry," she said, her eyes resting on Athena once more. Athena looked away.

The clapping started. "Not yet, not yet," Mr. Theo said.

That's when Horror, Dread, and Alarm rose to their feet and ambled toward the stage. Horror led the way, with the three sisters linking arms. They climbed the stairs while everyone watched in silence. Then Horror snatched the microphone from Mr. Theo.

"We are very impressed by the showcase," Horror said. I caught a glimpse of the tooth in her mouth.

"Yesssss. Inspired!" Dread lisped. "I *especially* liked the poems."

Maris squeaked.

Alarm took the microphone. "It's almost as if you all had some sort of . . . divine help!" she said, which sent them cackling.

Horror started digging into her bag. "Did either of you bring the checkbook?" she whispered, forgetting all about the microphone. Everyone in the audience started chatting at once.

They were going to do it! They were going to fund the school again! Corona Arts was saved!

The Gray Sisters were now *all* digging through their purses, tossing out chunks of stale churros as they looked.

"No matter!" Horror yelled into the mic, causing the speakers to screech.

Everyone covered their ears.

"The check will be in the mail," Alarm shouted into the mic next, followed by another squeal of the sound system.

"Well done, children," Dread shrieked. "Might any of you have a question for us?"

Everyone was quiet. "Oh my goodness," I heard Mela say.

"Ask them about the tenth muse!" Nia urged.

I raised my hand.

Horror scanned the room. "No? No? Well, we'll be going, then."

I waved my arms, but Horror, Dread, and Alarm were

already trotting off the stage and out the door, back to the Queens Botanical Garden, probably, and their favorite bench.

Everyone was cheering anyway, except for Ari, who looked like she might puke. Athena was busy sighing, rolling her eyes, and glancing at her watch.

"What a plot twist!" Mr. Theo said once everyone calmed down. "Congratulations to all. Now let's wrap this up with our contest. Winner gets a free ice cream, my treat, from the Queen of Corona!" He stood beside Athena and raised his hand over her head. "If you think Tina's tapestry is the winner, please clap!"

A handful of students applauded. Athena's smile faded slowly until her lips were set in a tight line.

I looked at the Muse Squad. They shook their heads.

"Wasn't us, I promise," Thalia said quietly.

Mr. Theo gave Athena a sympathetic pat on the shoulder. Then he moved over to Ari. The clapping began before he could even say anything.

Paola was the first to get to her feet, then everyone else followed like a wave. The smile on Ari's face could have lit up the whole school.

"Congratu—" Mr. Theo began to say, then froze. Athena was clapping slowly. One by one, everyone in the audience except for the muses froze, too. As she clapped, she stopped looking like Tina Olimpica, and started looking like herself again—all golden, tall, and imposing.

In the echoing silence that followed, Athena spoke. "I suppose that was to be expected. Tina was a stranger, and Ari was a friend. The results were flawed," she said. "Disqualified, Arachne!"

"YOU PROMISED!" Ari shouted. There were tears staining her cheeks. A gentle rustling sound filled the room, and I turned to watch as thousands of spiders trickled out from under the stage.

Athena noticed them, too. With a deep sigh, she snapped her fingers, and the spiders became butterflies that flittered in the air, landing in our hair and on the backs of chairs, before turning into dust.

Ari sat down with a thud and covered her head with her hands. "All for nothing," she said. "It was all for nothing."

"Come on," I said to the Muse Squad, and we leaped out of our seats and joined Ari on the stage, huddling around her. The other muses soon joined us.

"Be reasonable, Dread Goddess," Clio said. "She's just a child."

Athena shrugged. "It was a gift, don't you understand? She loves to weave so much. I gave her the ability to do so for an eternity. Webs for years and years! A human can't do what a spider can. And she'll live forever as a spider. Humans die. If you ask me, children are *ungrateful*."

A melodious voice boomed from the auditorium's balcony. "A human can love and be loved, Athena. A spider can't. And we all know love is the most powerful force there is." It was Aphrodite, sitting on the lip of the balcony, swinging her feet back and forth.

Athena groaned. "Not you! You cannot get involved, little sister. You know that."

Aphrodite jumped down, landing gracefully on her feet. She sauntered up the center aisle. "Yes, I know that. Nobody can stop you when you set your mind on something."

Athena laughed, but it wasn't a happy sound. "Usually that's the case, except we are in the presence of the storyteller just . . . now." Athena rolled her eyes.

My backpack suddenly felt a little bit heavier. I opened it up, and there was the book Tia Annie had shown me. My emblem. It had come to me when I needed it most. But now, I was afraid to touch it, scared of what it might mean.

Athena walked right up to me. I tried hard not to shake but couldn't manage it. She crouched down to face me. My arms were still wrapped tightly around Ari. Athena seemed to observe me for a moment, the way we look at interesting animals at the zoo.

Finally, she spoke. "You can force me to concede, storyteller. That's the gift you've been given, and the power you've been granted. End the story the way you see fit." Athena then rose, pouted, and kicked a churro off the stage. It bounced off the head of someone in the first row, but they didn't notice, of course.

Etoro and Paola were wiping tears off their cheeks.

"The storyteller," Etoro whispered.

"Such a blessing," Paola said.

Elnaz was clapping softly. "I always knew you were special, kid," she said.

"Mm-hmm, me, too," Tomiko added.

As for Clio, she only looked on with a sad smile on her face.

"Go on," Etoro said.

"No tengas miedo," Paola added.

Tomiko and Elnaz each squeezed one of my shoulders.

"Squad?" I asked, looking to Nia, Mela, and Thalia. "I didn't mention it, but apparently I get to finish this story. This," I said, holding up the book, "is my emblem."

Thalia laughed softly. "You're the captain, Captain."

"And we've always got your back," Nia said.

Mela sniffled and gave me a watery smile.

I pulled out the book and opened it to the end. There was a description of the contest, of Ari's tapestry, and Athena's. At the very bottom was white space. A silver pen materialized in the seam of the book.

Aphrodite clapped. "You're toast, Athena! Go on, buttercup! Tell my big sister what to do."

My hand shook as I gripped the pen.

"No," Ari said, looking up at last. She held on to my wrist. "If you force Athena to give up, it won't be real. It won't be just."

"But I can fix it. I can make it safe for you forever," I

whispered. "I know you don't like it when I use my magic on you. But this is different, can't you see?"

Ari only shook her head. "If it isn't real, then I'd rather be a spider."

I knew what I had to do. Ari wanted justice, not a favor. She wanted help, not a rescue. Tia Annie had told me that Ari was a hero whose story needed to be told. Not a hero who needed to be saved. Ari was in charge of the story, not me.

So I did what I could.

"Okay," I said to Ari. "Trust me?"

Ari wiped her eyes with the heels of her hands, sniffing and nodding.

I picked up the pen. With the shakiest, worst handwriting ever, I wrote:

Athena was fair.

And so Athena was.

Chapter 31
THE TENTH MUSE

The moment I wrote the words, I expected the book to disappear. But it stayed there, heavy in my hands.

Athena eyed me intently. She walked over to Ari's tapestry and started to look at it. Really look at it. "Come," she said to Ari, who rose on shaky legs and joined Athena, facing the artwork.

"How did you manage to hide the warps during the repair?" we heard Athena ask. Ari pointed to the tapestry here and there, and the two of them spoke quietly. "The discontinued wefts are particularly good," Athena said.

"What are they talking about?" Thalia asked.

"I don't know. Tapestry stuff?" I said.

After a while, Athena took a step back. Then another. "It's clear to me that Arachne has woven the superior tapestry. Well done, young one."

Aphrodite whooped and cheered, high-fiving people's foreheads up and down the aisle seats. "You can stay with me, Ari," she said. "There's no way I'm giving up the Queen of Corona. Business is too good."

And just like that, Aphrodite was gone.

"It's been very educational, Arachne," Athena said. What she learned, she didn't say. I didn't expect an apology, and she didn't give one. But it was enough. Ari would get to be a human forever. But more importantly, Athena had been honest, and a little less full of pride herself, if only for a moment.

"Thank you all. It was an enjoyable quest. I hope my monsters weren't too much trouble."

"Oh, no bother at all," Thalia said.

The rest of us looked at Thalia and shook our heads.

"What? I'm English. We're polite."

Then, just like Aphrodite, Athena was gone, too.

Mr. Theo was the first to stir back to life. His glittery microphone clattered to the floor.

"What happened?" he asked, smacking his lips together, as though he had a funny taste in his mouth.

"Headquarters," Clio said under her breath.

The muses and Ari hurried off the stage while everyone else was waking up. The students sitting on the aisle were rubbing their foreheads where Aphrodite had smacked them, but otherwise, nobody seemed to notice that anything strange had happened.

I could hear Mr. Theo thanking everyone for coming as we ran out. And from the corner of my eye, I spotted Maris, watching me go, her hands raised in a "What's up?" gesture.

We walked, hopped, and skipped to the Hall of Science, not worrying about entrance points. The muses chattered happily around me, while Ari and I walked together, our arms linked.

"Thanks for everything," she said.

"It was your story, after all."

"Yeah, but you didn't have to help. None of you did. You were all amazing." Ari gave my arm a little squeeze.

There is no real trick to taking a compliment. Sometimes, you just have to say thanks, which I did. "You were amazing, too. So brave! I would have totally pooped my pants back there."

Ari laughed and laughed, and it was the first time I'd heard her really crack up like that, which made me start snorting with laughter, too.

We slipped into the Hall of Science while Elnaz distracted the woman at the front desk with a song.

"Your powers are pretty handy," Ari commented. "Do you sneak into movies a lot?"

Mela gasped, scandalized. "We do *not*."

Back in the comforting blue light of the Great Hall, we took our seats on the beanbag chairs. Clio stood at the front of the room.

"Thus concludes yet another adventure, muses." She looked directly at Ari. "We trust you will keep our secret, as we will always keep yours."

Ari saluted, which made Clio frown. Ah, so Clio was back to her usual disposition.

Behind Clio, the muse finder clock still refused to budge, its arrow stuck on Queens. Clio laid a hand on the globe. "We still, however, have the question of the tenth muse to contend with."

Thalia gasped. She bounced in her beanbag until Clio looked at her. "Hang on! What if it really *is* Ari?"

Nia and Mela cheered. "Yes, more Muse Squad members!" Nia cried.

"Make sure you get a good entrance point, is all I am saying," Mela said to Ari in a whisper.

But Ari lifted her friendship-bracelet-covered arms and shook her head. "Nope. I'm *inspired*, not inspiring. I just want to be a kid again."

Clio agreed. "Ari is correct. She was clearly a Fated One from the very beginning, and I look forward to what your art will do for the world now that you are in it again. But she is not a muse."

Nia, Thalia, and Mela sighed.

"Worth a shot," Thalia muttered.

I heard a knock on the door to the Great Hall then. I turned and caught a glimpse of a face in the window.

That's when I knew, without a doubt, who the tenth muse was.

I didn't just know. Like Aphrodite had said, I would find the tenth muse when I *noticed* her, because she'd been there, all along.

She was kind. She was talented. She'd stopped a pair of curious kids from getting hurt by the lions at the library, and even helped me with writer's block a few times. But most importantly, when the time came, she inspired a Fated One who was struggling to get the right words out onstage.

Just in case, I opened my book and wrote:

Maris Emad was the tenth muse.

The muse finder clock began to chime again, just as Maris slowly opened the door.

"Hi," she said, wiggling her fingers.

Clio took a deep breath, her eyes falling on me for a moment. Then she turned to Maris.

"Welcome, Maris Emad, you are one of us."

Later I sat with Clio in her office and munched on a brownie while she paged through the book. Finally Clio asked, "How did you know that Maris was the tenth?"

"Remember when Ari was struggling onstage?" I said. "She was frightened. Maris started complaining of a headache, then she started rubbing her temples, encouraging Ari under her breath. In that instant, Ari got braver. I could feel it, the magic in the room. At first I thought it had been one of us. But it was Maris."

"If you'll recall, the muse finder clock located her at the beginning of the summer," Clio said.

"Aphrodite told me that the tenth muse was helping us all along. And she did! Maris helped me write a concrete poem on the second day of camp, she convinced all the campers to stage a protest, and she told me about the Nemean lion. She even saved two little kids at the library from becoming a lion's lunch," I said, excitement building in my voice as I listed each example. "Who knows how long she's been inspiring people?"

"Ah," Clio said. "She's a busy one, then. And talented."

She really had been helping us. Maris had been *my* muse all along!

She was going to rock this job.

Clio took a fresh bite out of a brownie. She chewed quietly. Papers were scattered everywhere. Two new boxes sat in the corner of her office. Each was labeled with the words "Tapestry—to be stored."

"We don't know what her specialty is," Clio wondered.

"She's a great poet," I said. "Better than I'll ever be." I stared at my hands. There was something else I was itching to do. One more line I wanted to write in the book.

It made sense. So much sense.

The gods on Mount Olympus had chosen a helper to assist Ari in her quest. Me. And I'd done my job.

They'd made me the Muse of epic poetry. The Hero Maker. But I didn't even know who Emily Dickinson was.

I thought of my family, who I was always running away from every time my bracelet warmed up. I was missing things, like playtime with Rafaelito and episodes of *Zombie Beach*.

But did I really want to say goodbye to the Muse Squad forever? Nia, Thalia, and Mela were my best friends, too.

Before I knew it, I was crying. Again. These ridiculous tears wouldn't ever let up, would they?

I heard sniffling. Clio was wiping her cheeks.

"Grief?" I asked.

Clio shook her head. "No, these tears are just the love that remains when you miss someone you are very fond of. Tears can be liquid love, you know."

I knew. It's what Tia Annie had wanted me to understand, too. I didn't know my purpose yet. Future-Callie would have to discover that. I'd spent the last year asking questions, searching for answers to mysteries, big and small. But now I felt okay with not knowing. In fact, not knowing what came next in life seemed like the best adventure of all.

But one thing I did know was this—I loved my family

with all my heart. And they needed me, probably more than the muses did. Maybe *they* were my purpose? After all, hadn't I been Tia Annie's purpose all this time?

I started to take off my bracelet, but Clio held my hand.

"Keep it. I'll make an entrance point for you wherever we go, Callie." She cast her eyes from side to side, as if she was telling me a secret. "We're headed to the Field Museum in Chicago next," she said in a whisper.

"Nia is going to freak out!" I shouted, and Clio grinned.

Then we were quiet for a long time, and we each ate another brownie.

My mom always said that "No" is a complete sentence. "Yes" was a complete sentence, too. I was saying yes to my old life, and to the new beginnings I would find in it. But I was still very sad.

"So there will be nine muses again," I said after a while.

"That's always been the way," Clio said. "I can put in the paperwork as soon as you're ready."

I thought about it. "No, I think I want to just . . . finish the story." I tapped the book with my fingers.

"I understand."

"Will someone else be the storyteller now?"

"Maybe. The storyteller always appears when we need her," Clio said.

"I'll miss you, Clio," I said, choking back a sob.

She didn't say anything. Instead, she came around her desk and wrapped me up in a big, brownie-scented hug, and cried into my hair for a little bit.

At last we looked at each other through watery eyes, and I got up to go. "I'll be waiting," I said, jiggling my bracelet.

"Leave the monsters to us, and I promise to call you for fun meetings only," Clio said. She put some brownies in cellophane for me and said goodbye.

That night, I called the Muse Squad over for one last muster. We met on the ship that was my entrance point in the Hall of Science. Maris was with them. She'd received a golden cuff bracelet etched with silver quill pens all around as her communication item. She kept one of the knit Wonder Woman cuffs on her other wrist. The bracelets made a mismatched pair, but it suited her.

"Why did this get so flipping hot?" she asked us when she arrived, pointing at her communication item, and we laughed.

"You've got loads to learn," Thalia said. "Listen to me, and you'll be fine."

Nia snorted. "Right. Listen to her, and you'll be in trouble quick."

"There are lots of rules," Mela said. "The first is—"

"Everybody, hold up," I interrupted. I sat down on the deck and pulled the book onto my lap. "I've made up my mind about something."

The others sat around and waited expectantly. I opened

up the book to the last page. The silver pen rested in the binding again. I took a very big, very shaky breath.

"I'm . . . I'm quitting the Muse Squad," I said all in a rush.

"No, you are not," Nia said.

"Unacceptable!" Thalia shouted.

"I just started here! I need you," Maris complained.

"This is absolutely tragic," Mela said.

I held up my hands. "Listen. I've done my job. This book came to me at the right moment, and now it's waiting for me to end the story. A muse always trusts her instincts, remember?"

Everyone nodded in agreement. Then we all started crying.

"Stop it, Mela," I said, through tears.

"I assure you that I have nothing to do with this," Mela said.

We cried it out for a little bit, because I had a new rule, Rule #978: Sometimes you've got to let the tears happen.

"Clio promised I could have an entrance point wherever you go next," I said. "So, it's not really goodbye forever."

Nia sat up straight as an arrow. "We're moving head-quarters again?"

Uh-oh.

"I—I didn't say that exactly," I stuttered.

A chorus of "Tell us, tell us, tell us" began, and when I did, Nia shouted, "YES! YOU ARE ALL GOING TO

LOVE CHICAGO!" so loudly that a guard came up to shoo us away.

Then Thalia made him catch a case of the giggles, and he left us alone.

"How did you *do* that?" Maris asked, her eyes wide.

I put my hand on her shoulder. "Poet, you've got a lot to learn."

I wrote the words down in the book later that day, away from everyone, sitting cross-legged on the pin-pan-pun. I didn't want anyone watching, really.

It was just me and the story now.

I picked up the silver pen.

I wrote:

Callie Martinez-Silva was a regular girl.

I closed the book with the pen inside and set it down. There. It was done.

Picking up my phone, I texted Maya.

Me: Hey Mission Control, what's up?

Maya: Apollo 13, I miss you! I was just about to text you. We got a puppy! Fernando and Mario have been saving up all summer for it! AND MAMI LET THEM KEEP IT!

Me: WHAT?! I thought they wanted to get a car?!

Maya: That's what I thought. I'm so glad they changed their minds!

We texted back and forth for an hour, with Maya sending me pics of the new puppy, which Mario had named Mr. Abominable, and looked like a cross between a German shepherd and a bulldog.

I couldn't wait to snuggle his smooshed-up face!

When we said our goodbyes, I looked over to where I had put the book down, and it was gone. Unlike everyone else's emblems, my book only came to me when I needed it. It made sense. The book was a powerful thing. Maybe too powerful for anyone to have all the time.

I ran my hand over the place where the book had been and tried to imagine who the next storyteller might be someday. Maybe they'd be a kid, like me.

As for my magic, I couldn't feel it all leashed up anymore. I couldn't feel it at all. I took a deep breath and felt really light. And happy.

I was happy.

The rest of the summer was waiting for me.

"Papi, Laura," I called from my room. "Let's go get ice cream."

Chapter 32
HOMECOMING

At the airport, Papi had hugged me a long time at the gate, and he dropped five loud kisses on the top of my head.

"Be good now," he said. "Listen to your mother. And here," he added, handing me an envelope. "Give this to your brothers, por favor."

"I will," I said. "And you should help Laura with the dishes, honestly. Set an example for Rafaelito and all that."

Papi chuckled. "Tienes razón, like always. Such a smart girl. How'd I get so lucky?"

"I love you, Papi."

"I love you, too, kiddo," he said.

I added another rule to my growing list. Number 999: Sometimes parents have to be far away, but they love you all the same.

In the plane, I watched the New York skyscrapers grow

smaller by the second, until the city was just a gray dot. Somewhere down there, the muses would be mustering, and a brand-new Muse of the epic poem would be learning what it takes to inspire a hero. I had a feeling Corona Arts would be brimming with poets next summer!

"Thanks, Santa Claus!" Fernando was saying as I unloaded the souvenirs I'd brought home for everyone:

—A book about video games for Mario, and a *Wonder Woman* comic (an issue that came highly recommended by Maris) for Fernando. I'd bought them both at Vision Books, where we'd escaped the cyclops.
—A small brass stargazer for Maya from the Hall of Science. She had squealed and hugged me when she saw it.
—A picture of me standing next to Fortitude at the New York Public Library, in a frame for Mami. "Bella," she'd announced, kissing my picture.
—And I bought a dog collar for Mr. Abominable, too, with the words "I love Little Italy" all around.

Later, I'd give Raquel Mr. Theo's bedazzled microphone, which he let me keep after I'd introduced him to Ari's Auntie A.

That night, Mami made arroz con pollo for dinner (my favorite), and we filled each other in on our summer adventures. Maya had been clomping around in astronaut slippers since she'd gotten home, apparently. They were white and fuzzy, with a little stuffed astronaut perched on the toe of the left foot, and a stuffed space shuttle on the right.

"Do you think I can wear these on the first day of school?" she asked, while Mami made a face.

"Please don't," I said.

I thought about Past-Callie a lot in the days after I'd given up my muse powers. Past-Callie would have inspired Maya *not* to wear her slippers to school. Now-Callie would just have to convince her the old-fashioned way.

As for Future-Callie?

Who knew?

I sort of liked not knowing, even if it meant not having magical powers, or seeing Tia Annie again. I still dreamed of her sometimes, but I always knew it was just a dream. One time, I dreamed that Tia Annie and I rode a roller coaster to Cuba. Another time, I dreamed that she'd come back to life, and was our neighbor. Once I dreamed of her face—just her face, really close up, telling me she loved me.

Maybe that one wasn't a dream.

As for my brothers, they read Papi's letter and, later that night, had a long conversation with him on the phone. I didn't eavesdrop, even though I really wanted to. Mario and Fernando had to figure this one out on their own, but I would be there to listen and to love them (no magic involved) if they needed me.

One last thing.

Every once in a while, my bracelet starts to warm up. Not too hot, because it's never an emergency. Muse problems aren't my problems anymore. But when the bracelet heats up, I make my excuses, slide under my bed, and close my eyes.

And when I open them, I'm usually staring at four pairs of shoes (one of them pink with a smiley face drawn on them), and the familiar voices of friends saying, "Welcome back, Callie."

Acknowledgments

Readers, thank you for joining Callie and the Muse Squad on this journey. I hope they've inspired you to think of the world in new ways and to seek the muse within!

To my editor, Kristin Rens—thank you for believing in the muses from the beginning. If there's a tenth muse, I think you might be it.

Thanks to the team at Balzer + Bray, especially Mitch Thorpe, Emma Meyer, and Joel Tippie. To cover artist Jonathan Stroh, thank you. The muses were definitely with you on this project. Thanks, as well, to Mary Pender for her efforts in helping me share Muse Squad with others.

To the writers of Las Musas, un montón de gracias por su apoyo y amistad.

To Stéphanie Abou, my agent, coconspirator, and friend, thank you for taking this leap and so many others with me—here's to many more.

Thanks to Hallie Johnston for being the Muse Squad's

first reader and a pal forever.

To Didi—this book is dedicated to your friendship, which means the world to me.

As ever, my real-life muses are my family. Sin ellos, nada. To Orlando, Penelope, and Mary-Blair—I love you all, times infinity.